clean lines

Cedar Tree series #4

FREYA BARKER

CLEAN LINES
(Cedar Tree, Book FOUR)

This book is a work of fiction and any resemblance to any person or persons, living or dead, any event, occurrence, or incident is purely coincidental. The characters and story lines are created and thought up from the author's imagination or are used fictitiously.

Cover Design:

RE&D - Margreet Asselbergs

Editing:

RE&D - Vanessa Leret Bridges - PREMA

DEDICATION

To Mariette, who for many years has given tirelessly of herself in her care for my parents. Because she was there, looking after their every day needs, I was able to move to a different continent and build a new life, within the comfort of knowing Papa and Mama were always looked after.

The women in my books are all strong, capable women, but none of them hold a candle to your abilities, you strength and your compassion.

You will always be my sister and I love you.

TABLE OF CONTENTS

PROLOGUE

"Is that gonna hurt?"

"Remember those pokes I had to give you a few minutes ago?"

The poor little guy nods his head furiously, tear tracks still staining his cheeks from his earlier encounter with my needle.

"Well, those pokes were to make your skin go to sleep. Wanna see?" I watch him look at me from under his thick lashes as he nods again, this time with a little less enthusiasm as I pick up a spare needle. "I'll do it softly first, and then a little harder and I promise I'll stop if it hurts, okay?"

"Okay," comes his timid little voice.

Five-year-old Matthew came into the emergency room with his mom after a spill off the swings, right into a broken beer bottle some idiots had discarded in the park's playground. Two good-sized lacerations; one below the other on his lower leg, with the bottom one deep enough to expose the bone. It was going to need a good cleaning and a fair number of stitches to close, but first I needed to freeze the area and that was not fun for the little squirt, who had already screamed bloody murder. I'm not about to traumatize him even further and am trying for his cooperation, which will be the faster way to go, if I can get it.

A few gentle pricks with the needle bring out a big smile on Matthew's face, and when I poke a little harder he even giggles.

"You are one tough little super kid, aren't you?" I smile at him.

"I didn't feel it!"

"Told ya. Now I have to squirt into the cut with that bottle to clean it up really well before I put some stitches in, but you know you can't feel anything, right? Are you gonna be able to help me out?"

I hand him a stack of dressings., "Here, hold on to these, and every now and then can you wipe my forehead? This is hard work, you know." A quick reassuring wink at his mom, who is observing from the side of the bed, and I snap on a clean pair of gloves. "Ready, Matthew?"

"Ready," he says proudly sticking out the dressings.

It takes me only twenty minutes or so to clean out and neatly stitch both lacerations and the only time the little guy complains is when I put a loose dressing over the stitches to protect them, because he can't show them off to his friends.

I have a smile on my face listening to his little boy chatter as he walks out the room with his mother, while I make quick work of cleaning up the discarded needles and gauze.

"You were really good with him."

The familiar deep raspy voice coming from the doorway startles me and I turn around to face its owner. Chief Deputy Sheriff Joe Morris is leaning his impressive frame against the doorpost, a small smile playing on his lips. *Damn.* That man does interesting things to my insides every time he focuses those baby blues on me. Tall, at least a good foot taller than I am, dirty blond hair sprinkled with the odd hint of grey and always a tad on the long side, making it curl at the ends; perpetual scruff on his chin and those long limbs he manages to move gracefully. He is a sight for sore eyes. He is also a persistent flirt.

"What are you doing here?"

"Some numb nuts thought it was a good idea to get behind the wheel after pouring a bottle of Wild Turkey down his gullet. He ended up in the ditch with a cut on his head when I tried pulling him over. He's next door getting a few stitches and I decided to look for you."

His smile widens. "And here you are, working your charms on the little guy."

I choose to ignore the fact that he came looking for me. Don't think he needs any encouragement.

"Thanks. I like little kids. They're so direct and straightforward. Don't give or take any bullshit. It's refreshing."

One eyebrow shoots up and his demeanor changes as he regards me with intense eyes. "Huh. Straightforward you say?" He pushes his body off the doorframe and slowly stalks in my direction, freezing me like a deer caught in headlights. "I think I remember how to do straightforward, if that's how you prefer it."

Busted.

Walking right up to me I can almost feel the body heat radiating off him and I have to tilt my head back to see his face.

"Have dinner with me tonight." He holds up his hand to stop me when I open my mouth to turn him down, again. "Don't. Hear me out. We've done this dance for weeks now; the flirting, the playful banter. Me trying to get you to agree to a date and you turning me down. It's been a fun game but I'm serious now. Have dinner with me tonight. I'm interested in you and unless I'm way off base, I think you might be interested too."

I'm struck dumb. Literally. Normally quick with the comebacks, he has taken all the wind out of my sails with this display of honesty. He's right. For weeks he has been coming in on occasion on official business, or I've bumped into him in town and we've flirted innocently. Or so I thought. I have turned down every semi-serious invitation he has issued, thinking I either wasn't ready to get on that ride again or that he wasn't serious. Maybe a combination of both. But this sounds genuine and truth be told, I am tempted. Do I dare? The man is one walking temptation and the simple fact he is asking plain little ole me should make me giddy, but instead it makes me apprehensive.

"Thinking hard there, sunshine," he says, lifting a wayward curl away from my face and tucking it behind my ear. Oh geesh...

"Okay then," I croak out, a big frog having taken residence in my esophagus. Clearing my throat I try again, "I'll go to dinner with you."

The full force of his white smile hits me in the gut and I suck in a quick breath at the impact. Handing over his phone, he tells me to enter my number and address. I only have a second's hesitation, figuring that being who he is, he could probably look me up if he put his mind to it, so I throw caution to the wind and do as instructed.

"I'll send you a text so you'll have mine," he says. "Pick you up at seven tonight?"

The few functioning brain cells I have jump into action, causing me to nix that plan. "Actually, why don't you tell me where I can meet you at seven?"

Joe tilts his head and regards me through his thick eyelashes.

"Okay, I'll give you that play this first time, Naomi, even if it is against everything I've ever been taught."

I attempt to hide my smile at his implication there will be more dates. We'll see. At least I'll be able to control when I leave if things don't go well.

When I drive up to Tequila's at a little before seven that night, I can't see Naomi's car anywhere yet. I have the choice to either go in and claim the table I reserved earlier, or wait out here and escort her in. Thinking it might be a nicer touch, I opt for the latter and pull my truck into a spot where I have a good view of the parking lot so I can spot her pulling in off Main Street right away. I spotted her last week getting into a brand new midnight blue Denali at Safeway, so I know what I'm looking for. Although the little brunette has somehow never had a problem grabbing my attention, from the first time I saw the back of her at the nurse's station at the hospital; her hair up in a ponytail, wearing generic scrubs that had me mistake her for a nurse instead of recognizing her as the new doc on the block. I snicker at the memory, because the little firecracker didn't take any time setting me straight. Dark brown eyes bright with irritation flashed as she took one gander up and down my body to finally settle on my face, a slight smirk on her face before she cut me down to size. Yes, a big challenge in a little package.

Ever since, we have built up a good rapport, with easy teasing banter and heaps of sexual tension, at least from my end. Yet she has consistently persisted in dodging my invitations. Saying yes this afternoon all of a sudden was a great surprise. I have a feeling it wasn't an easy decision for her to make. There seems to be quite a bit going on in that pretty little head of hers that I'm eager to discover, but I have to admit, she is the first one to have me interested in going on a date in many, many years.

I like to fuck as much as the next guy, but have managed to do so without any entanglements, and keeping them as far away from my home turf as possible. My life is complicated enough and it never seemed worth it to add to it, but for some reason Naomi makes me want to go there.

My phone rings just as I see Naomi pull into the parking lot. I quickly answer with a short, "I can't talk right now. I'm having dinner. Call you later." I put the phone back in my pocket and walk over to Naomi's ride.

"Gosh, you startled me," she grabs at her chest when she whips around, hearing my approach behind her. It's the first time I've seen her out of the drab hospital scrubs and the little black curve-hugging number she is wearing now, is doing amazing things to my libido. Who knew so many lovely curves were hidden under that shapeless green uniform? Her usually tied-back hair is flowing in loose shiny coffee-black waves just over her shoulders, and the hint of lip-gloss is the only make-up I can detect on her fresh beautiful face. At the risk of overstepping my boundaries, I lean in for a soft kiss on her lusciously shiny lips. The sharp intake of breath, followed by a slight sigh when I pull my mouth away tells me enough.

"You ready to go in?" I try to play it off as casually as I can, pushing down the urge to slide my mouth over hers and taste her properly. That little appetizer certainly had my entire body at attention. Hers too.

"What was that?" she blurts out, a blush on her cheeks.

"You look beautiful. I'm happy you agreed to come on a date with me, and I got rid of the awkward anticipation of how your lips would feel against mine. Now I know... that I will want to have another taste later."

Her blush only deepens and while she still seems a little dumbfounded by my straightforward response, I quickly grab her hand and pull her with me to the entrance of the restaurant.

No sooner had the waitress seated us at our table and taken our drink orders, my phone starts ringing again. One quick look at the screen tells me to ignore the caller.

"Do you have to take that? Are you 'on call' or whatever they call it?" Naomi asks.

"No, nothing like that. Just something I can deal with later. I'll turn off the sound. Don't want any more interruptions," I tell her, grabbing her hand over the table. I can see it makes her a little uncomfortable, but I'm not going to beat around the bush; I'm not afraid to have her know I'm interested. "So, tell me about yourself. How did you end up in Cortez of all places?"

"Oh my, now there's a question that has a potential heavy load. Let's just say we needed a change of scenery and a fresh start. Cortez seemed like the right place and I've always loved visiting Mesa Verde. Started with my parents when I was young."

I have to admit, I don't really register much after she says *we needed.* It implies another person in her life and I can't help but scrutinize the fingers of the hand I'm holding in mine. No rings, but a slight indentation that might be the remainder of one. When she pulls her hand forcefully from mine, I raise my eyes and meet her fiery ones.

"Sorry," I admit, "When you said *we*, I..."

She stands up out of her seat and doesn't give me a chance to finish before giving it to me with both barrels. "You thought I would flirt with you if I had someone waiting at home? You think I would say yes to an invitation to dinner if I had a commitment to someone else? What kind of person do you take me for? I have a son at home, for your information, not that I think it's any of your business at this point." Grabbing at her purse she is almost out of her seat before I can stop her.

"Woah. Wait. Stop. Don't run out of here angry."

She holds up and looks at me with hurt evident in her eyes. I'm pretty sure someone did a fine number on her and I inadvertently pushed a hot button. Not ready to have this date end so soon, I grab her hand and gently coax her back to her seat. I still want to learn more about this intriguing little package of a woman.

"I'm sorry for jumping to conclusions. I wasn't really thinking, just reacting. Sit, and tell me about your son."

With her wistful eyes looking at me from under her lashes, it's clear she hasn't quite made up her mind on whether finally going out with me was a mistake or not. I squeeze her hand to encourage her and with a deep breath and a small—albeit hesitant—smile, she starts telling me about her kid.

"Well, he's thirteen and he's two hand fulls. The move here from Phoenix was as much for his benefit as mine, 'cause I'm afraid the bigger city was going to swallow him up. Here he has more of a chance to be a kid." She shakes her head and laughs a little at herself. "He just doesn't see it that way. Yet."

Wow. A kid. I'm surprised to find it doesn't send me running the way I would've imagined.

"What about his dad?" Touchy question, I know, but I'd like to know the potential minefield I'm walking into.

"Oh God. Is this really what people talk about on dates? I'm so out of practice. It's no wonder I've been avoiding it like the plague."

The slightly panicked look on her face has me throw back my head and laugh.

"Relax. It's not routine for me either and if you don't want to answer, you don't have to. I simply wanted to know if he is still in your son's life."

Before she has a chance to answer, my phone starts vibrating again. Third time since I turned the sound off and put it aside on the table. I've been trying to ignore it, but apparently it has become too much of a distraction for Naomi.

"I really think you should answer that. It sounds like it might be urgent."

"Sunshine, I know who it is and I can guarantee the urgency has no basis in reality."

I'm gonna dunk that phone of his in my water glass. Already a bit of a nervous wreck, I don't need the buzzing every couple of minutes to shock me out of my concentration. Yes I am concentrating hard not to make an ass out of myself again. What is wrong with me? I almost stormed out of the restaurant all because of a valid concern the man had when I implied I wasn't alone. I've grown so distrustful and bristly. So here I am trying to steer clear of the sordid details of my failed marriage and my douchebag ex without appearing to be too uptight and I know I'm failing miserably. It would have been safer to stay at home with my grumpy kid and read a book over pizza. The company is so freaking tempting though. He seems genuinely interested; not put off too much with my knee-jerk reactions, and I really... really liked that kiss in the parking lot. It's been a long time since I've been looked at with such appreciation and been kissed so sweetly. And then there's the hand-holding. Oh my, I had no idea that the slight stroke of a thumb over my knuckles could be such a rich and erotic promise. He is a lethal combination of looks, dominance, ease and charm, and even if nothing ever comes of this, Joe will surely feature with top billing in my fantasies for a long time to come.

We've just been served our dinner and I'm digging into my seafood enchilada, suddenly ravenous after a long day with barely any breaks to eat. The waitress takes off with our orders for additional drinks--I'll have one more of their awesome margaritas before I cut myself off--when I see a tall, stacked blonde bombshell come stalking in the restaurant. She is obviously scanning the place for someone and when her eyes land on our table, she doesn't hesitate, but starts marching over with determination marking her face. A muttered *'fuck'* has me turn to see Joe, already half out of his seat, a dark cloud of anger covering his features as he watches the woman approach our table.

"What the fuck, Brenda?" he bites off when she is no more than a few feet away.

A sick feeling of dread, almost like deja vu, comes over me, and I put my cutlery down.

"There you are, honey!" the woman exclaims loudly. "Was wondering where you were, since you weren't answering your phone."

"Told you I was out for dinner and would call later. This is not cool, Brenda." The barely contained anger in Joe's voice is clear.

Then *Brenda* turns her attention to me. Oh shit. With a huge, albeit fake as hell, smile she sticks her hand out to me.

"Hi there, are you one of Joe's colleagues? I'm his wife, Brenda."

I don't remember how I got to the car, let alone home, but I end up in bed with a pillow over my head, crying at my own stupidity. Again!

I could hear him yell after me when I tore out of Tequila's on a run, but I wasn't about to stop and listen to another set of goddamn lies. Been doing that for too fucking long already. Once bitten, twice shy. Except I guess I needed that extra reminder that you can't fucking trust men.

CHAPTER ONE

"What do you mean, he can't stay with you anymore, and you're sending him home?"

"I just don't have the resources to look after him properly, Naomi. He makes life very difficult for me."

I can feel my blood start to boil. The fucking miserable excuse for a human being is talking about his son for crying out loud.

"Are you shitting me? You were all too happy less than a year ago when Fox decided he wanted to be with you; were full of snide remarks for me and lofty intentions of showing me up on the parenting field, and now you're just going to dump him? He's not a fucking sack of potatoes, James. You don't get to shove him out of your life because he's an inconvenience; he's your bloody son! Do you have any idea what this will do to him? He's sixteen years old and life is hard enough. You're gonna make it even harder."

The silence on the other end is a clear indication that James is done with this discussion. Typical. It was always his modus operandi to leave me hanging in silence, waiting for me to cave, and I don't disappoint this time either.

"Of course he can come home. This *is* and will always be his home, but listen to me carefully; I will not put this kid through another upheaval. This is it."

Other than to let me know where and when to get him off the Greyhound bus he is sticking him on, James doesn't seem to have any more to say to me. Miserable piece of shit.

Fox had been thirteen years old when I finally left James; something I should've done long before. But with my good Catholic upbringing, I had it ingrained in me that once you made your bed, you had to lie in it. James was my messy, rumpled and very dirty bed. One that many others were invited into; more than I would even venture to guess, I'm sure. He always had a tendency to belittle me, even early on in our relationship, but he was older and already a successful attorney, while I was still in med school and unsure of myself; of my position in his life. My parents, who were both still alive at that time, had been over the moon that their only child would not only become a doctor, but had snagged a high profile criminal lawyer for a husband. They died suddenly in a car accident in California just after my dad had retired; their first road trip in the new RV my parents had bought. My consolation was that they had had a chance to meet their one and only grandchild and died together, living their dream. Fox was only one at the time, and I was devastated. Looking back now, I know I lost myself for a while. A combination of what might have been postpartum depression and the grief over the loss of my parents somehow took the stuffing out of me. In hindsight, that's likely when James started playing the field again; or maybe he had done it all along and just became more lax in hiding it. Regardless, I had somehow become numb to the put-downs and blind to the betrayals over the years, until Fox started asking questions about the '*girls*' Dad would bring home for lunch. Turns out the sleaze-ball had been bringing his office interns to my house. To fuck in my bed. I decided to go home for lunch myself one day, after making sure Fox would be at school over the lunch hour, and found him in my bed banging two women. Two women! On the quilt my mother made me when we got married. That was it for me. And honestly, there was a part of me that wasn't surprised; a part that had been expecting this day to come.

Suddenly none of this was okay anymore; not the belittling I would endure, not the cheating, none of it. So I called it. I told him I was done and he didn't even fight me, just scoffed and said I wasn't ever gonna manage on my own. Fuck that.

I moved to Cortez three years ago, hoping to find a place to live where I could teach my son some proper values, where I would be able to heal and he could develop into a normal healthy kid. But thirteen is a tough age. As if the split wasn't hard enough on him, moving from bustling Phoenix to quiet Cortez had a huge impact. Not to mention the fact that suddenly the mother who had been mostly depressed and emotionally absent for most of his life, was now suddenly up in his face.

I tried to lay out some very basic ground rules without sweating all the small stuff, but in the long run, even that handful of rules was too much for Fox. At fifteen he decided to move back with his father in Phoenix, a move James seemed eager to try, so I gave in, wanting to give them a chance to improve their barely existent relationship.

Crap. I don't know what went wrong in Phoenix and I have no idea what state Fox will be in when he gets home, but I have a feeling the tension will be high.

The surly and oppositional, but very verbal Fox, is the one I expected to come off that bus; not this quietly angry kid in front of me, doing everything he can to avoid eye contact.

"Hey, Bub. Good trip?" I try for a neutral start, along with one of my big 'mom' hugs he has grown to hate over the years. He surprises me when he wraps his arms around me and hides his head in my neck. Not easy, since Fox outgrew my five-foot-two frame when he was barely twelve.

A mumbled *'fine'* from his ever-deepening sixteen-year-old voice reaches me, and my motherly instincts are screaming foul. I caution myself to patience; knowing my boy. If I start questioning him about what happened before he is ready to spill, I may never find out. So I tuck my curiosity and worry down and stealthily run my hand through his longish hair in a futile attempt to capture the little boy that was. Sensing more affection than he is comfortable with, Fox straightens up immediately. *Busted.*

"Come on. Let's get your gear and pick up some greasy Mexican before heading home. Sound good?"

Taking the barely formulated '*Whatever*' as encouragement, I hoist one of his bags over my shoulder and walk to the car.

Despite his typical bottomless appetite, the food from his favorite Mexican restaurant does little to lift his spirits.

"Have you stayed in touch with Miles at all?"

He shakes his head. "Nah, only for a bit on Facebook, but it was awkward."

"Well, I saw him yesterday at the clinic. He's doing volunteer hours there now. Told him you were coming, and he said he might pop by later? Maybe you wanna give him a call?"

The only response I get is a shrug before he takes off to his room and closes the door. *All right then.* I'd almost welcome the arguing and yelling from before to this boy I hardly recognize. What the fuck happened in Phoenix?

With Fox in his room and his music on loud enough to wake the dead, I step out on the deck to call James for some answers.

"Miller—"

"James, it's me. Just wanted to let you know I got Fox off the bus okay. We're home now, but I—"

"Not another word. I'll call you back," James cuts me off sharply and hangs up.

Looking at the phone in my hand in disbelief, I have to fight the urge to call back right away and tell him to fuck the hell off with his asshole behavior. What the hell was that all about? Something in the tone of his voice holds me back and I head inside to clean up the remnants of our take out from El Burro Pancho.

It's still early, only nine thirty, when I crawl into bed after a shower and quick peek in on Fox. Tomorrow is Monday and Fox has to start back to school, which he seems less than enthused about. I have to start a new shift that has me on four twelve-hour days, followed by three days off. Not a great way to start off with my boy back home, but it is what it is and I'll take the three days off in a row.

Just as I reach over to flick off my nightlight, I notice a missed call. James. I quickly call up the voice mail.

"Don't call me on my phone again, Naomi," he starts, his voice just barely above a whisper to where I have to strain to decipher what he's saying. "I've run into some trouble and it's best you don't contact me. Don't let Fox get in touch with anyone back here either. Make sure of it. If you have to, just tell him he was heard..." A click ends the call with a friendly voice asking if I want to delete or save the message. Instinctively I want to hit seven for delete, but at the last minute I change my mind and save it instead. I spend the night mulling over what kind of shit James got himself and our son into.

"Bub! Come get your breakfast. We're gonna be late!" I yell up at the bottom of the stairs.

Fox has settled in somewhat over the past week. He's still not talking much, and after trying to get some more information out of him the first morning about what happened with his father, I decided to give that some time after he cut me off sharply. I was still concerned though, especially since I hadn't heard another thing from James since.

When he drags his long lanky body into the kitchen and plops down on a stool, I go in for another attempt. Setting a plate of French toast in front of him, I cautiously ask, "Have you heard anything from Dad lately?"

Fox looks at me from under his eyelids still heavy with sleep and slowly shakes his head.

"Nothing?"

"No Mom, nothing. Can I eat my breakfast now?"

Against better knowledge, I decide to push a little. "I'm just wondering, honey. He left me a message after you first got home not to contact him, but I haven't heard from him. I'd hoped he would've at least talked to you."

His head shoots up at that. "He called here?"

"I'd called him and must've interrupted something 'cause he hung up on me, but called me back when I was in the shower and left a message. Haven't heard since and thought maybe he'd contacted you."

"Did he say anything?" Fox looks at me eagerly, but I don't want to go into details over the strange message. If it worries me, it's sure to worry him. So I lie.

"Only to say that he'll be busy for a while and not to call his phone."

His shoulders slump a little more as he shovels his food in his mouth, not saying another word. *Damn.*

The drive to school is quiet after that and I barely get a response when I drop him off, reminding him his dinner just needs to be heated up in the microwave.

"I'll be home around nine thirty," I manage to fire off after him as he walks away from the car.

I have half an hour before the start of my shift and am determined to put it to good use. I need some answers.

The moment I walk into the hospital, Jenna Stanley, the hospital administrator, makes a beeline for me.

"Naomi, can I have a minute?"

"Can it wait ten minutes, Jenna? I came in early to make a few phone calls first."

The stuck up Barbie never fails to try and flaunt the fact she's dating our new Sheriff in my face. *Whatever.* She can have Joe. Not like I ever had him to begin with. But word had gotten out of our one disastrous date, years ago, and apparently our somewhat antagonistic attitudes toward each other also have not gone unnoticed. Reason enough for Jenna to try and stake her claim. And apparently Barbie is not happy at being delayed in being able to do so, judging from the ginormous pout on her perfectly made up face. That's too bad. I firmly shut the door to the small office behind me, leaving her standing in the hallway.

"Bancroft, Leeds, Miller and Associates. How may I direct your call?"

"Hi, yes. I'd like to speak to James Miller, please? It's Naomi Waters."

"Ms. Waters, I'm sorry to inform you that Mr. Miller is not available. Can I take a message?"

"Actually no. I'm calling about our son and it's important I speak with him."

I can hear the rustling of someone putting their hand over the mouthpiece, a click, and then the familiar voice of Frank, one of James' partners, comes over the line.

"Naomi, how are you?"

"Frank? Hi. I'm good, but confused. What is going on? Something wrong with James?"

"Why do you think that? Has he been in touch with you?" Frank counters.

"I talked to him briefly about a week ago, but he hung up on me and he left me a rather cryptic message after that. But both Fox and I are getting a little worried."

"Fox is with you? Thank God!"

"What the fuck is going on, Frank? You are worrying me." A chill runs down my spine at the thought Fox might've been missing as well.

"We haven't seen James for over a week. He simply never showed up to court one day and we can't find him. We've been to his house, which has been ransacked. No sign of him or Fox so we didn't know where either of them were."

"Well Fox is here. James sent him back last week on the bus. Why didn't anybody contact me?"

"We didn't know where to find you, Naomi. James never told us where you had gone. He always kept things close to his chest. A habit we all get into, working in criminal law I guess, and there was no paperwork anywhere to even indicate your maiden name."

"Did anything happen? Any cases go wrong? Are the police on it?" I have so many questions I want answers to.

"We're looking into all of his recent cases and so are the cops. We just filed a missing person's report, but maybe you should give me your location so I can pass that on to them. They'll likely want to get in touch with you too."

I don't know what it is, but something about the slight eager edge to his voice makes me resist giving him my address or personal number.

"You know what, Frank? Just give me the name of whatever officer is in charge and I'll get in touch with them myself."

I can tell he's not happy, and after trying once more to push me for more information, he gives in and passes on the name I need. I'll have to hold off on calling until I have a break during my shift, because I just officially went on the clock. At least that's what I'm thinking Jenna means when she opens the door without knocking and starts tapping on her wristwatch. *Bitch.*

CHAPTER TWO

"So there's nothing you can tell me? I mean, I have his son at home and he's worried. We're both worried."

"Sorry ma'am, we've looked into the possible disappearance of Mr. Miller, but I have to tell you, it appears as though he may have left of his own free will, since all personal papers, his car and a good amount of his clothes seem to be missing. The apparent break in may very well have happened after he was already gone. We found no evidence of anything but property damage to the house. I'm sorry, there really isn't much else I can tell you."

The officer is starting to get on my nerves, so I try once again. "At least tell me you are looking into some of the cases he was working on? I told you, on the message he left on my phone he clearly indicated he was in trouble. Surely that would warrant a closer look?"

"Ma'am, as I mentioned, you're welcome to drop the recording off at your local PD in Cortez and they will make sure it gets to us in case there is ever a need to follow up, but in the meantime, I'm afraid that other than a breaking and entering, there is no evidence of any crime taking place."

Afraid I'll say something I regret, I hang up the phone, seething with frustration.

It's dinnertime and I worked all day without a break until now. A quick stale sandwich from the cafeteria is all I manage to grab before calling the Phoenix PD. One bite that tastes like sawdust and I'm no longer hungry either. I turn to toss the remainder of the sandwich in the garbage when a figure in the doorway startles me.

"Jesus! Katie, you scared the crap out of me. What are you doing here?"

I smile up at my newly married, very pregnant and annoyingly happy friend, Katie Whitetail.

"Had a session with Kendra and got a craving for a Harissa grilled chicken sandwich from the Farm Bistro and decided to bring one for you too. You mentioned last week you were working late shifts?"

She waves the paper bag in front of my nose and just like that my appetite is back. Snatching it from her with one hand, I wave her over to a vacant chair with the other.

"Sit. Take a load off. Where's your hunky husband?"

"Out on a job. Been gone for two days and already I'm sick of eating alone." She takes a big bite from her sandwich and continues with her mouth full, "Blue just sits there and stares at everything that goes in my mouth. It's starting to creep me out."

"So I'm it? I get to be your dinner buddy? Lucky me! I just tossed some three week old sandwich from the cafeteria in the trash fully expecting to go hungry, so this is very welcome." I reach over with my sandwich and touch hers with it.

"Cheers."

"Crud! I forgot napkins," Katie grumbles, trying to lick the Harissa aioli dripping off her fingers.

"Hang on, I've got paper towels here."

Plopping a roll on the table in front of her, I sit back down and start eating mine. Damn this is good. I groan with every bite I take until I hear Katie chuckle.

"What?"

"Sounds like a friggin' porn movie in here."

"Shut up and finish your sandwich," I tell her in between bites.

Ever since Katie moved to Cedar Tree earlier this year and I took over as her physician, we've become fast friends. Suffering from a brain injury, it took her a while to regain her mobility, but she is well on her way to a full recovery. Of course finding herself pregnant shortly after getting involved with one of her coworkers at GFI, has been the best motivator. Both she and Caleb are investigators and worked together long before their relationship turned into something more than just professional, but in short succession they went from colleagues to husband and wife. I'm tickled pink that they want me to take care of her through the pregnancy as well.

It's always been a dream of mine to have my own family practice. Nothing big, but something manageable. A clinic that would offer, not just straight medical care, but other types of health services as well. Kendra and I sometimes talk about where we would set one up. She's the physical therapist who's gotten Katie this far and still sees her regularly. Between Kendra and I, we could already offer quite a range of services.

Pipe dreams; that's all they are. The reality is the clock on the wall telling me I have five more minutes before I have to get out there again.

"That was so good. Thanks for bringing me dinner," I tell Katie, wiping the remnants off my lips.

"My pleasure. Now are you going to tell me what had you so upset when I came in?"

Wondering if I should confide in her, I decide to just tell her in great lines what has happened. Katie is one of the few people I've let in a bit on my background.

"I told you James sent Fox back here to live, right?" When Katie nods I continue, "Well, we haven't heard from him since he left a message last week saying not to contact him, that he'd be in touch. Nothing since, so I called his firm in Phoenix and they haven't seen him in over a week. Not only that; his house has been broken into. I called the Phoenix police, but they seem to be content assuming he must've taken off. Despite the fact his house turned up broken into. Go figure. Also, in that message he left me, he said something about being in trouble, but when I mentioned that to the cop I was talking to, he seemed less than impressed. I'm just getting a really weird feeling and I'm worried. I can tell Fox is too, although I haven't even filled him in on everything."

Katie grabs my hand over the table. "Want me to look into it? See if we can find anything out for you?"

I shake my head. "No. I don't want to cause any problems right now. I don't know what is going on frankly, but I have a nagging feeling Fox may be involved too, even though he still hasn't opened up about what happened between him and his dad."

I get up and gather the garbage and plop it in the bin before washing my hands at the sink. I'm surprised we haven't been interrupted yet. I should've been back in the ER almost five minutes ago.

"I really have to hustle but we'll be in touch later. I have a couple of days off coming up."

Katie gets up as well.

"Hang on, before you run off, Caleb and I are planning a pig roast at the barn in a couple of weeks. Are you game?"

"A pig roast?"

"Yeah. I wanted to do something country-ish... for the housewarming. It should be all finished by then. I've never done one before and Caleb said his brother would help cook. They used to do them all the time. I've invited the whole gang."

"Sure. Let me know the date when you pin it down. I want to make sure I have the day off. Oh, and I'll bring someone," I add, thinking I'll try to convince Fox to join.

Katie's eyebrows shoot up in her hairline. "Really? Do I know him?"

"Ha. Yes you do, in fact. Fox, you twit. Who else? You know I don't date."

"Damn. I was hoping... I mean, of course I'd love for Fox to come if he wants to?"

I roll my eyes at her, knowing full well she'd like nothing more than to have me find a man now that she's found hers. I have my hands full with my son right now though. Don't really feel the need to add more testosterone in the mix.

"I'll check with him. Gotta run now, honey. Thanks again."

I give her a little wave over my shoulder as I head down the hall toward the ED.

"So how come you're not asking me to that party, Sheriff?"

Fuck. I knew I made a mistake when I hooked up with Jenna. The woman grates on my nerves with her assumptions and her cutesy nicknames. It doesn't matter how often I tell her I'm not interested in any kind of relationship, it seems to go in one ear and out the other. She manages to zone in on me like some homing device whenever I'm within range of the hospital. It's creepy as shit. For the longest time, she'd been making eyes at me while I still had hopes to set things right with Naomi, but after she knocked me down once again, I turned around and found a willing Jenna ready to take me home. So I went. Not my proudest moment, nor were the moments that followed, when I went back to try and fuck away the frustration over a woman I couldn't have. Like a total moron I got sucked right in when guilt compelled me to take her out for a few meals. When she started spouting around that we were an 'item,' I called things off right away. Asshole move, I know, but I never promised anything more than that, and I've always been brutally clear about it. Today is no exception. I don't need that kind of bullshit and even though I was called away to help settle down an injured but unruly prisoner before I could set her straight, I waste no time when she corners me at the nurse's station the moment I walk back out.

"Jenna, for fuck's sake, how many times do we have to go over this? I've been straight with you from the start; there is no relationship. There never was and it's not going to happen now. I've held back before, not wanting to cause a scene in public, but you're not letting up with the inappropriate behavior in public. You're leaving me no choice. Drop it already."

I really feel like an absolute ass already, but I'm fed up from having to pry her off me every time she spots me. The look on her face is one of anger; surprisingly. I had expected maybe tears or hurt, but she's clearly pissed off. When she turns on her heels and marches down the hall, she almost knocks Naomi over. *Fuck.* I hadn't seen her there and she looks equally pissed. Isn't that great.

"You seem to have a way with women, don't you, Sheriff?" she hisses as she walks by me.

Fucking brilliant.

The woman who's been stuck under my skin like some kind of festering splinter; the one I haven't been able to banish from my thoughts for longer than a few hours at most since the day I first set eyes on her, has to be witness to yet another one of my *prouder* moments. I should pack it up and move to Alaska. Start the fuck over again, 'cause it seems no matter what I do, however well I do professionally, I manage to screw up my personal life like nobody's business.

Thank God I manage to avoid both angry women while I wait for my prisoner to get fixed up enough for me to take to jail. Next time I'll send a couple of deputies; be a long time before I set foot in this damn hospital again.

Two weeks later I'm breaking my own vow.

We've had some reports of vandalism near Crow Canyon Archeological Center come in over the last few weeks. Predominantly littering and a bit of damage at some of the excavation sites, which I suspect may be the work of teens. I've been checking around there after dark a few random nights without any luck, but tonight I can spot the unmistakable glow of a fire as soon as I pass the outer building of the center. Turning off all my lights, I pull into the brush on the side of the dirt road to call for some back up. They may be kids, but if they're hopped up on booze or drugs, my badge won't impress them much. Until I know what I'm dealing with, I'm not going to barge in blind.

"Dispatch"

"Carol, it's Joe. Any patrols west side of Cortez? I'm at Crow Canyon, at the Center. There's activity tonight."

"Sir, I've got Drew coming up the 160 from the airport. I'll send him through."

"Perfect. Tell him to cut his lights coming in. I'm going to check things out on foot."

"Ten-four"

I flick off the interior light before I get out of the truck. In the dark night, even a small light like that would stand out. Closing the door quietly, I try to take in my surroundings. It's probably easiest for me to stick to the path or at least the softer soil on the edges. I don't want to alert anyone to my approach. For now all I want to do is have a look at who is there and what they're up to.

I manage to stay on the trail until I can hear loud voices and laughter coming from the direction of the fire. In fact, I'm getting so close, I can hear the occasional spitting of wet wood. The occasional flicker of flames is visible through the trees. I start moving into the brush, careful not to make too much noise. Slowly circling around, I try to find a decent spot from which to observe.

I'm just settling in against the trunk of a good-sized tree, with a prime view of the small clearing where three young guys are drinking and smoking, when I hear crashing from the woods behind me. Before I even have a chance to react, a fourth kid comes stumbling out of the brush right in my path. *Fuck.*

"Shit! Run!"

At the sound of their buddy's yells, the three idiots by the fire take off, but my focus is on the tall skinny kid tromping through the undergrowth in front of me. I call out and identify myself, but the dumb fuck just keeps running, until I suddenly see him disappear before my eyes. Closing in, I notice we've reached the edge of another dig, this one about six feet deep, showing the remnants of what could be a kiva, and the kid is crumpled at the bottom whimpering, holding his wrist which is bent at an awkward angle. Stupid kid ran right off the edge in the hole.

I take my flashlight off my belt and shine it down in his face. *Dammit.*

"You Doctor Water's kid?"

I've seen him around town with Naomi a few times in the last few of weeks. Surly shit, from what I can tell. A timid nod is all he gives me. *Great.*

"What's your name?"

"Fox... Fox Miller," he tells me, his head hanging down.

I look around me to get my bearings and grab my radio, which only gives me static.

"Alright kid, I'm gonna have to get you out of there myself and then we better get you fixed up. Looks like you broke your wrist. May well be the least of your problems though, Fox."

With the help of a discarded ladder on the side of the excavation, his sweater and my belt stabilizing his arm and my body behind him to guide him up, Fox manages to get out of the hole.

Ten minutes and a short stop to douse the flames later, we get back to my truck where Deputy Drew Carmel has pulled up with his patrol car.

"You see the other kids?"

"Managed to chase down one; he's in the back of my unit. The other two were gone by the time we got back here."

"All right, take that one in. I'm gonna have to take this one to the hospital. He fell running away from me. Dumb shit broke his wrist. We'll be in after."

"Later, Sheriff."

CHAPTER THREE

"Fox? What the hell?"

As expected, Naomi is front and center when I bring her son in to the Emergency Room. A quick scan around the lobby shows no sign of Jenna; and thank God for that. One spiteful woman is enough for me today. Ah fuck, I'm lying. One look at Naomi and I remember, with vivid clarity, what attracted me to her in the first place. The glossy dark hair, gentle curves, big eyes, all wrapped in a tight little package that drab green scrubs can't hide. Happens only every time I see her. Maybe that's the real reason I've been avoiding her more and more. Fucking burns to hit your head against the same brick wall over and over again. And make no mistake, that brown-eyed little spitfire has built one damn fine brick wall around her.

Right now she's too preoccupied with her son to mind me, so I take a wall just inside the treatment room where she ushers him to just observe and listen. Naomi is carefully unwrapping my amateur sling, mumbling under her voice the entire time.

"Mom. Stop fussing."

Oh boy. Wrong thing to say, kid. I can see her back straighten as she rests her hand on the bed beside her son and leans her face in close.

"Fussing?" The low timbre of her voice would be all sorts of sexy if it weren't intimidating as shit. "You think I'm fussing? You be glad I am keeping my cool and am in my professional mode, Fox, because let me tell you, I'd like nothing better than to break your other wrist for you right now!"

The kid has the good sense to flinch, despite the fact that he is easily a head taller than his mom.

"I can't believe that for weeks you wouldn't talk to me, hardly do more than grunt actually, yet the first thing resembling a sentence I get is *'stop fussing?'* This after you are brought in to the hospital by the Sheriff...the Sheriff, I tell you, with a fucked up arm when you and I both know you were supposed to be at home doing homework. Yeah, I'll stop fussing. Let me get right on that!"

Turning around, she comes toward me and I have to fight to hide the grin that has crept up on my face. I'm only awarded a deadly glare before she slips past me into the hallway, leaving me with a miserable-looking Fox, whose head couldn't hang any lower. Save for a brief glance my way and a small smile I send him, the room stays quiet until Naomi returns with a nurse in tow.

"Stacy will take you to X-ray, but I can tell you right now that wrist is broken and out of position. I just need to know how badly."

"Mom, I'm—" Fox starts, but Naomi holds up her hand.

"I don't want to hear it right now. Give me time to cool off and talk to the Sheriff. I don't want to say shit I might regret, Fox. Go with Stacy; she'll take care of you."

Technically I should follow Fox wherever he goes but I have a feeling he won't be running off. I stick around to see Naomi deflate the moment Stacy wheels the stretcher out of the room.

"Hey. Come on, let's grab a quick coffee in the caf and we can talk," I offer, hating the tired and defeated look on her face.

I honestly didn't think she would go for it, but she shrugs her shoulders and pulls herself together and leads the way over to the nurse's station to let them know where she can be found.

My only excuse for following Joe to the cafeteria without argument is that I'm done. Stick a fork in me done. I'm about to lose my shit and I don't want to lose it all over the ER in front of my coworkers, thank you very much.

I've been on eggshells these past few weeks since Fox got home. He's been virtually unapproachable, especially since finding out his dad is missing. Several phone calls to the Phoenix PD have not brought any relief on that front yet either. No, if I thought it was tense between us before he left for Phoenix, it's ten times worse now. I've tried now, on several occasions, to get an explanation out of him on what led his father to send him home. Fox has continuously shut me down, each time more insistently than the last. The only thing that's given me some semblance of peace is that at least he hasn't been getting into any kind of trouble outside of the house. In fact, he has mostly stayed inside and hasn't even had his old friend Miles around. That illusion is quickly shattered tonight when Joe walked him in, with his arm in a make-shift sling. *Fuck me sideways.*

So here I am, sitting in the corner of the hospital caf with my hands wrapped around a hot coffee I probably shouldn't be drinking at this time of night. My son's in X-ray with what likely is an off-set wrist fracture, and across from me is a man who makes my skin crawl in the most grating and seductive ways equally. All I want to do is cry. I know I have to ask, or at the very least look up, but I'm afraid those last tattered threads that are holding me together will snap. So I do nothing but stare at the small puddle of coffee at the base of my cup, left from when I slammed it down too hard on the table.

"Doc..." he starts softly, and his use of the unimaginative nick name he hasn't used in the last three years tears at my last bit of resistance. A ragged sob breaks free, followed by another, and then the lid comes off. I hear the scraping of a chair and knees pressing in to mine as Joe scoots his chair to shield me from view as I lose it. With one hand on the table in front of me and one on the back of my chair, his big body has me boxed in, but rather than crowded I feel oddly safe.

Struggling to get a hold of myself, I grab a handful of napkins from the dispenser on the table and furiously start wiping my nose and face, all the while, Joe says nothing.

"I'm sorry..." I start.

"Nothing to be sorry for, and just so you know, whatever trouble you think he's in, it's not that bad."

Of course that sets off another round of tears and a few more minutes before I have those under control.

"Tell me what happened?"

"I was following up on some reports of vandalism at Crow Canyon; the Archeological Center? He was one of four kids partying at one of the digs. The fire they built tipped me off from a distance. I had no idea it was him. He saw me first and started running and I took off after him. He ended up falling right into another excavation. Tried to stop his fall with his hands I imagine, because by the time I got to him, he was sitting at the bottom cradling his arm. That's when I recognized him. Got him out and brought him straight here."

I'm sick to my stomach but I have to ask the next question, both as a mother and a physician.

"Alcohol and drugs? I thought I smelled some booze on him now that I think about it."

"Yeah well, you might want to take some blood and get a lab work-up done. I'll need it for my report too."

I just nod. I haven't looked Joe in the eyes yet, but when his hand slides down my back I turn to face him.

"What will happen?"

The genuine concern and warmth in his clear blue eyes is unmistakable and for a minute I wonder if I should just tell him all my worries, but just then Stacy walks in looking around.

"Dr. Waters? Your patient is back in his room and I took the liberty to have security stand guard when I couldn't find the Sheriff. The radiology report is at the nurse's station."

"Thanks Stacy, I'll be right there. Oh, and could you, or get the lab to come and draw some blood for a tox screen on him?"

"Sure thing."

With a curious glance at Joe after seeing what I'm sure is my tear-blotched face, she is off again.

"Well, I'd better get back and see what the damage is," I sigh, pushing back my chair, and forcing Joe to do the same.

"I'll stick around here to wait for results. We'll take it from there. He didn't have anything on him, so for now trespassing and mischief are his only issues. Maybe we can ask him some questions together later?"

I know Joe is being gentle with me, or rather for me, and I'm grateful, so I take the plunge.

"Yes. There are things I need to know too; things he hasn't told me. Stuff that may be important. There is so much I've tried to manage by myself but I think I might need your advice. But first let me look after him."

He's surprised, I can tell that much from the slight lift of his eyebrows. And no matter how much I want to stay angry with him, right now my son is in trouble and I am not above using my fucked up connection with Joe to get answers if I can.

I walk straight into the room and pull up Fox's scans on the computer, while Joe stays to chat with the security guard. Fox is lying on the bed, his good arm covering his eyes.

"How are you doing?" I ask him softly.

"I'm okay," he mumbles, but he doesn't move his arm.

"Hey Bub? They're gonna come take some blood in a minute to take to the lab; anything you wanna tell me before they do that?"

Slowly he drags his arm down his face and his eyes are brimming with tears. My baby is crying and it breaks my fucking heart. Swallowing the lump in my throat and blinking furiously I smile at him, letting go of all the anger and frustration I'm feeling. I carefully reach out and place my hand on his cheek. Instead of shrugging me off, he presses his face into my palm and another little tear cracks my heart.

"Just tell me, babe—like ripping off a Band-Aid—then we'll deal with it, and with that messed up wrist of yours. Come on, be brave."

I can hear Joe has entered behind me and a quick look over my shoulder finds him once again leaning against the wall. Fox looks at him too and then at me.

"It was stupid. Just hanging out. At first it was a few beers and some laughs. Then one of them started bringing hard liquor and weed. Last night this new guy came and he brought meth. I told them I didn't want it." He focuses his eyes down on the floor as he continues, no longer willing to look either of us in the eye. "But they gave me a hard time, so I inhaled some to try it anyway. The stuff made me sick and when I went in the trees to throw up, that's when Sheriff Morris saw me."

I have to swallow hard and take a minute. Fear and anger threaten to make me lose my cool but in the end I manage to maintain my composure. I need to keep him talking and continue in a moderate tone. "Okay. Okay... I guess it's good it made ya sick. But Bub, we're gonna have to sit down and talk about why at some point. Why you stick your neck out and do stupid shit you are too smart for. Now I know Sheriff Morris will have some questions for you, but first we're gonna have a look at these scans of your wrist and see what's what. That okay with you, Joe?"

I turn around to Joe, who simply nods in response.

The news is not so good for Fox. He has a complex fracture of his distal radius, the end of the larger of the bones in his forearm, and will likely need surgery. I've put a call in to the orthopedic surgeon, but he won't be in until tomorrow and with the alcohol and the meth in his system, I'm going to have to admit Fox. He won't be happy, but I'm hesitant to give him any pain medication without very close supervision. The end of a fucking perfect day.

Joe managed to get a little bit of information out of him and left a short while ago, telling me he was sorry he had to leave, but that he had another one of the boys at the station he wanted to have a talk with. I don't know whether it's fatigue or what, but I can't quite figure out what he has to be sorry about.

It's after midnight already and well past the end of my shift. I manage to snag one of those fancy sleeper chairs and pull it into the room next to Fox's bed. Might as well crash here.

I must've fallen asleep myself at some point, watching the rise and fall of my child's chest, still seeing the little boy in the lanky almost-man crowding the hospital bed. A noise behind me startles me awake and I turn to find Joe standing in the doorway.

"Sorry, Doc. Didn't mean to wake you. I was just backing out," he whispers.

"S'okay. I just dozed off."

I watch him make his way in the room and pull a stool up beside me.

"What are you doing here so late?"

"Just on my way home from the station. Decided to see how he was. How you are."

I take my time scanning his face, the day's growth of beard, the hair curling up at his ears, his straight nose and firm jaw, before those expressive blue eyes drawing me in.

"Doing alright. The surgeon will be in in the morning to assess him and we'll take it from there. I'm still waiting on the lab work to come back, but he already confirmed what he took, so it's almost a moot point. I'm just at a loss where to go from here."

"Wanna tell me what you were referring to earlier? The advice you were talking about?"

I peek over at Fox, who appears to be sleeping deeply and pull my legs under my body, settling deeper in the chair.

"Fox went to live with his dad when he didn't like the rules I expected him to follow. James was a shit husband but hadn't been a bad father, and I knew any judge would've given a fifteen year old kid the option."

I continue giving Joe as much background as I can before outlining the events since Fox has been back. When I tell him about my conversation with James' partner, Joe interrupts. "Did you tell him where you were?"

I shake my head. "No, something felt off so I told him I would get in touch with the Phoenix PD, but they are writing it off; saying he appears to have left voluntarily and the break-in looked to have occurred after. I've called them a few times since, but am getting nowhere. Then last week, Fox asked about his dad and wanted to try and contact a buddy in the neighborhood. I finally told him what his dad had said to say; that he had been heard…whatever the hell that means. He turned white as a ghost and if he wasn't speaking to me before, he surely isn't speaking to me now. I can't get a damn thing out of him. Now this. I'm at a loss. I know something is going on, something that started in Phoenix and has to do with James, but I can't get to the bottom of it."

I'm surprised to find Joe handing a box of tissues over, and only now discover tears falling down my chin. *Great.* Second time in one day I let my emotions show in front of this man.

Almost angry, though mostly with myself, I snatch a handful and wipe my face.

"What's your husband's full name," he asks curtly.

My eyes shoot up at the short tone and I instantly bristle. "It's James Thomas Miller and he's my ex-husband. We've been divorced for nearly four and a half years now."

"Point taken," he says, lowering his eyes for a moment, before refocusing on mine. "And I will have a look if I can find out anything, but you and I, we really need to have a long overdue talk about some persistent misunderstandings. Ones that I have been trying to clear up for years, but have never been given a chance to. If nothing else, I want us to be able to work together, be real and straight with each other, and not hide behind snide innuendos and bitter retorts. All based on false impressions and misinformation."

Now it's my turn to lower my eyes, embarrassed, because I'm the one who refused to listen to any explanations for years. I haven't wanted to listen to anyone, too hurt by what seemed so obvious to me at the time. It's clear to me from the edge to Joe's voice and the hurt evident in his eyes that I've been unfair to him.

"You're right. Long overdue and I'm sorry for my part in that."

Joe blows out a puff of air before making a valiant attempt to smile at me.

"Get some sleep. We're both exhausted. I'll be in touch, okay?"

I simply nod as he returns the stool, and gives my shoulder a squeeze on his way out the door.

Damn.

CHAPTER FOUR

"Drew! Can you come in here?"

"Sheriff?"

As one of my youngest deputies, Drew Carmel for some reason hasn't been able to bring himself to call me by my first name yet, even though I make a point of it every time he calls me 'sir' or 'Sheriff.' I'm not big on adhering to the strict and out-dated hierarchical protocols, especially since we have a small crew and work closely together both outside and within the confines of our offices.

"Joe please, Drew," I remind him once again. "Have you had a chance to run that name through the system again? James Thomas Miller?"

"This morning, Sir." He blushes when he sees me flinch at the '*Sir.*' "Sorry"

"No problem. Hard habit to break, I know."

"Anything?"

"Nothing. No flags, no tags, no call outs, nothing."

"Damn. 'Kay, thanks."

Since leaving Naomi sitting by her son's hospital bed in the dark a few days ago, I've been trying to get some information for her on the boy's father, but so far I've come up empty. From what I can tell there is no active missing person's case, and the only thing open is a breaking and entering at his address in Phoenix. Not something that generally has particularly high priority in the busy Phoenix police district. This morning I put in a search with the Maricopa County Court Docket for any cases that list Miller as the representing attorney for the last year. Not sure what I'm hoping to find, but there may be something that sends up a flag. Being a criminal attorney is sure to have ruffled some feathers over the years, and it won't hurt to see if anything bears looking into.

I was back in the hospital the day after I picked up Fox and brought him in to check in, but when I popped my head in, the surgeon was with them discussing the surgery Fox apparently was going to need, so I couldn't go in. Not my business. Instead I picked up a copy of the lab results at the nurse's station, left a message for Naomi that I'd been by and headed out.

The toxicology report shows only minute traces of meth in his system, meaning he likely barely took a hit. Just like he said. Thank God for that. But his alcohol levels had been far above the legal limit. I'm torn. Part of me wants to back off and call it lesson learned, given that the kid likely will have a lengthy reminder of his fuck up, and if it wasn't for the chat I had with Michael Vincent, the second boy we picked up that night, I might let it go at that.

Michael's involvement makes the whole thing a bit more complicated, though. Not only was he the one who brought the kid with the meth, but before I'd even gotten back to the station that night, his father was already raising a stink in my office. Young Michael turns out to be the son of Les Vincent, chairman of the Montezuma County Board and technically my boss.

When Frank left mid-term last year, the board appointed me Sheriff on an interim basis, to serve out his term until the next election. A local business man, Les has many years on the board and a fair amount of clout in the community, and I have no doubt he could make things difficult for me. Something he doesn't hesitate to point out the moment I walk in.

I fucking hate politics and I don't waste any time letting Les know I'm doing the job he appointed me to do—no more—no less—and that he's welcome to sit in while I ask his son a few questions.

Unfortunately, Michael isn't very forthcoming with information. Claims he didn't know the kid's name, only that he met him at the arcade earlier in the week and they struck up a conversation. It stinks to high heaven, but with Les looming in the room, there's little I can do to push for more, and I end up releasing the boy to his father's care, letting him know I'll be in touch to follow up. Something I aim to do soon.

Sick of being cooped up inside, I grab my hat and make for the door, when Carol stops me.

"Sheriff, call on line two."

Instead of walking back to my office, I grab the phone on the front desk.

"Morris."

"Sheriff Morris, this is Deb Blake. I'm a clerk at the Maricopa County Court. I understand you were interested in the listings of attorney James Miller on our docket?"

"Yes, I am."

"Sir, he was recently replaced on all active docket listings by one of his associates. A Mr. Frank Bancroft is now acting defense attorney on all open cases."

I take a minute to process before asking, "Can you tell me what the last case was Miller saw through trial?" I figure perhaps not a current case, but a prior one that hadn't worked out so well and left a disgruntled defendant, could have put Miller in the situation he appears to be in now.

I realize I'm grasping at straws until I hear the clerk's sharp intake of breath.

"Oh my, I didn't realize that was his."

"What's that?" I prompt.

"Sorry... A month and a half ago a key witness for the DA's office was found dead. He was scheduled to testify in court the next day in the murder trial of Tad Jackson. James Miller is Mr. Jackson's defense attorney. It caused a lot of unrest in the community, especially since just a week or two after that, following numerous attempts to delay by the District Attorney, Mr. Jackson was acquitted by a jury of his peers. What should have been an ironclad case became nothing but a collection of circumstantial evidence without the witness account to tie it all together. I can't believe I didn't place Mr. Miller's name sooner."

The clerk's chatty personality supplies me with some very interesting information. Judging by the timeline and the events, this may well have something to do with James' disappearance; voluntary or not.

I ask Deb if she can send over summaries of the court transcripts and thank her for the call, noting her name for future reference. It never hurts to make new friends in useful places.

"Carol, keep an eye out for a package from Maricopa County. It's personal. Just plop it in my office, will you?"

"Sure thing, Joe."

On my way out the door I wave at the almost seventy-year-old woman who's been running this office and the dispatch since I was in diapers. Carol has survived eight sheriffs and will most likely survive me as well. Her coffee is like engine oil, and will strip your eyelids off your eyes in a heartbeat thus serving its purpose, or so she says, and her grit and wisdom is unequalled. I love that woman. She makes coming into work every day that much better.

Dean Edwards offered me to scrub in on Fox's surgery, but I declined. In hindsight, the OR might've been less unnerving than the waiting room was. A humbling experience to say the least, to experience events on this side of the fence.

Half an hour into what was supposed to be at least a two-hour wait, I find myself too restless to stick around any longer and wander off to find some action in the ER, letting the nurse know where I'm off too and leaving my pager number.

It's been three days since Joe brought Fox in and the poor kid has been in agony the whole time. Dean showed up early the next morning and confirmed my suspicions that surgery would be necessary to stabilize his wrist, which appears to be broken in two different places, but was hesitant to schedule him any sooner than today because of his tox screens. With the residual effects of alcohol and meth in his system, he didn't want to subject him to anesthesia to soon, and opted to instead keep him hospitalized, and his system flushed with fluids before taking him to the OR this morning. Fox hasn't said much, except to apologize once again; this time I let him. He still won't open up about Phoenix, stubbornly turning his head whenever I bring it up, which is about every time he asks whether I've heard any news on his dad. Whatever happened is eating at him. Big time.

No word from Joe either, other than a message that he'd been by to pick up the lab report on Fox. I have to admit, I'm disappointed. I thought for sure we'd maybe turned a corner. Friendship sounded better than the cold war we'd been waging the past few years. Although it would be difficult keeping this damn persistent attraction to him under wraps, which had not waned one bit, not even when I hated his guts.

I swallow down the bitter edge of disappointment just as I turn the corner into the Emergency Room and bump right into the object of my musings.

"Joe..." escapes me, rather breathlessly, followed immediately by a betraying blush I can feel burning on my cheeks.

Joe holds me steady by the shoulders as he takes in my flushed face with a hint of a smile.

"Hey Doc, I was just coming to look for you." His deep rumble washes over me like a soothing balm.

"You were?"

"Heard from Stacy that Fox just went in for surgery. I'm sorry. I wanted to come by earlier, but got caught up with a phone call."

He rests his hand on my shoulder and the heat it generates radiates all the way through my body and sends an involuntary shiver down my spine. *Oh damn, Naomi. How inappropriate!*

"Were you on your way somewhere or can we sit down? I'd like to know about Fox and I have some stuff to share with you too."

"I was gonna kill some time in the ER but I have nowhere to be. I hate to say it, but how about a coffee at the cafeteria? Not my favorite place but I need to stick close by in case..."

"No need to explain. Let's go."

With his hand finding its way from my shoulder to the small of my back in one long stroke, setting off even more inappropriate bodily reactions, Joe guides me in the right direction.

On my second cup of coffee while toying with the remnants of my appropriately named 'Morning-glory' muffin, since it was starting to wreak havoc on my stomach, I try to tie in what Joe tells me with what I already know.

"So you're thinking that this murder trial James was working on may have somehow been the *'trouble'* he was referring to?"

"Look, I'm just guessing here, and I might know more once I've had a chance to look over the transcripts. But it seems highly coincidental that a high-profile murder trial, which goes completely off the rails after the suspicious death of a key witness, and the disappearance of the accused's defense attorney within days of the resulting acquittal, would not be connected somehow." Joe regards me carefully, gauging my reaction. I simply nod. Having him confirm my suspicions makes me feel better, even if he just painted a disturbing picture.

"I can see that. What I don't get is if you can see that, and I can see that; how come the Phoenix PD isn't seeing that? Especially when you add in the break-in around the same time?"

My mind is spinning with all the possible scenarios and frankly, it's scaring me to death. I've always known that James was sticking his neck out for some of the vilest creatures on God's earth, but he always preached that everyone deserved his day in court and I had to admit that I was of a mind that you were innocent until proven guilty. Most of the time. But then my mind jumped from murderers to Fox and the fear that his abrupt departure from Phoenix and these events also coincided, suddenly caught my breath.

"Doc? Naomi? What's wrong?" Joe's voice barely penetrates all the terrifying thoughts that are jumbling through my mind.

"Naomi. Look at me." The stern tone and the two firm hands grabbing hold of my face and bringing me nose to nose with him help me focus.

"Fox," I manage and I see confusion, then realization settles in Joe's eyes, right before he rests his forehead against mine.

"First we get him through surgery, then we have a talk with him. In the meantime I'm going to have a talk with Gus Flemming. There is only so much I can do on my own time and this is way out of my professional jurisdiction, but with his private security company he has much freer reign. Okay?"

He looks me in the eyes intently and even though I am now even more of a nervous wreck, I give him an affirmative nod. With a kiss on my forehead he releases me.

"Well, well, well. Isn't this sweet. Although a little tacky, I have to say, with your son in the operating room, to be sneaking off for a little private time with someone else's boyfriend. You're lucky I'm not the jealous type."

Oh, she did not just... I'm half out of my chair to deck our hospital administrator when Joe puts a firm hand on my shoulder and pushes me back down.

"Once again, Jenna... so out of line and far off the mark. Not to mention outrageously inappropriate and insulting to Naomi. Every time I think you couldn't possibly drop that bar any more, you manage to lower yourself even further. Don't you have any pride? Any fucking common decency? Nice display of professionalism for a hospital administrator. Oh, and a quick reminder—since you seem to need it—I am not, nor was I ever your boyfriend. If you have a beef with me, you take it up with me, but leave Naomi out of it." The venom is unmistakable as Joe's voice rises during his tirade in Jenna's face.

Jenna's face is turning beet-red and her mouth has dropped open, primed for a response surely. Her hand comes up and reaches for Joe's arm, but taking one look at the forbidding expression on his face, she drops it quickly, lifting her chin in the air instead. With a glare through slitted eyelids in my direction, she turns and marches straight out of the cafeteria, without another word. Joe sits back down in the chair beside me, running his hands through his hair.

"Jesus... I'm sorry, Doc."

I'm still reeling at the little shit storm that just played out in front of me, and suddenly the scene I walked into in the hallway a few weeks back comes through a little clearer. *Shit.*

"It's a like deja vu all over again, isn't it?" I try to lighten the sticky weight that's left behind, but the flare of Joe's eyes tells me I may have missed the mark. It's then I remember our dinner date a few years back, interrupted by his *wife* and I cringe. *Fuck me.*

"I meant to the run-in in the hallway a few weeks ago... I wasn't talking about... shit, Joe. Just let me get my boot off so my foot fits better in my mouth," I mumble, but Joe bursts out laughing.

"What's funny?"

"You. Us. This. It's all pretty messed up; like the universe is conspiring against us. Good thing I'm up for a challenge."

He grabs my hand and looks me straight in the eyes.

"Promise me, Doc, that I'll have a chance to explain everything to you. There never seems to be a good time, and now is not one either, but I really need a chance to clean the lines of communication. Starting with the history of my very *ex*-wife, Brenda."

I'm too rattled to do anything other than agree without argument. Too many questions are bouncing around and I really don't have time for this right now. I should have one focus only, and that's my son.

Joe promises he'll call or pop in later before walking me to the waiting room, where I am greeted by not one, but three sets of arms around me.

"Hey girl, we were wondering where you were off to. Thought it might've been an emergency, just didn't think it was one so *fine.*" Arlene throws her head back and laughs as Joe throws up his hands and backs out of the room, mouthing *'later'* at me. Emma is punching Arlene in the arm telling her to behave, while Katie gingerly lowers herself into a chair, trying to hold her big pregnant belly in place. My girls have come to hang with me.

I met Emma first when a truck tried to run her down in the streets of Cortez a couple of years ago and she was brought into the ER. She's married to Gus Flemming, owner of GFI, the security company Joe is hoping to call for help. Arlene is her best friend and owns the diner in Cedar tree. She had her own emergencies that brought her to the hospital, and even though I had met her through Emma already, she and I became closer then. Arlene belongs with Seb Griffin, amazing cook and co-owner of the diner. Not to mention a gorgeous walking art canvass of a man.

Katie is my special girl. She's pretty kick ass and worked free-lance as a private security specialist for GFI for years before she incurred a devastating brain injury that landed her in a wheelchair. Her road was long and dreadfully painful but she was able to regain almost full mobility with the help of an amazing man, and now husband, Caleb; with a bonus baby on the way.

These girls have all been through so much and yet have stayed so strong. They amaze me every day. I've never met a bunch of more loving and genuine women.

"I love you guys," I tell them through my tears, so very grateful for my friends.

CHAPTER FIVE

"Joe! Been a while. You here to see Gus? He's in the window booth."

Beth has been at the diner for about as long as I can remember. I remember crushing on her when I was a teenager, and my parents would bring me here for lunch on Sundays. She was working the kitchen then. My parents have both since died and the old owners of the diner left for warmer Florida years ago, selling the place to Arlene, even the diner itself is not the same after the renovations earlier this year. Heck my crush disappeared the same way my pimples had but Beth was still here. Still loud, still in your face and still always cheerful.

"Hey Beth, good to see you. Yeah, I'm meeting the big man. I'll just have a coffee and whatever Seb's cooked up for special today. I don't even need to know. Surprise me." I smile at her.

"Coming right up."

"Joe. How's life?"

Gus and I have been friends for over twenty years. As far back as the Denver Police Academy, when we were both new and bright-eyed recruits. We worked for the Denver Police Department for a few years as uniformed cops, before we both got fed up with big city politics. I found my way back to my home ground and into the Montezuma County Sheriff's Department and Gus ended up going private, doing security detail, investigations and bail skips from Grand Junction. He relocated to Cedar Tree in the last two years, moving his main office here, while leaving a small crew behind in Grand Junction.

"Complicated. How about yours?"

Gus laughs. "I hear you, man, although I can't complain. The last few months have been fairly quiet. I'm almost bracing for the next shit storm to hit."

Beth walks over and sets down my coffee. "Seb's got some fried rice thing for lunch. Indonesian. He calls it Nasi Goreng. I think he's making that shit up. You sure you still want some, Joe?"

"Sounds good to me. You order yet?" I ask Gus, chuckling.

"I'll have some of that stuff too, Beth, please?"

"Two Nasi Goreng coming up. Your funerals," she mumbles as she walks away, sticking her pencil behind her ear, as always.

"So, you mentioned something about needing my help?"

Gus never was one to beat around the bush so I quickly outline the events of the past couple of days, Naomi's description of the message left by her ex, and her findings from his place of work and the Phoenix PD. Then I tell him what I've come up with so far.

"I'm walking a fine line here, Gus. Aside from a very faint connection to a vandalism case that her son happens to be involved in, I have no business looking into this stuff in any official capacity. I've pushed the limit as far as I can by requesting the trial transcript be sent to my office, even if I asked them to be addressed to me personally and not the county sheriff. But something is off here. I can sense it, and that boy of hers knows something or saw something, but he won't open up to Doc.

I saw her this morning and she's terrified, though she hides it well."

"Doc, huh?" Gus lifts his eyebrows. "You finally set her straight? 'Bout fucking time you did. I still don't understand why you let that drag on for so long."

"Made a start but I wasn't gonna go there with her son in surgery, Gus. Made her promise to hear me out this time though."

He had been on my case for a long time, trying to get me to clear the air with Naomi, and being one of the very few people always aware of my situation, he's been frustrated. He finally gave up trying to push me but with Naomi becoming one of his wife's friends, I guess it must've been awkward at times. *Fuck.* Can't believe I never really considered that.

"I'll set it straight. This situation has gotten way out of hand. Sorry man."

Gus waves his hand.

"Just finally go get the damn girl."

"We're aiming for friends, Gus. Just friends," I emphasize, trying to ignore the part of me that's always craved more from her. The asshole across from me just snorts.

"Alright. So I will put out some feelers for you. Might be a couple of days, but we'll keep an eye out for your girl."

My glare doesn't have any impact on a snickering Gus. Asswipe.

The rest of our lunch is spent in relative quiet, eating this Nasi Goreng-shit Seb cooked up. Rice, chicken, diced vegetables, fragrant with spices and spicy enough to leave a nice glow, topped up with a fried egg. Damn that's good.

I tag Beth to get me an order for takeout; I'm thinking dinner tonight.

I'm halfway to my office, when I spot Michael Vincent, the kid we picked up with Fox at Crow Canyon, running across the road and into Cortez City Park. I look at my dashboard clock and see it's just one forty-five in the afternoon. No way in hell he's done with school already and the high school is on the other side of the Walmart Plaza. I check for traffic and cross the lanes, pulling into North Park Street where I know kids like to hang out at the water fountains. Parking my truck, I can see Michael meeting up with two others just outside the washrooms and duck inside. Fucking kid. I knew he was into some shit. I quickly radio in to Carol who will send a head's up to the Cortez PD, but I'm not waiting around.

Just as I get to the public washrooms, the door slams open and the two unknowns take off running. I'm tempted to pursue, but am more concerned with Michael, who's not coming out. When I push open the door, I see him lying curled up under the sink, in a rapidly spreading pool of blood.

"Jesus!"

"Carol!" I yell into my radio, "Got a kid down. Get an ambulance down here, STAT!" before dropping down and scanning the boy for injuries. The garbled moaning coming from his battered face is encouraging. He's still alive at least. I try to calm him down.

"Michael. Ambulance is on the way, buddy. You're gonna be ok, I've got you."

But I'm questioning the truth of my own words when he tries to roll back and I see the large hunting knife stick out of his abdomen.

I call Carol back on the radio. "Carol. Get hold of Les Vincent and tell him I'm bringing his son in to the ER. Have him meet us there. Make sure you talk only to him. No messages."

"Oh Joe... Yes, yes of course I will." A smart woman with too much experience, Carol knows exactly what it is I'm not saying. I don't know if this boy is gonna make it.

I manage to change into a spare shirt I carry in my truck, before Les storms into the ER, but there's nothing I can do about his son's blood spatter all over my uniform pants. He takes one look at me and freezes on the spot, all color draining from his face.

"Hey... They're taking care of him, Les." I'm trying to reach him but he seems to be stuck staring at the fucking blood on my pants. "Les! Snap out of it man. Michael is alive and they are working on him; okay?"

No matter how much I dislike the guy, this is not something I'd wish on anyone, so I walk up to him and carefully grab his arm, guiding him over to the waiting area.

"What happened?" His voice cracks and he needs to clear his throat.

I tell him exactly what I saw, not leaving out a single detail. I also explain that since this happened within Cortez town limits, it will likely be a Cortez PD investigation, but that we'd probably join forces if it turns out this was in any way connected to the incident up on Crow Canyon. His eyes flick to mine at the mention and he quickly looks away again.

"I'll never forgive myself if that turns out to be the case," he says quietly.

"What are you saying?"

"I warned him not to talk to you, not to get in the middle of an investigation with an election year coming up next year. Maybe if I'd have let him talk..."

I interrupt him here, "Look, you don't know that. First focus right now is your son and you can't afford to waste time on guilt. He needs you. So focus."

"Right. Okay." He seems to get himself together just as one of Naomi's colleagues comes into the waiting area.

"Sheriff?"

"Yes, this is Les Vincent, Michael's father."

"Good. Mr. Vincent, your son has some facial trauma that we are not as concerned with right now as we are with the injury to his abdomen. An ultrasound shows that the knife has done substantial damage to some of his organs and he is bleeding into his abdominal cavity as well. We have to operate on him to see the extent of the damage and repair what we can. The OR is being prepped and the anesthesiologist is ready for us. All we need is your consent."

"Yes, do whatever you need to do to save him. Can I see him before?" The man is close to his breaking point, and as he walks away with the attending doctor, my heart aches for him.

"Mom?"

Fox's raspy voice pulls me from my thoughts.

"Hey, baby. How are you feeling?"

He's been slowly waking up from the anesthetic for a few minutes now, struggling to cling to consciousness.

His surgery took a little longer than expected and by the time Dean came to give me a report in the surgical waiting room, I was starting to get a bit worried. Luckily the girls were doing their best to keep me distracted. The delay had been caused by some bone shards that had travelled, and needed to be removed before he could properly set the bones and affix the plate and screws to keep everything in place. Fox might have to have another surgery in a month or two to remove them again, once the bone has sufficiently healed, but for now he was good to go. The girls left with promises to check in later when I come to see Fox in recovery.

"Sore... Thirsty..." he croaks.

"The thirst we'll call the nurse in for, she's in charge of your medication, but I can give you a bit of water."

I push the call button to get one of the nurses' attention and bend the straw in the water cup so he can take a sip.

"Not too much at once, love. You don't want to bring it back up," I caution him when he starts gulping it down.

When the curtain around us opens, I expect it to be one of the two attending nurses, but am surprised to find Jenna poking her head in.

Seriously?

"What can I do for you, Jenna?" I know I sound bitchy, but come on. After this morning's scene in the cafeteria, I thought for sure she'd leave me the hell alone.

"Just wanted to inform you of a change to the schedule you may have missed. You're on overnights, starting at nine tonight. And also, that request for time off? I'm afraid that won't be possible on such short notice."

At that she pulls the curtain shut and disappears, leaving me stunned. Then I get mad and am about to haul ass after her when Fox pipes up beside me.

"She just fucked you over, didn't she Mom?" his voice still raspy from drugs. "What did you do to her?"

"First of all, watch your mouth and secondly, I'm breathing, and that apparently ticks her off. I have no idea, Fox, but I'll fix it. Get some rest."

I put my head down on the bed beside his hand and close my eyes, fighting the urge to cry. Fox was coming home tomorrow and I had planned on spending a week at home with him. I should have plenty of vacation time banked, but I guess our wretched hospital administrator is intent on making my life even more difficult. It's ok. I can deal. I've dealt with other people's shit all my life; this isn't new. I just need a few minutes to pull back from this looming depression I feel myself sliding into. Once I do that, I can tackle anything again. *Right.*

I feel fingers scratching my skull and know it's Fox. He used to do this a lot when he was little, run his little fingers in my hair and scrape the fingertips over my scalp. Even as a toddler it was his way to soothe himself... and maybe me. *Oh baby.*

"What's wrong with her?" Joe's voice stops the fingers on my head and I miss their magic already.

When I lift my head, he's crouched down beside me, his hand on my knee and his face so close, it wouldn't take much to put my lips on his. *Jesus.*

"I'm ok, Joe," I answer before Fox has a chance to say anything.

"You're sad."

"Nah. Just a little worn, that's all."

"Why don't you go home for a bit?"

"Can't. Your girlfriend just informed me not five minutes ago, she changed the schedule so I have to work overnight, starting at nine tonight. Not to mention she nixed my time off to look after Fox so I'll have to make some sort of arrangement for that." I can't help the bitter bite in my tone, thinking he is at least in a small part responsible for pissing the bitch off. But when he drops his head down looking like the weight of the world is resting on his shoulders, I feel guilty for laying it on so thick.

"I'm sorry, I..."

"No. Don't apologize, although she never was, nor will she ever be, my girlfriend. I do take full responsibility for not seeing her for the vindictive shrew she is sooner. I'm sorry to have put you in this position. Let me talk to her, I—"

I stop him. I'm not about to let him do that. It would only make things worse.

"Don't think so Joe. You jumping in for me one more time would only add fuel to the flames. No thanks. I'll handle it," I say with much more conviction than I feel.

"What brought you back here anyway?"

His eyes flick over to Fox before coming back to me. "I was planning to check in on you guys anyway at some point, but eh... there was an incident in the park earlier and Michael Vincent, the other boy we picked up at Crow Canyon the other night? He was injured."

My hand automatically seeks out Fox's, which is clenched in the sheet.

"What happened?" Fox almost whispers.

"He was attacked at the public washrooms in the City Park. It's pretty serious, bud, but he's in good hands now and I'll keep you up to date. Promise. Listen, I know you just got out of surgery and I'm not going to bug you now, but do you think maybe tonight, before your mom starts her shift, I could come back and talk to you? I know you told me as much as you could that night, but I know a few more things now, and would like to pass those by you. Think that'd be okay?"

Joe looks at me, even though the question is directed at Fox and I see deep concern etched there. My balanced life is just crumbling to dust between my fingers when I realize his concern is for my son. I nod my assent.

"I need your mom for a sec. Promise she'll be right back."

With a small nod in the direction of the hallway, he indicates he wants me to follow. I turn to Fox, try to give him a reassuring smile and a quick kiss on the top of his head.

"Two clicks, Bub."

Out in the hallway, Joe pulls me in a quiet corner where he grabs my shoulders.

"Michael was severely beaten and stabbed. They have him in surgery but he's critical. I saw the two guys going into the washroom with him, and also saw them run out. One of them was there at Crow Canyon, Doc. Fox has seen him, knows him, has talked to him. We need to make sure Fox stays safe."

CHAPTER SIX

"Hey, honey! So glad you're coming to stay with us. Finally someone who I hope will appreciate my cooking."

"Shut it, woman. Don't tell me I don't appreciate your cooking; in the past two years you've grown me a potbelly."

Fox finally cracks a smile, even though his face has read thunder since he found out we would be staying with Emma and Gus for a while.

Between my new schedule change and the myriad of uncertainties in our lives right now, settling in under the roof of a well-known security specialist gives me some peace of mind. Well... technically we'll be in the guesthouse and Fox will be there alone overnight, which is partly why we are doing this. I wasn't going to send Fox to school this coming week anyway, since he is still recovering and when Joe suggested moving in with us, or us moving in with him, I had to put my foot down. No way. Too close for comfort. I'm just getting used to talking to the man again, let alone having to share my morning coffee with him, or God forbid, having to watch him parade around the house half naked after a shower. Yes, my mind just went there. *Fuck.* Anyway, the guesthouse at Gus and Emma's had been refuge for quite a few of our friends already, so it felt okay to accept the offer when it came last night. Both Gus and Joe feel that with the attack on Michael, as well as the question marks around James' disappearance, this is the safest route, until we have more answers.

Emma already had Fox set up on their huge sectional couch with a plate of muffins that he was eagerly chowing down on.

"Slow down, Bub. You just started eating solids this morning. The bathroom in the guesthouse is something special I hear, but not hanging around the toilet bowl, I'm sure."

A roll of his eyes, but my kid isn't stupid; he knows I have a point and leaves it with the one muffin, putting the plate with the rest of them on the coffee table.

"Didn't know you had a go at the shower in the guesthouse too?" Emma snickers when I walk into the kitchen on the hunt for a cup of coffee.

"Shut up, you awful woman!" I laugh at her. "I never did, but one hears things; doctor privilege and all that."

"Oh phooey. You are no fun. Everybody's *done* that shower. That's why Gus had it put in."

I stick my fingers in my ears and blow raspberries at her.

"What did I put where?" Gus asks as he wraps his arms around his wife with a chuckle.

"Hush, we've got kids in the house."

"You are unbelievable Emma. You started with the sex shower and now you're scolding Gus?" I smile at her.

"Hello! Right here... and eh, not so sure I want to even have a shower in this amazing bathroom at this point," Fox pipes up from the living room, where he obviously was able to follow the discussion word for word. We look at each other and burst out laughing.

I'll have to get used to not driving to my house after my shift, which I almost do this morning. The night was relatively quiet, as weeknights often are, so I was able to check on Michael. I've never met the kid but Fox said he was 'okay,' which in sixteen-year-old speak is a seal of approval. He made it through his surgery, now minus a spleen and a portion of his liver, but he can grow old without those. Lucky kid. So far, no signs of infection which is the next major concern to look out for since his bowels were nicked and there was waste in his abdominal cavity. He was put on intravenous antibiotics right away and is being monitored very closely.

Joe never managed to come back to question Fox, but called me yesterday to let me know he would be by today. Things were hectic, he said. I bet. It's not everyday someone is attacked so violently in the middle of the day in Cortez. He sounded tired.

I love this drive to Cedar Tree. After exiting the 160 and turning onto County Road G, the scenery immediately changes. My thoughts immediately start wandering to the occasional chats I've had with Kendra about basing a clinic in Cedar Tree. I hadn't actually considered moving in that direction for quite a while yet, but given the atmosphere at the hospital and the shitty shift changes I've been handed, I'm thinking maybe I should keep my eyes open for opportunities. Maybe I could see how Kendra would feel about actually moving forward on those plans. Sure, it would mean getting Fox back and forth to school in Cortez, but that shouldn't be too difficult to manage.

With my mind going a mile a minute, before I know it, I'm pulling into the driveway to Gus and Emma's house, and the guesthouse that is our home for at least the next week. I'm surprised to see Joe's truck sitting out front. It's barely nine thirty in the morning.

I take the path alongside the house to the back, where the guesthouse is located and find the door unlocked. Fox must be up and about. A quick check in the bedroom confirms he is gone. Probably at the main house being stuffed by Emma. She has a tendency to love everyone to death with food. Not that you'll hear much complaining; she's a good cook and a kick-ass baker. Bakes all the pastries for the diner, since Seb prefers to stick to cooking and is happy to leave the muffins and pies to Emma.

Fox and I share the bedroom, since the guesthouse only has one. With me working overnights, we don't have to get in each other's way. I don't mind sleeping on the couch either, if it comes to that, because Emma and Gus have a thing for huge sectionals. There is one in the living room here too.

Stripping out of my scrubs, I grab a clean towel, toss it on the vanity and turn on the hot water in the shower. The infamous shower. Shower heads coming out of the walls in all directions make for a full-body massage and what was supposed to be a quick rinse, turns into a much longer session, with me moaning and groaning at the effect the jets of water have on my tired and aching muscles. When my stomach starts rumbling from hunger, I reluctantly get out, dry off and dress in some comfy yoga pants and a tee. Wet hair still up in a towel, I walk out of the bedroom, only to be startled by Joe standing in the middle of the living room.

"Oh, wow, you scared me."

"Yeah. I could tell you didn't know anyone else was here," he says with a smirk on his face and a pointed look toward the bathroom.

"What do you mean? I was just..." Suddenly it hits me. "How long have you been standing here?"

"Long enough."

"I... I was just... I wasn't... Ahhh! I was just enjoying a relaxing shower!" With every stammer, he starts chuckling harder until finally I pull the wet towel off my head and toss it at him when he starts laughing out loud. *Bastard.*

"Easy there, Doc. Assaulting an officer of the law with a wet towel is not helping your case."

"Oh shut up, you ape."

"Mom? Sheriff Morris?" Fox walks in and throws me a worried look that gets me laughing.

"Nothing, Bub. We're just goofing around." I risk a quick glance in Joe's direction, who still wears a smug grin but has lost some of the sultry fire in his eyes.

"That for me?" I point to the plate Fox carries in his hand.

"Oh. Yeah, Emma loaded some food up for you. Man, she cooks a ton."

"That she does," Joe says, "and she does it well too, but always for an orphanage. Hope you don't mind gaining a few pounds, 'cause I can guarantee you will."

"No thanks," I jump in, "my body carries plenty already. I'll try and avoid her kitchen."

"I wouldn't mind bulking up a bit. Dad said I'm too skinny."

I look at Fox and see a hint of sadness in his face. Was this something James did to Fox too? Put him down? And on physical appearance? Fuck, that hurts my heart. To think I voluntarily let him walk into that.

I can sense Joe looking at me from the corner of his eye, before he turns to Fox. "You know, there's a really good gym not too far from your school I sometimes work out at. Not like those big chain gyms where all you see is rows of machines. This is much smaller, with a few guys that help out with training programs and keeping you on track. Even some punching bags and a ring, if you're interested in trying some mixed martial arts, you know? A bit of everything."

Fox's eyes had shown increasing interest as Joe was talking, but at the last minute his face shut down.

"Not for me," he muttered avoiding Joe's gaze. Besides, you have to be eighteen to sign up for those places."

I'm just picking at the plate of breakfast, sitting back to see how this is going to play out, because for years I've wanted Fox to do something physical, something athletic, but whenever I've suggested anything, it's been shot down. Looks like maybe Joe's suggestion was going to go the same route.

Joe throws me a little wink. "You've got a point, but I know the owner of this place, and he's ok with underage guys as long as they come with supervision." Before Fox has a chance to interrupt, Joe adds, "And it just so happens I go three times a week, usually around four or so in the afternoon, before it gets too busy. It's nice and quiet but frankly, I tend to have trouble finding a spotter. So you'd probably be doing me a favor if you tagged along once or twice. When you're feeling better of course. Although, you could get started on your legs I guess. But... I totally get it. If it's not your thing, it's not your thing." And with that he turns his back to Fox and faces me, a little smile playing at the corner of his mouth.

"Were you going to eat all that?" He points at my plate.

"Nope. I've picked at it enough. Have at it." I smile. Smart man. Over his shoulder, I can see the wheels in Fox's head turning, while Joe leisurely finishes off Emma's breakfast.

"You know..." Fox starts, "I could probably help you out a couple of times a week. After school or something? If you really need a hand."

I have to turn around to hide the smile on my face.

"Yeah. That'd be great. How about we see about next week? Just so you can have a look around, get comfortable with the place. We'll sort the details later." Joe is very low key in his approach and I marvel at how a man who, by all accounts, has never been a parent, can be so smart at handling the most difficult of ages with such ease. When he looks up at me I mouth a 'Thank you,' and am rewarded with another wink.

"Now on to a much less pleasant subject before your mom hits the sack. I don't know if she told you how Michael got hurt? I never got into details when you were in recovery."

"She said he was stabbed by a couple of guys in the park."

"Beaten severely and then stabbed in the stomach, yes. And he is very lucky. According to your mom, he came through surgery ok and as long as he can fight off any infection, he should be ok. His face will heal too. But Fox, these guys? I saw them. I saw them come out of the washroom and run off, and from what I could tell, at least one of them was at Crow Canyon with you guys."

All color seems to drain from Fox's face and I hurry to sit next to him on the couch and put my arm around him.

"What... Who?" he stammers.

"Well, that's where I need your help. I didn't get a great look at all of them down at the dig, but you would have. So if I describe the kids who were in the park with Michael, can you tell me if you've seen them before? Either at Crow Canyon or even somewhere else?"

"Not sure I want to... " Fox is suddenly quiet in his response and Joe sits down on his other side, but I jump in first.

"Look, Bub. I get it. I get you don't like to squeal. Hell, you probably don't want to talk after what happened to Michael, but the reality is, those guys know you were picked up, just like Michael. If they were afraid Michael was going to talk, you would be just as much of a threat already too. Baby, I'm not trying to scare you on purpose, but I also don't want you to stick your head in the sand and tell yourself that as long as you stay quiet you'll be ok. Keeping this kind of stuff to yourself is never a good idea. Let Sheriff Morris do his job, Bub. Please?"

"And you can call me Joe, but your mom is right. I can't do much without your help."

"Is that why we had to come here?" Fox wants to know looking at me. "You think they'll come after me? That's just great." He sinks back in the couch and runs his hand through his dark brown hair, in need of a cut. He looks scared with a wide-eyed glance in my direction, as if hoping to find the answers with me. But his problems aren't a scraped knee or a bad dream this time. I'm as lost as he is and am relieved when Joe jumps in.

"Look," Joe points out, "I don't know anything for sure at this point. Certainly not until I've had a chance to talk to Michael, which will hopefully be sometime today, but it would be smart to be a bit more cautious."

"I guess, although I'm not sure what else I can tell you about the guy I haven't already told you."

A bit of defiance returned to his demeanor and I was almost glad to see it instead of the worried and dejected look on his face. Joe just chuckles.

"I'll ask and you just answer what you know. You'll be surprised how far we get."

My questions start simple with clothes, a print on a T-shirt he might remember, brand of shoes; those kinds of things, before moving to actual physical descriptions. By that time, Fox is so concentrated on details, he's able to provide a much clearer description of the guy than he did a few days ago in the hospital.

"Wow. I can't believe I knew all that. Cool."

"It's an easy trick. When you ask someone for a description of anything; a person, a book, a movie, their brain often doesn't know how to sort through all the information it has stored, but when you break it up into smaller sections and then collect all the bits at the end, you get a more complete picture. What we have now is a young man wearing Etnie skate shoes, dark blue with grey lettering, worn jeans with a chain hanging from his belt loop to his pocket, a dark old Creed shirt, has short-cropped dark blond to brown hair, light colored eyes, and is somewhere between eighteen and twenty. Oh, and likely around five foot ten or eleven, because you said you could look him straight in the eye. I'm guessing that's your height?" I ask him.

Fox nods with the hint of a smile on his face.

"So is it? The same guy, I mean."

Damn. He isn't gonna let me get away like I'd hoped, and from the eager look on Naomi's face, neither is she.

"Sounds like one of them. Down to the T-shirt actually," I grudgingly admit. "Now the other guy I saw also had dark hair, but it was a bit longer, and he looked Hispanic. Also was a little lankier. He had a goatee, looked to be early twenties to me. Was wearing a football jersey and I could barely tell what kind of pants he had on, they were hanging so low; I think they may have been dark jeans. Know anyone who wears his jeans around his knees?"

Fox chuckles, and I have to say I like hearing that; the kid is in a potential shit load of trouble and I think he knows it. And we haven't even started on the events in Phoenix yet.

"No," he says, "I'd remember."

"Okay, good. Now I have one more thing," I look at Naomi to see if she is falling asleep on me, but she still seems to be hanging in, curled up in a corner of the couch but quiet and attentive, keeping a close eye on her son. "Gus and I are trying to help you and your mom find out a little bit more about where your dad might have gone and there are a few things I'd like to know."

There is hesitancy in the look Fox throws me, but I push on.

"See, there was this case your dad was working on. A rather high-profile case that hit the newspapers at some point. It's the last one he worked on before he disappeared and we're trying to figure out if it's somehow connected. One of the witnesses died during the trial and it caused quite an uproar. Did your dad ever mention anything at home?"

I can pinpoint the moment when Fox shuts down. His eyes glance over to his mom quickly before coming back to me and at the mention of the death of the witness, I see fear before he averts them.

"Can't remember. Never paid much attention to his work," he says pushing up from the couch. "I'm gonna lie down now though, I'm beat."

Won't talk. He knows something, has heard or seen something but fear is holding him back. Must be something substantial, but I've pushed the kid enough for one day.

"That's ok, buddy. You did good and I'm glad for your help."

"Want me to come check on you in a bit?" Naomi asks.

"Nah, I'm good." And with that he disappears into the bedroom, shutting the door behind him.

CHAPTER SEVEN

Naomi lays her head back on the couch and groans.

"How did we get into this, Joe? I mean a year ago I thought everything was starting to balance out, work and Fox, living here. Heck, even the temporary rebellion and moving to live with his dad seemed like a small glitch, something we'd be able to iron out. But now I find out James was belittling Fox too…I can't let that happen. Not only that, but fuck, look at the outcome; I should never have let him go. God this is all kinds of fucked up and I feel totally useless."

I don't say anything, just lift her feet in my lap and start working my thumbs into her insteps. The moans coming from her mouth don't do anything for the growing pole in my uniform pants and I carefully shift her feet in my lap.

"You're a great mother, Doc. You're letting him grow up. A lot of parents don't give their children the chance. Sure, the knocks can be hard and he's run into some shit that neither of you are responsible for, but you're here ready to catch him, to support him. Not pressuring, or suffocating him, but allowing him to make the right decisions on his own. That takes a lot of guts on your part, and will go a long way to making him into the decent man I'm convinced he will be. Give yourself some credit. We'll sort this stuff out; I promise. And keep him safe in the meantime."

I'm so focused on her cute toes, I almost miss the muffled sniff. When I turn to look at her, I see two big deep brown eyes full of tears looking back at me. *Well shit.*

"Thank you..." Her chin wobbles and the first tear rolls down her cheek. Ah damn. I cup her cheek and brush it away.

"I seem to be crying around you a lot," she smiles through her tears, making me chuckle, and just like that my dick is trying to show me who's boss again and I'm fighting the urge to take her in my arms. Not the right time to go there; not without clearing the air first. And what better time than right now?

"I had a crush on Brenda all through high school but she never paid me any attention." At the mention of Brenda's name, Naomi tries to pull her feet from my lap, but I hold them fast, continuing to stroke my thumbs down her soles.

"She was your typical, popular girl; a cheerleader, homecoming queen and I was just a scrawny kid with pimples who sucked at sports. After high school, I left for the Denver Police Academy and worked for the Denver PD for a few years. That's where I first met Gus. When I decided the big city wasn't for me and returned to Cortez to join the Montezuma County Sheriff's Office. I was ready to settle down. At least that's what I told myself when I bumped into Brenda again. I had bulked up some over the years and my face had cleared up… Brenda hadn't changed much; she was still a knock out. I was pumped she showed interest and was in a hurry to tie her down. Two months later we were married… but it took me about as long after to realize my mistake. By then, Brenda was pregnant and more than anything I wanted a family, so I stuck in. I figured maybe motherhood would settle down her erratic behavior, the mood swings, her tendency to get physical. I was deluding myself. She lost the baby while staying with a friend for a few days, while I was working an important case. We tried again after, but she never was able to get pregnant again. Her behavior became even more outrageous than before, and I ended up hiding in work to escape the house…the constant fighting."

I rub the back of my neck, not looking forward to the next part. This is where it gets painful, but I'm determined to clear the air.

"One day I came home late from a shift to find a party in full swing at the house. People all over the place, none of whom I'd ever seen before, drunk—trashing my house. I was livid. Brenda was half-naked dancing on the coffee table. We had a huge fight and somewhere in there she blurted out she hadn't had a miscarriage, that she'd aborted our baby…that she never wanted to be tied down with a kid."

I take a deep breath against the sting of opening up that wound again. *Fuck.*

"Oh my God, Joe. I'm so sorry..." Naomi whispers, her hand clapped over her mouth.

I clench my jaw to get through this hardest part of the story without losing it.

"She had gone to a clinic while staying with her friend, who had chosen to cover for her. I have never hurt a woman, could never hurt a woman, but in that moment, I wanted to kill her, I swear. Kicker is, she not only had the abortion, she had her tubes tied at the same time too… That did it for me. I walked out; told her I was filing for divorce."

I feel Naomi's hand sneaking into mine, but I keep my eyes straight ahead. I don't think I've ever gone so far as to tell this entire sordid tale to anyone in such detail. Not even Gus knows all the bits and pieces. If I want to move forward though, I have to clear up the past. Leave it behind.

"That was her first suicide attempt. I got a call from the hospital. She'd been found by a downstairs neighbor when water started leaking through the ceiling. She was in the tub with her wrists cut. She went into a six week inpatient treatment facility where she was diagnosed with BPD, borderline personality disorder. It was only the first time, there were several more. Brenda lost her parents fairly young and had no remaining family; it was difficult to turn my back on her."

I turn to face her on the couch, and see I've made her cry again. Wonderful. Grabbing both of her hands, I look her in the eyes because it's the next part she really needs to hear.

"When I met you, I had been living on my own for four years, just flying under the radar and keeping my peace. I'd check in on Brenda. She was still living in the same apartment. I would do stuff for her if something needed fixing, but generally tried to steer clear of the rest. She was unstable though. She would go off her meds constantly. I never dated." I squeeze her hands in mine to make sure she hears me clearly. "Oh, I'd hook up from time to time—I'm not ashamed to admit—but mostly out of town, far away and preferably as anonymous as possible. Sleazy, I know," I add when I see her wince, "but it worked for me at the time. Until I met you, and all rational thought seemed to disappear. Doc, I was so far gone over you, I wasn't thinking straight. Or I would never have risked taking you out to a restaurant in town, when you finally agreed to a date with me. Brenda seems to have a sixth sense when my attention is taken up by someone else. She had become needier from the moment I started making a play for you. I knew I shouldn't have mentioned I was out for dinner when she called me on the way to the restaurant, but I wasn't thinking. I was just eager to get to our date. It also never occurred to me to explain my situation to you. Stupid. I know that now. But other than Gus, nobody really knew I was still married. Hell, I'd forgot most of the time. It was nothing but a mere piece of paper that only existed because every time I wanted to put an end to it, Brenda would go off the deep end. There were also her medical expenses to consider. It just became a status quo I learned to live with. When she stormed into the restaurant and put me on the spot, I should've said something; shouldn't have let you run out like that, but Brenda was in a manic state, making a scene and I was torn. Believe me, there hasn't been a day in the past three years that I haven't regretted that spur of the moment decision. I hate that the opportunity I thought I would have to set things straight and explain my situation to you, never materialized."

And just like that, Naomi is up and off the couch and out the door in her bare feet, and she's…running. Whoa, where the hell is she going? *FUCK.*

By the time I get out there, Emma has her head out the backdoor of her house.

"Is she alright? Did something happen?"

"Nothing I can't fix, Emma."

"If you say so," she says with a smile.

Turning the other way, I can just see her disappearing into the cornfield behind the house. *Jesus, girl.* I take off after her, before she gets too far.

But she doesn't. About ten steps into the corn, I find her on her knees in the dirt, curled over, just ripping my heart up with her crying. In two seconds flat, I'm down in the dirt with her on my lap, secured in my arms, and despite the fact that she sounds like her heart is breaking, mine feels oddly at peace for the first time in a long time.

"Naomi, babe, look at me," I try to coax her face up but she just burrows it further into my neck, so I just rub her back and let her ride it out.

"I'm just gonna finish my story here then, because there's something more you should know, honey. That incident in the restaurant and you walking away was a good thing."

When she shakes her head in my neck and mumbles, "I was stupid—" I stop her.

"It was a *good* thing. Wanna know why? 'Cause it made me realize even if I was ready for a relationship emotionally on some levels, I wasn't on others and not near ready enough from a practical point of view, that's for fucking sure. It took me a year after to work toward a divorce with Brenda with the help of a psychiatrist. She still ended up having to be hospitalized for a while, but has been living in Boulder in a supported living facility for the past year now and even works. She's the one who ended up wanting to move away to start fresh. If not for you, Doc, I would still be living in limbo. I'll be forever grateful to you for that."

The shuddering has stopped underneath my hand that was stroking her back and I move it to the back of her head and urge it back so I can look at her. Even wet-faced, red-nosed and blotchy, she still takes my breath away.

"I must look a mess," she mumbles.

"Yes, you do," I smile, and when I see her mouth fall open I add, "but you're still a gorgeous mess."

The smile still on my lips, I bend down to fit them over hers, tasting the salt of her tears. The slight hitch in her breathing spurs me on to lick my way into her mouth and her full-bodied flavor hits me like a fist to the gut. Deep, visceral and with an involuntary physical response that has me groan my passion into her mouth. The feel of her arms sliding around my neck as she moves around to straddle me, and the slight tug of her fingers in my hair, has my hips rolling underneath her. Christ, I can feel her moist heat through the fabric of my uniform slacks. Our tongues tangle and slide, probing and teasing. The fresh scent of the corn, the earth, Naomi's soap and her warm arousal stimulates every last one of my senses. I find myself with a hand under her T-shirt, palming her plump breast, wanting to draw it in my mouth as deep as I can suck it, but not wanting to let go of the intense fusion of our mouths. The feel of her soft flesh in my hand makes me want to roll her over, right here in the dirt, and strip her of all her clothes. And just then…my fucking phone rings.

"Morris," I croak out, barely remembering my name as I reluctantly release her luscious mouth and manage to pull out my cell. Any other time, I would've ignored it, but I am technically working. Not that anyone would know, by looking at me right now.

"Sheriff, it's Carol. Got a call from Les Vincent; Michael's awake."

"Thanks Carol, I'll head straight over there. Be in after."

Naomi has crawled off my lap and is standing in front of me—flush bright on her face and chest—straightening her clothes. I stand in front of her and pull her close.

"That exploded way faster than I had hoped for," I tell her.

"Uh... that was *very* friendly, for *just friends*."

"Yes. I don't think the 'just friends' label is gonna work out so well for us. What do you think?"

She squirms a little in my arms and keeps her eyes downcast. "I'm... I can't deny you do all kinds of things to me Joe. I mean, I about mounted you just now, but so much is happening at once. And I... what you told me... the time wasted. I just need to catch up. I haven't slept in going on twenty hours and I'm scared, turned on and exhausted. I don't know what to feel right now and if I don't see a bed soon, I'm gonna cry again."

"Fair enough, Doc. Let's get you to bed. I have to run and see if I can get my mind off you and on some work anyway."

I walk Naomi back to the guesthouse, pop inside to grab my hat and give her a quick kiss before heading out. In my truck, I try to focus on the upcoming questions I have for Michael Vincent, and how best to approach him. It serves to be a difficult task though, not to replay this morning's events. I think about how I managed to coax Fox out of his shell a few times and got him to give up more information than he thought he had or wanted to part with. About how good it felt to finally, after three years of pent up frustration, be able to clear the air with Naomi.

And I think about how close I came to fucking her in the dirt, in the middle of a cornfield, on a weekday morning.

CHAPTER EIGHT

"Aww, Mom, why'd you have to go and pick up homework? I'm so close to beating this level of 'Call of Duty' one-handed."

Walking in the door from my fifth consecutive twelve-hour overnight shift, and a stop at Fox's high school to pick up some work for him so he can try and keep up a little, I am not in the mood. I'm tired, and cranky, having had to deal with filling someone else's shift, who had a 'family emergency' last night. The irony of it didn't escape me. Jenna's smirk this morning as I passed her at the nurse's station, exhausted and I'm sure bedraggled on my way out the door, was proof enough the vindictive bitch was out to run me down.

"Fox. Please don't argue. If you feel good enough to play on your Xbox all day long, surely you can find some time in your busy schedule to try and keep up with a bit of schoolwork. Or are you willing to blow off an entire year for the sake of a stupid mistake?"

Low blow, I know, but I have no patience right now for calm negotiations. I feel bad though, when I see guilt mark his face, before he puts down his controller and picks the folder up off the coffee table where I dropped it. I walk over and drop a kiss on his hair, and try to soften the sting of my words. "I just don't want you to get so far behind that it's going to take too much to catch up again, Bub. Easier to do a little bit now and then, than it will be to try and tackle it all at once when you get back."

"Yeah, I know, Mom," he agrees softly, leaning back into my touch. "I brought you back some breakfast from Emma's."

"Thanks, baby, but I'm so tired. I'm half-asleep on my feet. I think I'm going to try and get a few hours in now. Off the next two days before I go on afternoon shifts. So I'm going to try and adjust my sleeping routine."

"Wow. She really has you flipping on a dime, doesn't she?" My son is nothing if not observant. "What's her problem anyway?"

"Don't know." I'm not about to share with my child that I think the hospital administrator is jealous of me over the town Sheriff. Nope. Gonna keep that one to myself. "I do know that I'm seriously thinking of making a move forward on those plans I had for the distant future."

"You talking about that clinic idea? The one with Kendra?"

"Thinking about it."

"But Mom..." How a sixteen-year-old, who already has gone through a substantial voice change can sound like a whiny child is beyond me, but there it is.

"Bub, don't worry about it now, okay? We'll talk about it when I get up. I have two whole days to spend with you. Isn't that wonderful?" I joke, ruffling my hand through his hair.

All he does is roll his eyes at me before I blow him a kiss and take myself to bed.

The past few days have been a little surreal. I'm out of my element; living out of a suitcase in Gus and Emma's guesthouse, not having my own stuff around me. No regular schedule, so I feel like I'm flying by the seat of my pants most of the time. And Fox is home so there isn't even his schedule to depend on, to help keep me grounded. I feel adrift and sinking. It doesn't help that I haven't seen Joe since our little escapade in the cornfield. Good grief what an explosion of pent up frustration that was. All wrapped in about two minutes of lips and hands, but two minutes that left a deep impression. A deep craving for much, much more of *that*. But despite a phone call to let me know he had received some good information from Michael and would likely be busy until he had a handle on these guys, there hadn't been much from him. A daily drag into work, which is becoming more and more taxing—despite the love I have for my job—and one trip to Arlene's Diner with Fox, to meet Katie and Caleb for dinner before I had to leave for Cortez again. Also, still no word on James. When I saw Gus in the driveway yesterday morning, he mentioned his buddy with the Phoenix PD was being extra cautious, checking some 'stuff' out; whatever that means. So yeah, I'm spinning... in a downward spiral and I don't like this feeling at all.

"Mom! Joe's on the phone."

I shoot up straight in the bed. Must've finally fallen asleep after all. Still groggy, I grope around the nightstand for my phone but come up empty.

"MOM! Phone!"

Right. I left it on the kitchen counter on purpose when I went to bed. I pull on some yoga pants and pad into the living room, where Fox is making a sandwich in the kitchen, my phone on the counter.

"Please tell me you weren't hollering into the phone?"

He just shrugs. Great, Joe must be deaf by now. I pick it up and sink down on the couch.

"Are your ears ringing?"

The low chuckle on the line has an instant effect on my lower belly.

"I'll live."

"Good to know."

"Doc," his voice suddenly turns serious, "We received a report from one of your neighbors this morning."

I sit up straight, tension immediately clamping down on my body.

"Why? What's wrong?"

I notice Fox throwing me a concerned look and lightly shake my head, but it apparently, I'm not convincing enough to throw him off because he's now glaring.

"They knew you were gone for a couple of days..."

"Yes. I told them we would be until next week."

"Right. So when they saw some debris on the back lawn and blinds hanging out from a broken window on the upstairs level, they called it in. I went and checked. Wanted to do that before calling you in, because I know you just got off shift. I checked to see if you were still at the hospital first. Honey, it looks like someone broke in and vandalized your house."

I'm already on my way to the bedroom to get dressed, the phone still plastered to my ear.

"I'm on my way."

"Actually, no. *I'm* on my way. I'm turning onto County Road G now and will be there shortly. I think it's better if Fox stays there though. Trust me on this." His voice sounds so solemn, it's making my chest compress with fear.

"I've called Caleb and he's heading to your place now to take him to the shooting range for a distraction. He'll love it."

"Okay."

I'm too stunned to object to the prospect of my son handling an actual gun. Something I'd be dead-set against under normal circumstances. God knows I fought against that stupid Xbox long enough before finally caving. But this wasn't the time. Plus I was fast becoming scared enough to think maybe having Fox able to handle a real gun was not such a bad idea after all.

"Babe?" Joe's voice breaks through my running thoughts.

"Yes?"

"I'm hanging up now. Be there soon. Go talk to Fox and prepare him?"

"Okay."

I pull on some jeans, sneakers and a T-shirt, not even checking to see if it's clean or dirty. Who the fuck cares? When I walk out of the bedroom, Fox is still in the kitchen looking at me.

"What happened?"

Trying to pull myself together, I plaster as neutral of an expression as possible on my face.

"Well, seems someone thought it was a good idea to make use of the fact that we're not home and broke in. Joe doesn't know what exactly is missing if anything, so he's coming to pick me up to go check it out. But the best part is that Caleb's apparently on his way here to pick you up. He's going to the shooting range to practice and thought you might like to go."

The play of emotions on his face is almost comical, changing from shock to anger to excitement and finally settling on suspicion.

"Why are you okay with that all of a sudden? What's going on? You hate guns, hate me around guns. You've told me often enough. You don't even like me playing 'Call of Duty.'"

Yup. My son is not stupid. That and sixteen-year-olds are not as easily distracted as three-year-olds are; not by a long shot.

"Look, I don't know exactly what's up with the house. Joe didn't say, so I'm going to check it out with him, but I think you heading out to the range with Caleb isn't such a bad idea. You've been cooped up here long enough. You could do with some 'man-time' or whatever, and I really need to check this out without having you worry about me, or me worrying about you. Fair enough?"

After a long stare, he finally nods and then a slow smile spreads over his face. "You're gonna let me shoot a gun?"

I suppress a full-body shudder. "Just don't look so happy about it."

He fist pumps his good arm in the air. Still a kid after all.

"Holy shit, Joe."

He warned me the place had been ransacked, but I'm not quite prepared to see the utter destruction of all my belongings. Not to mention some substantial damage to the house itself. This goes light-years beyond vandalism. Whoever has done this has no interest in stealing any property; they were out for devastation. I'm sure once the shock wears off, that's exactly what I'll feel; total and utter devastation at the loss of my home, my things. Little fragments of recognition peek at me from the ruins of my living room. The torn corner of a picture of Fox riding his first bike, a shard from a replica of Ute pottery I bought at Mesa Verde years ago. I could go on, as I step around the broken bits and pieces of my trampled life around me.

"I know, honey. Try not to touch anything. Cortez PD lab guys have gone through briefly already, but we want to keep everything as is for now. Is there anything here that jumps out at you?"

"Just that this doesn't look like any ordinary burglary to me. Looks like a wrecking ball came through."

"Yeah. Looked that way to us too. Okay, let's head upstairs."

The landing is deceptively untouched and I'm thinking maybe they left the second floor untouched, until we step into my bedroom. This is obviously the window the neighbors saw broken out, since my blinds are bouncing in the wind, against the siding on the outside of the house. My beautiful rustic queen-sized canopy bed that I bought at an estate sale four years ago, has two of the four posts splintered and broken. The gauze canopy is shredded, my bedding ripped and tossed around the room and the nauseating smell of bleach alerts me to what I'm likely to find in my drawers and my closet. No piece of clothing seems to have gotten away unscathed. When I look into the bathroom, it's in no better state.

I'm numb and am barely registering what my eyes are seeing. Self-preservation, I'm sure. If I let the full impact of what happened here penetrate, I will lose it. I will. I will lose my ever-loving mind for good this time.

I turn to Joe. "What about Fox's room? His things?"

Joe winces. "This is where it gets weird," he says before he opens the door to Fox's bedroom.

I stand in the doorway, stunned. After everything I've seen in the past ten minutes, this one has me floored. Fox's room is completely untouched. Nothing. Wait... there's something written on the wall over his bed.

Feeling guilty? Good. Be glad your mother wasn't here.

"Holy shit..." is all I manage as cold child ripples down my spine.

"Yep... this is why I didn't think Fox coming here would be such a good idea," Joe mumbles behind me.

"No shit, Sherlock."

"Let's get out of here..." Joe urges my numb body down the stairs, out the door and into his truck.

I take a look back at the house that has been so welcoming to me for years, now suddenly a place I can't imagine returning to. Not ever.

"Take me away from here, Joe"

I thought the almost cold detachment Naomi showed inside was worrisome, but the shaky little voice asking me to drive off really has me concerned. She's holding on by a mere thread. I had questioned whether bringing her here would be a good idea, but those were my feelings talking. I know it was necessary 'cause she is the only one able to know for sure if anything's been taken. Besides, she has a right to know what is done to her home.

My mind is going a mile a minute, trying to flit through the possibilities of who is behind this. The intended message is clearly for Fox, there's no mistaking that, but the threat is against Naomi and it makes the blood run cold through my veins. My first thought had been the punks who were trying to build a drug network in our relatively quiet town and apparently were not afraid to use deadly force to get their way, but it almost seemed too contrived for them. I would expect a more direct and physical approach. Then there was the Phoenix case. Still no word from Fox's father, but I've had a chance to go over the trial transcripts and Maxim Heffler, the guy he was defending, is a scary piece of work. Never had anything stick to him, but the list of suspected involvements is a myriad of major crimes; including kidnapping, rape and murder, were enough to make you shudder. This was the second time in the last ten years he was acquitted of murder charges. The first time, two material witnesses for the prosecution changed their testimony on the stand, throwing the prosecution's case completely off course, and this last time, the witness ended up dead. All testimonies leading up to this witness had been circumstantial and setting the stage for him to tie it all together, but without his testimony, the case fell apart like loose sand. Within days Maxim walked out of court; another acquittal to his name.

I have to get Fox to open up about Phoenix, because if this man, this Maxim Heffler, has anything to do with James' disappearance—has anything remotely to do with the reason Fox left Phoenix in a hurry—then Naomi and her son may well be in deep trouble. And what is giving me heartburn right now is that the kind of sick little mind game that was played in Naomi's house back there, is probably just the kind of thing a psychopath like Heffler would get off on. Fuck what a mess.

When I look over at Naomi, I notice that while she is staring unseeingly out the window, tremors are starting to go through her body. I put my hand on her leg yet she barely responds.

"Honey? Naomi, look at me."

When she finally lifts her eyes, they are dull. I pull the truck over to the side of the road, put it in park and turn to her, taking her face in my hands.

"Talk to me. You're worrying me."

She opens her mouth a few times to speak but can't seem to form words.

"That's it. I'm taking you to the hospital." I turn around, intending to turn the truck around to Cortez Memorial, when I feel her hand on my arm.

"No hospital... please." The plea in that little voice, so unlike the feisty Naomi I know, breaks my heart. The tears collecting in the big brown eyes she's turned to me don't make it any better.

"Dammit, honey." I press a quick kiss to her head and grab my radio off the dash.

"Dispatch. Carol?"

"Sheriff?"

"Yeah. I'll be home the rest of the day, in case of an emergency. If Dooley from the Cortez PD calls in, tell him to get me on my cell. Drew can contact me there too. He can run the patrols. Okay?"

"Ten-four, Sheriff."

I toss back the radio, unclip Naomi's seatbelt, reach over and slide her all the way next to me and clip her into the center belt. With my arm around her shivering body, I turn the truck toward my house.

CHAPTER NINE

"Where are we?" Naomi mumbles from my neck, where she hides her face the moment I lift her out of my truck.

"My place."

"Why?"

"Because you don't want to go the hospital, I can't have your boy see you like this and you are at the end of your tether. I'm drawing you a bath, feeding you something and then you're having a nap. In that order. Then maybe you'll want to talk... or not. We'll play it by ear. Just let me take care of you for a bit. I have a feeling your load is getting a little heavy."

I manage to shift her weight to one arm so I can get the door open and slip us inside, closing up behind us. I walk straight through upstairs and into the bathroom, where I sit her on the counter; keeping hold of her with one hand while I turn on the taps and give the water a chance to warm up. Turning back to her, I see her eyes are clearer now, watching my every move.

"What?"

"I'm not used to this," she confesses.

"Used to what, honey?"

"Being taken care of. It feels... odd."

I chuckle. "I hear you. Feels odd to me too, wanting to take care of someone, but here we are. Lift up." I have the hem of her shirt almost across her waist when she lifts her arms obediently, seeming to not give much thought to what she's doing. Good thing too, because I'm doing enough thinking for the two of us. The sight of her creamy olive-tone skin makes me want to lick and taste her flavor, but my role here is to be her friend. If she got wind of where my thoughts were drifting, she'd rip a strip off me. I throw her shirt on the overflowing laundry basket in the corner and lift her up by the waist, putting her carefully on her feet.

"Hang on to the counter behind you."

One by one, I take off her sneakers, undo the buttons on her jeans and strip them down her legs, doing my best not to gawk at her. Giving myself a minute, I turn to the tub and put the plug in; the water now warm enough to draw her bath.

"Do you want bubbles or something? Don't know what I have but maybe my shower gel will work." I start rummaging through the bottles on the side of my tub.

"It's okay," her timid voice sounds behind me and I turn to face her.

Fuck, even in her plain white bra and panties, she's a compact wet dream. Round in all the right places and not a protruding bone in sight. Just lush creamy skin and white cotton. I close my eyes and swallow down the overwhelming urge to bury my face in her soft belly and breathe her in.

I have to get out of here before I manhandle her.

"Do you think you can manage from here, Doc?" I ask, lifting my eyes with determination to her face.

"I'll be alright. Thanks."

Still too compliant for her. Not natural and not to my liking.

"I'll be right downstairs, just checking in with Caleb and grabbing something to eat, okay? I'll leave the door on a crack, unless you want it closed all the way?"

"A crack is fine," she mumbles.

Yeah. Definitely not normal, I think as I slip backward out the door and leave it open a bit.

Downstairs, I quickly call Caleb and give him an update. He's still at the shooting range with Fox and says he'll take him to the diner to meet his brother Malachi and Katie there later. He even suggests taking Fox back to their place, saying Fox would get a kick out of Blue, their dog. I thank him before hanging up and checking my fridge for food. Thank God I have the makings for a sandwich and, if I'm not mistaken, I have some half-way decent canned soup I can warm up later too. For now, I just grab some crackers and cheese, plus a bottle of ginger ale. A quick look around my living room to see if it needs any straightening up, but other than some newspapers and a bit of dust, it's not so bad. I stop in my bedroom to change out of my uniform and am just about to pull on my sweats when I hear soft crying. Quickly tying the string at my waist, I slip into the bathroom and find Naomi sitting on one end of the tub, her knees pulled up all the way to her chest and her arms wrapped tightly around them. Her face is pressed into her legs and I can see her back heaving as she pulls in big gulps of air.

I slide down on the floor beside the tub and stroke her back. Her skin wet and silky under my coarse fingers. Damn. She surprises me when she turns and throws her arms around my neck, offering me a glimpse of her full breasts and large dark nipples, before pressing herself against my chest, the hard side of the tub wedged between us.

Not the way I expect our first skin-to-skin experience to be, but damn if those perfect lush tits pressed against my chest aren't the best thing I've felt in a long fucking time. My cock is instantly hard enough to nail boards, but the now gut wrenching sobs pulled from her trembling body are enough to keep my baser urges at bay. This woman is coming apart at the seams and holding her is all I can do to keep her together.

"Let it go, honey. Let it all out. I've got you."

I'm mumbling nonsense in her hair, sitting in a cold wet puddle, which is getting bigger by the second. When her gasps seem to grow a bit more controlled, I tell her to sit tight for a second, while I get up and quickly grab a stack of towels, putting them on the counter. Reaching around Naomi, I pull the plug on the tepid water and help her up and out of the tub. She seems uncaring, almost unaware as she stands gloriously naked before me. I'm trying hard not to notice the heavy globes of her breasts, the slight swell of her stomach, the distinct flare of her hips and the dark patch of curls hiding things I shouldn't be craving right now. *Right.* Like that's possible. Without wasting too much time to think about what I'm doing, I quickly dry her off the best I can, while she appears to withdraw into herself again. Pulling my bathrobe from the back of the door, I wrap it around her, lift her up and carry her to my bed, where she curls into a ball the moment I remove my hands. *Fuck.*

"You gotta talk to me, honey. I'm worried about you and if you don't talk to me, I'm taking you to the ER, whether you like it or not," I warn her while I strip out of my now soaking wet sweats and pull on some dry boxers before turning back to the bed to find her looking at me.

"No hospital."

I'm scared. Scared of myself right now. Scared of this out of control feeling I'm having that the world is closing in on me. It's so familiar. I've been here before and I don't want to be here again. I don't want to deal. I want to disappear where nothing can touch me. This overwhelming panic paralyzes me. I haven't experienced anything close to it in many years. I just want to feel the safety of those arms again.

When Joe threatens to take me to the hospital, I have to speak up. I watch him as he takes off his wet pants and am apparently not too out of it to notice his fine ass. But his boxers are in place before he turns around when I speak and he walks over and crawls into bed beside me pulling me to his chest. A chest I felt earlier but didn't get to admire. Now I can and I can't help but trace my fingers through the soft light chest hair that covers a large tattoo that runs the width of his pectorals. I'm not about to lift my head and examine it closer, because the steady beat of his heart under my cheek is comforting as is the soothing hand he's drawing through my hair. When he starts talking I can feel the deep rumble of his voice come from his chest.

"Please talk to me, honey. Whatever is eating you up in silence right now, is much better dealt with out in the open. Try and put it to words so I can help you."

I try a few times, eager to get myself out of this endless spin, but it's so hard finding words.

"I'm afraid..." finally bursts from my mouth, but that's all I can get out.

"Okay. I get that," Joe murmurs calmly. "I'm thinking there's a lot of shit going down all at the same time, and although I have no kids, I imagine there's nothing like fearing for your child. Am I right?"

I simply nod against his chest, my heart rate settling with every beat of his steady one.

"I haven't had one in a long time."

"A what? A panic attack?"

I'm only mildly surprised he pegs my breakdown correctly, considering he's dealt with an unstable ex before. Pretty sure he'll be backing away soon enough now, so I might as well come all out.

"There was a time I had them frequently, but I haven't had one in a long time; not since I left Phoenix."

"What triggers them? Do you know?"

"Can be different things, but usually something that overwhelms me... a feeling or a situation. When I feel trapped by circumstances or emotions or even by lack of control. I don't really know. It's so hard to put my finger on it. I guess trying to manage what is happening around me right now, and trying to ignore the desire to run and hide. It's just so much..." I start crying again, pissed at myself for doing it but not able to stop all the same.

"Shhhh, let's deal with logistics first, alright? Always easier to work with concrete stuff and maybe the edge will come off. I can see a few concerns, but let me know if I miss any."

Listening to Joe helps me sort my thoughts into better focus as he lists safety, housing, work for me, and school for Fox, as main areas that need to be addressed.

"Since we don't know who exactly is behind this or why, although we could hazard a guess or two, I think we should talk to Gus and see if we can't find a way to keep you and Fox looked after. Although you're safe enough at the guesthouse for now, , your house will be inaccessible for a while, until I can be sure that whoever was behind the break-in wasn't from out-of-state. Because if that's the case, that might involve the FBI. So I'd like to leave everything as is should they need to come on board."

The mention of the FBI has me sitting up in bed. "Are you serious? What are you thinking? Is this about the trouble James mentioned?"

Pulling me back down, Joe explains his suspicions about the outcome of the last case James was involved which indeed sounds very fishy. Combined with Fox's impromptu return to Cortez and James' disappearance, it's been more than enough to send up alarm bells for him.

"We need to talk to Fox, Doc. We need to let him in on what happened so he realizes how important it is we know everything. We've got to know in order to protect both of you properly."

I have to agree with him. Ever since Fox has been back, it's been eating at me that he won't talk to me about that.

I suddenly realize that I left Fox earlier and he must be worried out of his mind that he hasn't heard from me. I scoot out of bed, looking around me for my purse, so I can call him.

"Hey. Where are you going?"

"My phone. I need to call Fox. What time is it? He must be wondering where I am."

I'm pulled back against a solid chest and two arms slide around my waist, holding me tight.

"He's fine, Naomi. I called just a little while ago and they're probably only just leaving the shooting range now. Caleb is taking him to the diner to meet up with Katie and Malachi and was gonna take him to meet Blue at the barn after. Settle."

"Don't tell me to settle. I have every right to be worried about my son."

Who the hell does he think he is, telling me to settle? *Ass.* Bristling with indignation I worm out of his arms and turn around to face him, finding him smiling from ear to ear.

"What?"

"There you are. The you I recognize. It's good to have you back," he says, taking my face in his hands and sweetly kissing my lips. At first. I can't help my tongue sliding through my lips to take a taste, but as soon as I do, the mood of Joe's mouth changes from tender to hungry. Tilting my head, he plunges his tongue between my lips and claims ownership of my mouth. *Yowza.* Good thing I'm not wearing any panties, 'cause they'd have spontaneously combusted. Somehow my hands know their way to his hair and tangle there, while Joe's seem to have slipped inside the robe that is wrapped around me. With firm fingers he kneads the flesh on my ass and my hips, before hoisting me up. I wrap my legs around his waist, shuddering when my bare slit slides down over the coarse hairs of his treasure trail and encounters his unmistakable erection. Holy crap.

"Fuck, Naomi. I'm starving for you," Joe pants as he peppers kisses along my jaw and down my cleavage, sucking a mouthful of breast so hard into his mouth, I almost come on the spot.

"Feeling that wet pussy slide down my stomach makes me want to bury my face between your legs and taste your need for me."

Never before one for crass or dirty talk, but Joe's words turn me on so much, I grind my core against the crown of his cock. With a groan he turns around and has me on my back, legs wide open and him on his knees, on the floor between them, lowering his head with his eyes focused on mine. The first touch of his warm, wet tongue on my clit is feather-light, but has me nearly coming off the bed. So fucking long since I've felt the intimate touch of a man, I'm primed for it. I don't even care that I haven't waxed in donkey's years, and Joe doesn't seem to be bothered.

"So fucking good..." he groans as he strokes his tongue along my folds, opening me up further by pulling my legs over his shoulders and pulling my core deeper onto his face. And I help— oh boy, do I help. I am shamelessly grinding my hips on his mouth and the fingers he has slipped into me, pumping leisurely when I want him hard and fast. Joe's eyes never leave mine as he steadily sets the pace while I lose my mind. When he starts sucking on my clit, in little gentle pulls, I am done.

"Please, Joe... " I plead with him, grabbing his hair by the handful, trying to find that final edge that will spill me over.

"Ready?" he asks, pulling back, his mouth wet with my juices.

"Ahhhh..." I grunt out my release instantly as Joe clamps down on that bundle of nerves he's been teasing into a frenzy with his teeth and he curves his fingers deep inside me, hitting the ignition button. Because, *holy shit!* I'm blown to pieces as he manages to drag my climax out.

"Beautiful," he murmurs, placing a gentle kiss between my legs, causing another little shiver through my sensitized body.

Before I know it, I'm enveloped in his big body, one hand on my ass and one in my hair, my head on his chest. When I open my eyes I can't help but notice the massive hard-on he's sporting in his boxers.

"What about you?"

"Don't worry about me. I'm glad I was able to help you relax."

"Excuse me?" *Wait, what?* "I think I'd like to go back now. I need to see Fox."

I scramble off the bed, haphazardly pulling the robe around me and making a beeline for the bathroom where my clothes are, shutting the door behind me before I lose it completely.

The first time in years I let a man touch me and he did it to help me relax. I am now officially a pity fuck. My day couldn't be more complete.

CHAPTER TEN

I'm not sure, but I think I may have fucked up.

One minute I'm being all magnanimous, denying myself any gratification, only interested in hers, and the next she's out of bed and locked in the bathroom. I'm missing a step somewhere.

We are on our way back to Cedar Tree. Naomi insisted and there was nothing I could do or say to sway her. The moment she came out of the bathroom, completely dressed again, I knew she was retreating. Oh, she's friendly enough, pretending she didn't just have a massive panic attack or came apart under my mouth and my fingers, but the tightness at the corners of her mouth tell me a different story. Fuck. I can't just let this go.

"Naomi, what just happened?"

"Not sure what you mean? I'm all relaxed, just like you planned, and now I'm ready to deal with Fox. Why?"

The false cheery tone and fake smile are starting to piss me off.

"*Like I planned?* I didn't plan anything, I certainly didn't plan on virtually attacking you right when you were feeling vulnerable. I'm sorry if that pissed you off, but it wasn't easy trying to keep my hands off you all naked and gorgeous and... well, naked."

I glance her way to find her face one big question mark.

"But... but I thought... never mind," she stammers as she turns her face away and stares out the side window, her hands clutched in her lap.

We're coming up on a cut off onto a farmer's field and I pull in, fed up with these confusing messages I'm getting. I turn off the engine and turn sideways in my seat.

"Naomi... look at me."

She hesitates a second too long to my liking and I cup her chin with my hand, turning her head so she has no choice. I'm frustrated as fuck, have no idea what's going on in that pretty head of hers, and have no patience for playing games.

"Gonna ask you one more time, honey. What happened back at my place to shut you down like this?"

When she tries to lower her eyes, I tighten my grip on her chin and they open back up to reveal fresh tears filling them. Damn, this woman can cry.

"I don't like being a pity fuck," is what comes out of her tight little mouth.

What in Jesus' name?

"Who said anything about that?" I growl at her.

"You did," she spits out, gathering steam from what I can tell. "You said you were glad you were able to *'help'* me relax." She even makes quotation marks with her fingers for emphasis. "Well, thank you for that, but a massage at the spa would've worked wonders too."

Her tears are starting to spill over, but I get a feeling she's more angry than sad, especially when she pointedly folds her arms over her chest. I can't help myself, I start laughing.

"Are you shitting me? The only reason I'm not pounding your ass into my mattress right now with your legs over my shoulders, why I'm not having you scream my name over and over again all afternoon till you end up hoarse, is because I don't want to create a situation *you* might regret later. I want you so bad; wanted you so much all afternoon. I've been trying to recall every foul-smelling drunk I've ever had in my truck, every disgusting crime scene I've ever witnessed and each and every glimpse of my fourth grade teacher, Mrs. Winkler's panty-hose when she was wiping the blackboard, just to get this fucking hard-on I'm toting for you to go down. Nothing works!"

With both hands I pull the hair on my head and let out a frustrated groan. A snort has me glare in her direction, but that only makes her laugh harder.

"I'm sorry," she giggles, "Mrs. Winkler's panty-hose?"

Growling I unclip and slide way over into her space, crowding her against the passenger door.

"Give me your hand."

The stubborn little minx shakes her head, a smile still on her face.

"Your hand, babe."

Not waiting, I grab her hand and flatten it against the crotch of my pants where she can clearly feel the full length of my very hard, very hot and very hungry cock. Her eyes pop open and I lean in so my nose almost touches hers. "That. Is what my cock thinks of your idea of a *pity* fuck."

"Okay." Her voice is so soft, if I hadn't seen her mouth move I'd have missed it.

"Baby, don't doubt me, please. Clean lines of communication, okay? If I say something that confuses you or pisses you off, you tell me. I may not be the most sensitive guy around, but I'm not an asshole. Don't wanna waste more time on misunderstandings, not with you."

I kiss her hard on her full lips, but when she starts rubbing her little hand on my dick I grab it and pull back.

"Doc? You keep that up, and I'll be coming in my pants. Don't have an extra pair on me and I don't wanna get caught on the side of the road by one of my deputies with my dick out."

I slide back over to the driver's side, put the truck in drive and pull out, grabbing her hand in mine as we turn toward Cedar Tree. I can see a little self-serving smile steal over Naomi's face from the corner of my eye. *Wench.*

"So what's going on with you and Joe?"

I'm giving Katie a hand getting some food and drinks together in the large open kitchen of her and Caleb's huge barn-house. Joe and I just got here after finding they'd just left the diner. Since neither Joe nor I had dinner yet, Katie suggested making some sandwiches.

I'm mentally preparing myself for the heart-to-heart we have coming up with Fox, because I know that won't be easy. Not telling him about the house, or pushing him for more information, but I agree with Joe that it has to be done.

"I seem to cry a lot around him."

"Well that's not good. I haven't known you that long, but I know you're not a crier." Katie turns to me with an eyebrow raised. "I may be eight months pregnant, but I'm pretty sure I can still take him."

I chuckle at the picture her words paint in my head. "No, it's not his fault. In fact, in a weird way, I think it's probably a compliment to him. I mean, you said it, I'm not one to cry and yet I do it a lot when I'm with him."

"Hmmmm, I remember that. I remember Caleb doing that to me; making me *feel.*" Suddenly she's smiling wide. "Thinking it might not be such a bad thing after all."

"Of course in the meantime, my life is running off the rails like nobody's business. The bitch at work won't let up, Fox getting in trouble and hurt in the process, and now this break-in on top of James going missing," I point out, picking at a piece of cheese.

"Whoa... hold up there. What's this about a break-in? James missing? I mean I know I suffer from pregnancy brain, but when did all this happen?" Katie has turned me by the shoulders to face her and I have to tilt my head back a little to look her in the eye.

"Sorry. There just hasn't been much time... Life's been a bit crazy, out of hand even. Let's go sit down. You'll hear it all soon enough since we have to talk to Fox and Joe suggested that Caleb sit in on it."

In the big open living space, the guys are spread out over the various couches and chairs that are grouped around a ginormous stone fireplace, with Blue, Katie's dog, lying on his bed in front.

Fox is gesturing as he very animatedly tells Joe about his time at the shooting range, with Caleb simply nodding here and there. When I put the plate of sandwiches down on the table, he immediately snatches one up and starts eating, while still talking, now with his mouth full. So I cuff the back of his head.

"Hey. You have food in your mouth and by the way, did you not just eat a meal at the diner? Those are for Joe and me," I tell him, hiding my smile.

"Sorry," he mumbles around another bite, "still hungry. What happened at the house? Did they take a lot of stuff?"

My eyes meet Joe's and I give him a nod. Better let him do the honors, because the way I've been going, I'll just end up blubbering again.

"So I won't sugar-coat it. Your house was pretty much trashed," Joe says to Fox, clearly not pussyfooting around. Fox tries to keep his face impassive, but I can see the news is impacting him from the clenching of his jaw and by the way he plucks at the seam of his jeans with his fingers.

"Doesn't look like anything was taken according to your mom, but it seemed to be intended as a warning. A message was left; a warning that was directed at you, but the threat was clearly against your mother." When Fox tries to speak, Joe stops him. "Let me finish what I have to say and then you can have your turn. As I see it, there are two possibilities. One is our little meth-distributor, who is trying to scare you into keeping your mouth shut, which we both know it's too late for anyway. Or two, and this is the more likely option, whatever had you leave Phoenix in a hurry has caught up with you. And buddy, if that's the case, then we are working blind here." Joe sits forward with his elbows resting on his knees, looking Fox straight in the eye. Meanwhile, I am squirming to keep my mommy urges in check that come with the overwhelming need to interfere. I need to trust Joe to have this one.

Fox is fidgeting, his eyes going between me and the others in the room, only to finally settle on Joe. "I can't," he finally says quietly, "It could put everyone in danger."

"Listen to me, kid. Right now? Your mom is a target. Her room was ripped to shreds, Fox, and the threat was crystal clear. And you are not any safer. The reason I'm putting you on the spot here, with Caleb and Katie present, is that the more people know this *'secret'* you've been carrying around all this time, the less power it will have over you. Think about it. If whoever is doing this is trying to get you to keep your mouth shut, that incentive is gone once you've talked. The more people who know, the less likely it is they'll do anything about it. It would just point a bigger arrow at their ass. Right?"

When he finally gets a timid nod from Fox, I breathe a sigh of relief. Finally. "Go on, Bub. Let's get this shit dealt with," I give him an encouraging smile and get a weak one in return, but I'll take it.

"Well, uh... this summer, Dad was working on this case. Some kind of murder case. He was gone almost all of the time and then when he was around, he was stuck in his office with the door closed. He kept saying 'later' whenever I wanted to ask something and would forget about shit all the time. I was supposed to have a school form signed by him, something about a survival trip that was scheduled for the seniors that I'd signed up for. They needed his credit card information and signature that day or I couldn't go. So I went home for lunch hoping to catch him, knowing he was working from his home office. When I walked in, his office door was open and I heard him on speakerphone with someone." He stops talking and looks at Joe. "If you have to take me to jail, will you look after my mom?"

Without batting an eyelid, Joe responds, "Never doubt it, but I don't think you have to worry about jail, buddy. Just tell us the rest."

His eyes downcast, he picks up where he left off. "I heard Dad say something about not liking the way a murdered witness would look on his track record, and the guy on the other side laughed, saying... saying it was a bit too late for Dad to get squeamish. That it was done. I think I must've said something out loud then, 'cause dad looked up and swore at me, telling me to close the effing door. I never went back to school, locked myself in my bedroom. Dad knocked on my door later and told me to pack up all my shit, that I was getting on the first available Greyhound back to Mom. He said my stupidity may have cost both of us our lives."

This is where my big, strapping sixteen-year-old son loses it, but before I can get to him, Joe has him in those big comforting arms and lets him sob on him. My poor baby, such a burden to carry. And if that fucking asshole comes anywhere near *my* son again, I'm gonna put my scalpel skills to good use on his hide. Anger, fear and pain for my child battle it out in my chest and I feel like throwing up when Caleb comes over and pulls me up of the couch.

"Come on you girls, let's give these guys some time," he says, urging us to the back deck.

"That's my son in there. Wait a minute!" But my protests fall on deaf ears as I find myself pushed into one of the big loungers on the deck.

"Yes. Your son, who was treated like shit and put in danger by his asshole father and who would probably feel like even less of a man if his mother were to shed tears over him now. Let Joe take care of him."

"He's just a boy," I protest.

"I spent an afternoon with him, watching him empty clip after clip into a pile of targets, scratching his balls and getting high off adrenaline. Your son is a man," Caleb says firmly.

"Fine, but did you have to mention the ball scratching? I could've done without that visual," I mumble, causing Katie to laugh.

CHAPTER ELEVEN

"Neil's coming down for the pig roast this weekend anyway, so I had Dana book him a room at the motel while Naomi and Fox are still in the guesthouse. He's finishing up on a file this morning and will hit the road this afternoon. I have to go on a short run next week, but with Katie so close to her due date, Caleb's gonna stay close to home and Neil will hang around. Of course we have Mal now too."

"Sounds good, Gus. Thanks. Makes me feel better knowing they're covered while I try to dig through this shit heap."

Since Fox finally told us about the reasons he was sent back to Cortez, I've been in constant contact with the Phoenix PD. One of their detectives is scheduled to get down here early next week to take Fox's statement, but it had taken me a day and a half of dealing with their threats of obstruction of justice if I didn't immediately hand deliver Fox to them, as well as a phone call from Gus to one of his many contacts, before they toned down and agreed to meet at my office instead. No way in hell was I going to step back and let them work that kid over. Especially not after I could feel every guilty tear he shed work into my heart. Neither he nor his mom were going to be without my protection at any time. Besides, those idiots still haven't been able to tell me the whereabouts of Maxim Heffler.

I haven't seen Naomi since I kissed her on the porch at Emma's when I dropped her and Fox off. I'd briefly spoken to Gus and she was waiting for me outside when I left, just like I'd asked. I didn't think Fox was ready to see his mom make out with the sheriff and I needed to have my mouth on her before this case would suck me up. And suck me up it did. I've only managed to talk to her on the phone twice and haven't been back to Cedar Tree yet.

Just as I thought things with the Phoenix PD were under control, I got a call from the Cortez police chief, giving me a head's up that a partial fingerprint had been found on a red crayon found in Fox's room. Since the message on his wall was done in crayon and no other crayons were found in the house, the assumption was whoever wrote the message brought the crayon and must've accidentally left it there. A stroke of luck, 'cause getting prints off paper is always a hit or miss. They ran it through AFIS and it came back belonging to a small-time crook from Grand Junction who had done some time in juvie before getting hit with his first felony charge for drug trafficking two years ago.

I've been on the go since seeing his mug shot. It was the goatee guy from the attack on Michael. I had been absolutely wrong in dismissing them for the break-in at Naomi's. Apparently our young friend is more refined than I'd given him credit for. Felipe Rivas has been front and center on my mind ever since, and I'm eager to get my hands on him. Underestimating him was a mistake I won't make again. He may be a small time criminal, but that was a sophisticated mind-fuck he left for Fox, and something about it still didn't smell right.

For now, Fox and his mom would be safe in Cedar Tree and I'd like to keep it that way. Gus is instrumental in making sure of it.

"So has Naomi mentioned anything about those places she was planning to check out yesterday?"

"I heard her mention to Emma last night that one of the places looked promising, but she wants to show Kendra first. Why don't you give her a call yourself and find out?"

"I might. You haven't mentioned anything yet about Wednesday's meeting with the detective from Phoenix, have you?"

"You said you would handle it, so I didn't. You gonna handle it?" Gus wants to know.

"Yeah. I'm gonna handle it."

"Sometime before Wednesday?" Gus is testing me now and he knows it, judging by the barely concealed chuckle I hear.

"Fuck off. I said I'll handle it."

Truth is, I don't want to do this over the phone. I want to look her in the face when I tell her, because I have a feeling she might freak. Either at the fact that Fox is now considered a person of interest by the Phoenix PD, or the fact that I've risked my badge trying to keep her and her son tucked away in Cedar Tree for now. I'll have to though. Today, because as far as I know, she is back on shift at the hospital this week, and wouldn't be hard to track down there. I'll have to convince her to call in sick, or try and figure this the fuck out before then. With so many loose threads in my hands going in different directions, the latter seems more and more unlikely.

Carol holds me up on my way out the door.

"Joe, a Frank Bancroft called for you when you were on the phone. Says he's from some law firm in Phoenix?"

I recognize the name, although what James Miller's law partner wants to talk to me about is beyond me. First priority is to get Naomi up to speed, before I get bogged down even further.

"Leave his number on my desk, thanks Carol. I'll catch him later," I tip my hat at her on my way out to the parking lot.

In my truck I quickly dial Naomi. "Hey Doc, are you home?"

"Joe." The way she says my name, like she wanted to hear my voice as much as I wanted to hear hers, does something to me.

"Say my name like that again and I won't be able to drive straight." I smile when I hear her chuckle. It's a good sound and there's been too little of it lately. "Heading over. Any chance you're alone?" I add, living in hope and earning another laugh from her.

"Sorry. I wish."

"Fuck, woman. You're making it hard on me," I grind out, shifting to relieve the growing pressure against my zipper.

"I think that's the nicest thing someone's said to me in a long time," she plays my words back at me and the sultry tone that has slipped into her voice makes me want to slip my hand in my pants and palm my ever-growing erection. Parking lot of the County Sheriff's Office. Right.

"Honey, unless you want me to lose my job for indecent exposure, you better let me go so I can get on the road. See you soon."

All I hear is her soft giggle as she hangs up.

With an uncomfortably hard cock crowding my pants, but a big dumb smile on my face, I pull out of my parking spot.

I have no idea why I'm so giddy today. Actually, that's a lie; I have a pretty good idea.

The past few days have been pretty intense, with Fox freaked out, asking questions I don't really have answers to, and Jenna Stanley on the phone trying to make me pick up extra shifts again. Guess she hasn't heard the word *'no'* much in her life, because she just will not let up. On top of all that, I haven't seen Joe since that scorcher of a kiss on the porch. A kiss that left me feeling highly unsatisfied, and no way to relieve it with Fox sleeping a few feet away in the bedroom.

This state of limbo is not agreeing with me, edging me ever so close to either a repeat anxiety attack or that dreaded pit of despair I don't want to end up in. So I'm done feeling out of control and am grabbing the bull by the horns. Fox may not like it—yet—but something tells me this is the right time, when life is upside down already, to see how I can make some of those ideas I've been toying with a reality. We need a new place—because there is no way in hell I'll ever feel at home or secure again in my house—and I need to look for a space suitable for a clinic. If the two can be combined, even better.

Now Cedar Tree isn't that big, with a population of maybe 1200 or so, but I know with the neighboring Ute reservation and the abundance of even smaller towns dotting the area, I can make a go of this. One of the reasons the emergency room at the hospital gets overrun so often is because there are few other options around for medical care. Sure, there are some clinics in Cortez itself, but it isn't easy to even get an appointment, and most those doctors are affiliated with the hospital and split their time. No. I want a clinic that is set up like a more old-style family practice. Where people can come in for anything that ails them and only when needed will they be referred through to the hospital or a specialist. A lot of the simpler treatments, I can handle on the spot. With Kendra on board to offer PT, and hopefully a nurse practitioner at some point to help with the daily clinics, this would be a dream come true.

Arlene actually came up with a few suggestions, one of which I really love. The old feed-store has apparently been empty since 2010, when the much bigger farm and ranch supply place in Cortez opened and slowly killed the smaller business. The owners stuck around for another two years in the attached farmhouse, but ended up finally moving away. The place has been vacant ever since. Just south off the main thoroughfare right before hitting the town line of Cedar Tree, it sits on a decent parcel of land visible from the road. At least the storefront and the parking lot are; the house itself is set to the back and shielded by old grove trees.

I wish Joe had been with me. Fox refused to come, preferring to mope around the guesthouse and play on his Xbox, so I went with Emma. But I think Joe's insight might've been helpful. Kendra would have to see it too. Emma can turn grits into caviar and was excited about the possibilities for the place, but I don't have that kind of creative vision. She did get me all worked up and enthusiastic, but I need Joe's voice of reason to balance it out. We spoke briefly the other day and I told him about my plans to have a look around. He seemed to like the idea, and said he would've loved to tag along, but he was tied up with work.

I've surprise myself at the way I've slid into this supposed *'friendship'* of ours. I mean, I hated the man for years. Okay fine, not hated exactly, but just seeing him or hearing his name would piss me off. Now here I am, suddenly wanting his input.

I shouldn't be surprised that the phone rings right then and seeing that it's Joe, I already have a smile on my face. A little bit of sexy banter later along with the knowledge that he is on his way, and not even Fox's dark scowl from the couch can burst my giddy bubble. I so badly want to get horizontal with that man; that is if I haven't forgotten how by now. Having a broody sixteen-year old man-child around, makes that a bit of a challenge though. I do slip outside, leaving Fox to get sucked back into his game. The pathway that runs along the cottage to the guesthouse in the back is pretty sheltered on the side of the garage, so I lean against the stucco wall there. Waiting for that familiar truck to pull up.

The truck barely comes to a stop before the door flings open and Joe comes barrelling towards me. He must've spotted me in the glare of the headlights, because his eyes are on me until his body is pressed up against mine, my back against the wall.

"Had to see you." His voice is low and gruff and his hands cup my face before his mouth descends on mine, kissing me with such passion it draws the breath from me. I hang onto his neck and curl a leg around him, trying to draw him as close as I can to me. His lips leave mine feeling bruised and swollen as he places kisses along my jaw and down my neck. Lifting my breasts in his hands he presses them together as he dips his face in my cleavage, breathing deep.

"You smell so fucking good. I could stand here all day, breathing you in."

"I missed you."

At my words his head pops up and a slow smile spreads over his face. "You did?"

"Yup."

"Missed you too, Doc," he says, planting a kiss on my lips, "And I would like nothing more than to continue this and end up buried so deep inside you I'll never want to leave again, but I know your son is inside and we have stuff to discuss."

I try on a pout to hide the impact his words have on me, but it only makes him chuckle. Untangling himself from my limbs, he grabs my hand and pulls me to the guesthouse.

"Bub, you want something to drink?"

"Ginger ale, Mom."

Joe's asking Fox about the game we find him playing, while I get some coffee going. I figure Joe's trying to put Fox at ease a little because the tension was visible on his face the moment we walked in together. God only knows what is playing through his head and frankly, although I trust Joe, I'd like to know what is up.

After putting everyone's drinks on the coffee table I sit in the club chair and face Joe and Fox on the couch.

"Right," Joe clears his throat. "As you know, I've had to contact the Phoenix PD to let them know what Fox heard. Like I mentioned might happen, they've insisted on talking to him themselves. Now I'm not willing to tell them where you are until I know who I can and cannot trust. They weren't too happy about it, but with a bit of help, we managed to arrange a meeting in my office for Wednesday."

Fox is sitting very still next to Joe and other than nervously playing with the buttons on the controller in his hand and bouncing his leg, he's showing very little emotion. My own heart is pounding in my chest though, so I'm sure he's not doing much better.

"Am I in trouble?"

Joe quickly looks at me before turning his attention to Fox again. "You could be, but I'm not going to let anything happen to you. I hope you don't mind, but I have asked a lawyer friend to be present at the interview. Your mother and I will be there too, if they let me. I don't think you should worry about anything. You have some friends with really good connections who have experience dealing with stuff like this. Just trust us, okay?" He gives Fox's jumping knee a squeeze and throws me a reassuring smile.

I'm trying to decide whether to be angry at him for being presumptuous in making all these arrangements without consulting me first, or whether to be grateful for making sure we were taken care of. Guess the struggle is visible on my face, because he ends up sitting on the coffee table, his face inches from mine.

"There are a lot of things I'd like to do to lighten your load, but I can't. It's your life and you have to make decisions yourself. This though? This happened to be something I'm better equipped to handle, so I did. You can be mad, but it wouldn't make a difference. Let me shoulder this."

"You know you're sneaky when you're being all reasonable like that, right?" I tell him, lightly stroking my thumbs over the calloused palm of his hand I find myself holding. The light abrasion of his rough skin on the pads of my fingers has my nerve ends buzzing. The thought of feeling those rough hands skimming over the swells of my breasts, turns my nipples hard and I gasp audibly.

"Naomi," comes a low warning growl from Joe, right before the loud slam of the bedroom door that has the windows rattling in their frames.

Fuck. Guess my son just had a front row seat on the chemistry between the sheriff and his mom. Works just like a cold shower.

Joe leaves shortly after that with a lingering kiss just outside the door, but not before cautioning me.

"Look, I'll try to pop in again, but for sure I will see you tomorrow at the pig roast. Oh, before I forget; please stick to Cedar Tree. I need you to try and get some time off work, call in sick if you have to. Apparently no one knows Maxim Heffler's whereabouts."

When he sees the confused look on my face at the name, he clarifies, "The guy who was on trial? He's the one we think Fox overheard his dad talking to. He's in the wind, and there is still the threat on you from the message left at your house. It's easier for Gus and the guys to keep an eye out when you are both here. If you drive back and forth into Cortez, even with someone looking out for you, it would be too easy to track you back here from the hospital."

"But what about you? When you come here?"

"First of all, why would anyone assume I have a personal connection with you? And secondly, even if they did, all they would see is a sheriff doing what he's always done. Even when it comes to visiting here. Look, I know it's a pain, but try to lay low for a little, okay?"

No, I'm not okay with it but I'll deal, because I know I have to.

CHAPTER TWELVE

"Let's go, Bub. Don't want to keep Emma and Gus waiting."

Fox is dragging his ass getting ready and it's getting under my skin. We were supposed to be getting a ride with Gus to Caleb and Katie's for their housewarming pig roast, but at this rate we'll be late. Grabbing my phone, I send a quick text to Emma to let her know to go ahead. I'll take my own car and be right behind them. My phone rings almost right away.

"You sure?" Gus wants to know. I should've known the uber-protective man would want to hear it directly from me before trusting a text message.

"Yeah. My son is being a pain in my ass right now. We won't be long. Just let them know we're on our way."

"Okay. Naomi? Just in case, keep the phone handy and lock the car doors from the inside."

"Will do."

Way to make a girl feel safe. I was gonna jump at shadows now.

I'm excited about tonight, or at least I was until Fox started being a pest. Even dressed up a little; put on the best jeans and a slinky top I found in the bottom of my haphazardly thrown together bag. I'm really going to have to do something about our clothes. We can't keep washing the same stuff over and over again. Even put on some make-up, all because it almost feels like a date tonight. With Joe.

I haven't seen him today, but he did call last night to say goodnight. That was pretty sweet of him. Fox had come out of the bedroom the moment Joe had left earlier and ignored my attempts at talking to him, so I'd let him be, but when I walked into the bedroom with my phone after I identified Joe as the caller, he rolled his eyes at me. Brat. Joe's voice tempts me, even over the phone, but having your son in the next room with a disapproving scowl on his face is a very effective reality check. So short and sweet it was, nothing more, but I did get a promise that somehow, some way, we would find some time alone. I can't wait.

I did call the hospital yesterday afternoon and told them I had a family emergency and wouldn't be in until at least after next Wednesday, thinking that would give us some time. I was too chicken to deal with Jenna directly though, and left the message with the secretary. I tried to ignore the calls from Jenna that started flooding my phone after and haven't listened to the messages yet. Nothing I can do, or rather, want to do, about it now.

Funny, where before I would try and rebuild my life on securities, now it seems to have turned into one big risk. Both dangerous and scary, but also exciting. Kinda liberating to let go of the reigns, make a few contingency plans and then just see where it takes you. That's how I feel now, a little like floating on threats and possibilities. A weird state for me, but one I decided to run with for now. Not like I had much of a choice, and to be honest, as far as work goes, I wouldn't be too upset at this point if I lost my job, although I'd rather leave on good terms and of my own choice.

So I'd wear my slinky top, despite the chilly evening, and pretend I was going on a date. Well I did, until Fox gets a load of my get up and finally decides to speak.

"It's a pig roast, Mom. Not a club. And if you're going all dolled up desperate to try and catch the first guy that looks at you twice, I'm not coming."

Boom. That's the sound of my ass landing firmly back on earth. Just for a moment, I feel the tears welling up, but I force them down.

"I will ignore that deliberately hurtful crap you just spouted, because I don't want to believe you mean it, but Fox, if that's the way you treat people? Don't expect to receive any better treatment yourself. I may not have been the best mother these past sixteen years, but I've tried. Lately I've laid everything on the line and there isn't much I wouldn't do for you, but I won't stand by and let you belittle me. Not after the way I was treated for years. Did that make you feel better?"

I wait for an answer, looking at my tall son standing in front of me, his head now turned away, unwilling to meet my eyes. An almost imperceptible shake of his head tells me enough.

"Didn't think so. This is what you need to know; I like Joe, and he seems to like me well enough too. So for now, we'll see where it leads. That's all. I have that right and I don't need your approval for that, although it would be nice if you gave the man a chance, given the trouble he has gone through for us—for you. Now I'd like you to get ready. We have a party to attend."

With that I turn my back with my fingers crossed, hoping I somehow got through. Knowing words or even gestures might be too much to ask from a teenager, I'm pleased to hear his heavy footfalls make for the bathroom. Which is where he's been holed up for the past thirty minutes.

"Fox! Come on. You're taking longer than I do to get ready."

Finally the door opens and Fox comes out. Dressed in clean clothes and obviously showered with his hair wet, but a persistent scowl still in place. I can live with that. I hear it's all the rage with the teenage crowd. What I don't expect is the big bear hug my boy wraps me in, pinning my arms to my side. With his head on my shoulder I can barely hear the muffled *'Sorry,'* but it's there. Wrestling one of my hands free, I stroke his head and press a kiss to his hair.

"Forgotten," is all I say.

Pulling up to the big barn Caleb and Katie have converted into a gorgeous home, I see half of Cedar Tree is already present and accounted for, but the one truck I'm scanning for isn't there. I'm a bit disappointed Joe isn't here yet, but the night is still young.

Most of the crowd is concentrated around the kitchen and outside on the big back deck. Looks like Malachi is in control of the pig, with Neil hovering nearby. Like a moth, Fox ventures over to the flames as well, where Mal seems to take him under his wing after throwing me a wink. I don't know the man well, but I know he is trustworthy.

I spend some time mingling and chatting with Arlene, thanking her for the tip on the old feed-store, when I hear Caleb's voice from an upstairs window.

"Mal! Get Naomi and come up here."

The urgency in his voice has me jump up and make my way towards Mal who is obviously looking for me.

"I'm here," I tell him and together we make our way inside.

I know what we'll find. I've seen Katie grimacing a few times with her hand pressed against her lower back. I told her last week when I examined her that her cervix was already dilating and had even started thinning, which is pretty unusual in a first timer. So I'm not surprised to find her in a bed soaked with amniotic fluid, when I quickly have to begin rattling off my demands. One peek tells me this baby is ready; its little head crowing, showing us a shock of black hair with each contraction.

This is my passion, I don't think, I simply operate on what I know. This is almost instinct; muscle memory from my favorite year interning on the maternity ward in Phoenix. With a few reassuring words for the parents and Mal acting as gopher and nurse, this birth was as smooth as any woman has a right to give birth. By the time Katie and Caleb pull their newborn son on her chest, my slinky top is a sticky mess and I'm sure my make-up is smeared all over the place, but I wouldn't trade this night for anything. When Katie asks Malachi, her brother-in-law, to cut the cord instead of Caleb, the moment is so emotional, I almost lose it. This is what family should be. This is what I dreamed of having all those years ago, when I was young and hopeful. But now there was just Fox and I, no one else. Not really.

I slip into the bathroom to wash up as best as I can and compose myself before heading back in to check on Mom and baby.

An hour and a half later, Katie is lying in a clean bed, with little Mattias at her breast. She only needed two little internal stitches for a tiny tear, since Mattias wasn't a particularly tiny baby, despite being born a bit early. Mind you, one look at the paternal side of his family and you wouldn't be surprised. Those Whitetail men are massive.

"Here's a clean shirt," Caleb walks up and hands me a T-shirt, something I desperately need.

"Thanks," I smile at him, but he just looks at me with an impassive face before lifting me up in a bone-crushing hug.

"No. Thank you for... for everything. Just thank you." The normally level and contained Caleb can't hide the emotion pouring out in his voice.

"My pleasure and my privilege," I whisper to him, my eyes on Katie.

A kiss on my forehead and Caleb lets me go, turning back to his wife and child. Mal went back downstairs to 'man' the barbecue and the bar and I'm about to head down when Katie calls from the bed. "Would you take Emma and Arlene aside and send them up in the elevator when you go down?"

"Sure thing, honey. Call down if you need me."

I make quick work of my shirt in the bathroom and am about to start down the stairs when I hear Katie's voice behind me.

"Naomi?"

"Yeah?"

"Love you, girl."

That does it. I barely make it down the stairs to find Arlene and Emma already waiting—figures—manage to invite them up, and next I'm out the front door.

I'm drained when I drive to the pig roast. The phone call I received just hours ago from the Phoenix PD is causing this case to become a real threat to my career. A brief consultation with Gus gave me a little peace of mind, but the knowledge I carry that will have to be shared with Naomi is weighing heavy on my shoulders.

The moment I spot her slumped over at the picnic table in the side yard by herself in the dark, I know I won't be able to do this tonight. Not sure what happened to cause her to be out here, but I'm thankful to have a few minutes in private with her. I quickly park my truck and make my way over. She must hear my approach and lifts her head, but when I see her tear-streaked face, I'm convinced she somehow found out already. I barely have a chance to brace myself when she gets up and closes the distance, throwing herself in my arms.

"I'm so sorry—"

"It's a boy—"

We both start talking at the same time.

"What boy?"

"You missed it by about an hour and a half. The baby, Katie had an unexpected home birth," she tells me, smiling through her tears. I tuck her hair behind her ear.

"A boy huh? Is that why you're crying?"

"Been doing a lot of that lately. I'm sorry, I promise I don't usually cry this much. I'm not sad... not really. Just felt a little melancholy with the adrenaline letdown, you know?"

I can tell she is playing things down, and I don't like it. "You sure that's all it is?"

"Maybe suffering a little bit of envy, having that feeling of family is not something that worked out so well for me." Pulling out of my arms, she wipes her face on the hem of some man's T-shirt she is wearing, wipes her hair off her face and presents me with a forced smile. "Anyway, let's go join the gang. You must be starving. Long day? I know I am. Haven't eaten yet either," she babbles as she pulls me along the side of barn to the back where the mouth-watering smells of barbecue are making my stomach groan in anticipation.

Definitely not a good time for my news. I'm going to have to shelve it for tomorrow. I'm not about to mess with the celebratory atmosphere at the party, nor am I going to upset Naomi tonight. Looks like she may be barely hanging on as it is.

Gus spots me rounding the corner and walks toward me, but before he mentions anything, I give him a little shake of my head. He claps me on the shoulder instead.

"Glad you could make it. Did you hear this one here saved the day?" He turns and lifts Naomi right off her feet, making her squeal. "Cool as a cucumber to hear Mal tell it. Took over like a general ordering two of my operatives around. Three if you count Katie."

A small crowd has gathered around us and Naomi sidles closer and closer to my side, a bright blush on her cheeks at all the praise directed at her. I casually slip my arm around her shoulders.

"Come on, Doc. Let's grab some food. I think we need the reinforcements." And with a little nudge she walks beside me to where Mal and Fox are carving the pig and handing out plates. Fox has kept his eyes on his mom the entire time, I notice, and when we get close enough, he puts down the plates he's holding with his good hand and gives her a hug. A small smile plays over her lips and only gets bigger when he says, "That was pretty awesome, Mom."

"Thanks, Bub. It *is* pretty awesome. It does mean I'll have to stay the night here though, to help out with the baby."

"I'll be ok. I'll just catch a ride with Gus and Emma."

"Actually," Neil, Gus's youngest employee and resident techie, walks up behind him, "remember that game we were talking about earlier? I actually have a copy on my computer at the motel. If your mom doesn't mind you hanging with me tonight, we could head over now and you can crash in the second bed if you get tired."

Don't think I've ever seen Fox smile before and man, it's like a punch to the gut. I couldn't see it before, but without a scowl and his face wide open, suddenly he's the spitting image of his mother. Squeezing Naomi's shoulder, I lean and say softly, "He'll be safe."

"Alright, fine. Have at it." She smiles at the exuberant high fives the two exchange before they take off, yapping about their upcoming night of gaming.

The food is fucking amazing. I'm just cleaning off my second plate when Emma and Arlene come over.

"I gotta say, I normally think babies look like little old men, but this baby actually looks good. Almost cute," Arlene volunteers, stealing a piece of pork off my plate and popping it in her mouth. Naomi snickers as Emma elbows Arlene in the ribs. "Would you shush? Of course that baby is cute. All babies are cute."

"Let's agree to disagree on that. This particular baby is cute... almost, but mostly because he smiled at me."

"Arlene, he did not smile at you. Babies don't smile until they're about eight weeks or so old. Only in some cases earlier. Right Naomi?"

Naomi just raises her hands. "Not getting into that one. Sorry, girls."

"Anyway, we were thinking you must be tired, right? So what about if Arlene and I take first shift here tonight, after you make sure they're ok, of course?" The pleading look both women throw Naomi is almost comical and I can't hold back the chuckle. What's with women and babies? But when Naomi starts voicing some concerns, I quickly cut her off, seeing with sudden clarity the possibilities this arrangement may bring.

"Doc, you're tired. Why don't I go say a quick hello, while you check Katie and the baby out and then I'll make sure you get home safely. Get some rest."

I try to put as much sincerity in my voice as possible, but from the looks on all three women's faces and Mal's chuckle beside me, my ass is busted. So I do what any mature, self-respecting man does in such a situation, I shrug my shoulders and grin.

"Jesus, Joe," Naomi mumbles, rolling her eyes. "Okay, fine. Let's go see if they're up for a quick hello."

Letting her lead, I try to contain my smile—with difficulty—as we make our way upstairs. Things have certainly looked up tonight. While Naomi does her thing with Katie and the baby, I wait in the hallway, congratulating Caleb, who looks equal parts stunned and deliriously happy with his new fatherhood status. I'd be lying if I said I didn't feel a small pang of something that might've been jealousy, but I force it down and concentrate on being happy for my friend.

Katie is just beaming. This soft, nurturing and openly happy person so different from the woman I first met a few years ago. That woman would've looked odd with a baby in her arms, but on this new Katie, it fit.

"You did good, girl," I tell her, kissing her on the forehead, saying our goodbyes.

Downstairs, Naomi tries to convince me we have to go let everyone know we're leaving, but I disagree. "Not going back there, Doc. It'll take us another hour to get out of here. They'll figure it out."

With my arm around her waist I pull her with me out the front door and to my truck.

"Wait—" she stops me. "I have my car over there."

"Leave it."

"No. What if I have to come back tonight?"

"I'll drive you."

"But what if you get called out? Then I'll be stuck."

Fuck. "Good point," I admit, walking her over to her ride, but when she tries to get in I flip her around and press her against the driver's side door. "Gonna be right behind you. You okay with this? Now's the time to send me packing, 'cause I don't know I'll be able to turn away later."

She snakes her arms around my waist and grabs my ass, pulling my cock—which has been hard since driving up here—against her belly.

"And let all this go to waste? Joe, I've been wet for you for three years. Didn't matter if I was angry or not; it never failed. I've all but forgotten what it's like to let a man inside me. These past weeks, I've dreamed of nothing but you filling me."

With a growl I slam my mouth down on her, pushing my tongue inside and tangling with hers, while my hands slide down to grab her ass and lift her up. Her legs wrap around my hips almost instinctively and with her back against the car, I grind myself against the heat of her pussy, about setting myself off in the process.

"Joe," she mumbles against my mouth, as her hands find purchase in my hair, but my name is just enough for me to realize I need to get her home, before I have her naked in our friend's front yard. I pull back with difficulty, causing her to whimper. Leaving my forehead against hers, I rest a minute to allow our breathing to slow down before I slide her down my body until her feet touch the ground.

"That was by far the best fucking thing I've heard in a long time. And beautiful? I can't wait to get up inside you, but not here. Get your ass in the car. I'm gonna be right behind you and soon I'll be all over you."

I pull open her door, lift her inside and go for my truck.

CHAPTER THIRTEEN

And let all this go to waste? I've been wet for you?

On the short drive home, with Joe riding my bumper, I still have way too much time to think. And what I'm thinking is that I've gone and lost my mind. Who says shit like that? I behaved like some two-bit sex operator and sounded no better. If I didn't need both hands on the steering wheel, I'd have my face covered right now; I'm that embarrassed. Emotional. Too fucking emotional. It's either flat or deep with me and it's exhausting. Why I have to be this emotionally unbalanced *every* time around Joe, I have no idea, but I'm sure the man's had enough of crazy women for a lifetime.

When I park the car, I turn off the engine and drop my head on the wheel. Maybe this is not such a good idea. I probably should've stayed with Katie and the baby and not just gone running off with Joe at the first opportunity. Well, not exactly the first opportunity but still. It seems inappropriate. Doesn't it?

The door beside me opening startles me, but even more so does the feel of Joe's firm hands pulling me down from my seat.

"Don't. Don't sit there and talk yourself out of something we both know is going to happen," he says talking to the top of my head because I am studying the tips of my toes.

"Naomi?" He leans in and I can feel the heat of his words penetrate my skin as he speaks. "I need you. I need to feel your fingers tangle in my hair, your tongue in my mouth, your skin under my hands and your pussy squeezing my cock. I need it all, honey."

Slowly raising my eyes, I find his burning with lust and something more. Need? I trace my fingers over his lips and along his jaw before whispering, "Let's go."

We barely make it inside the door, which is quickly kicked shut by a boot, when he has me up against a wall. His hands frantically moving over my body, his mouth covering mine. I'm tearing at his uniform shirt, struggling to get the buttons undone, when he gets impatient, grabs it behind his back and pulls it over his head, flinging it to the ground. With both hands he lifts my shirt right off me before his mouth is back, bruising my lips. Before I know what's happening, he has my bra off and my arms up over my head, held firmly in place; his lips never leaving mine. My bared breasts are stretched up and the friction of my nipples against the light dusting of hair on Joe's bare chest creates an added flush of sensation causing me to whimper in his mouth. I move to get more of it. Grabbing both my wrists in one hand, Joe moves his other down to cup and lift one of my breasts letting go of my lips to track an open-mouthed path down my neck to fit his mouth over my nipple.

"Yesss," slips out as I arch my back to feed him more. A fresh flood of arousal soaks my already wet panties with the hot suction of his mouth, when he lets the nipple pop out and lifts his blue eyes to me.

"Your tits are glorious. So fucking sweet, babe."

His hand already found its way to undo my jeans and starts working them down my hips. With my arms still held over my head, Joe has me naked against the wall and I can't think about anything but feeling him inside me. I'm aching. I don't recognize the sounds coming from my mouth. When I hear the sound of his zipper, my eyes close in anticipation.

"Please."

The sudden release of my arms almost makes me stumble.

"Arms around my neck and hold on tight," he growls, before he lifts me by the back of my legs, up against the wall. I can feel the head of his cock sliding through the wetness gathered between my legs and I shift to get more of it. So hard—so hot. In one thrust, Joe slides himself inside me with a grunt.

"Jesus, baby—so fucking tight. Are you alright? Doc?"

I can feel him leaning back and taking me in. My eyes squeezed shut against stinging tears that want to escape. My lips pressed tight to hold back the cry of pain at the sudden burn.

"I'm ok. I want this, Joe. I'll be ok."

When I open my eyes I see the concern in his.

"Taking you to a bed. Where I can take proper care of you."

With that he slides out of me and I almost cry at the loss. Kicking off the pants around his ankles, Joe leans down, picks me up and walks into the bedroom where he drops me on the bed and lays down beside me.

"Didn't mean to hurt you, babe," he says stroking the hair out of my face. *Oh God!* I am mortified.

"So much for my big mouth, huh?" I try to joke it off, but he doesn't look amused.

"How long?" he wants to know.

I hesitate and start tripping over my words. "Really Joe? A while, okay? I'm... I just... I've been busy."

He chuckles, "I know you've been busy. How long, Naomi?"

I try glaring at him, but it doesn't have much of an effect when you're lying naked in a bed, in the dark.

"Four years, give or take," I mumble, starting to pull the covers around me, but Joe rolls partially on top of me and lifts my arms over my head again.

"That's a fucking long time, honey."

"Yeah, well—"

"Pleased as shit you'd let me in. I am," he leans in and kisses me sweetly.

"Now let's see if we can do a better job of honoring that privilege."

While one hand holds my arms in place, the other starts stroking down my body, his keen eyes following its moves, slowly making my skin tingle. Fingers tracing the curves of my breasts, gently rolling my nipple between two fingers and trailing down to my stomach, tracing the outline of my bellybutton. It isn't until his fingers trace the fold of skin left behind by the C-section that produced Fox, after thirty-six hours of labor, that I suddenly become aware of how exposed I am. The small bedside lamp was left on and everything is out in the open. I start struggling against his hold on my wrists, but Joe holds me fast, with his hand and his eyes.

"Trust me."

Seems such a simple request, but with so many layers.

"Stop thinking, Doc, and feel. Feel this," he says pushing the hard ridge of his cock into my hip. "That's what you do to me. Now trust me."

I try to relax while he explores every flawed inch of my body with his fingers and eyes, and when he leans in to kiss every part of me almost reverently after his scrutiny, I find myself relaxing into his touch more and more. When he finally lets go of my arms and lets me touch him in return, I'm putty in his hands. My legs fall open without reservation as he slides down to taste me.

When he finally slides into me, his hands holding my head so he can look me in the eyes, I'm languid and pliant from a few orgasms from his mouth and fingers. This time, the stretch when he fills me, is nothing short of bliss.

"So much better than I ever could've imaged," I tell him, my voice husky. The concern in his eyes is instantly replaced with a smoldering heat as he starts moving carefully. But when my hands take a firm grip on his stellar ass and encourage his movements, he scoots a hand under my hips, lifts me for a better angle and starts pistoning his hips in earnest. It doesn't take long before I can feel an unbelievable third climax building. My hand slides between our bodies and almost without thinking, I work that bundle of nerves to a crest before tumbling over, wrapping myself around Joe.

"Fuck!" his body jerks as he pumps his release inside me and collapses on top, his head buried in my neck.

When he tries to roll off, I hang on. "Don't go yet," I mumble.

"I'm too heavy."

"I like you on me—in me."

Joe pushes up on his arms and the smile he gives me takes my breath away. After a minute, he's rolling off me with obvious reluctance to clean up in the bathroom. He comes back with a washcloth and a towel, and I'm so far gone, I let him clean me.

"You're right you know," he says.

"'Bout what?"

"Reality *is* much better than the imagination. Now that I know what you feel like, I wish I'd never wasted my time on anyone else."

"So why did you?" I whisper.

"Because I never thought I'd get a second chance," he says, stroking my hair away from my face.

I can feel the blush staining my cheeks and try turning away when Joe leans down and whispers against my lips.

"You. Are. Beautiful."

Waking up with Naomi's warm soft body tangled up with mine is my new favorite part of the day. One I'd like to have on repeat indefinitely. Her body half splayed over mine, legs entwined and her cheek pressed to my chest, puffing little breaths through her parted lips is not something I'm likely to tire of.

After she let me clean her up last night we didn't say much, just curled up together and fell asleep, exhausted by the day's events and sated by each other's bodies. Sure, I feel guilty for keeping information from her she has a right to, but I figure after the day she had—fuck, after the day I had—we both deserved this.

The harsh light of day has a way of bringing realities back to the forefront, and I know I have to clear the decks with her. A quick peek at the alarm clock on the nightstand tells me it's early yet—only five thirty in the morning—but I don't want to take any chances. Detangling myself under her sleepy protestations and sliding out of bed, I go in search of my pants and some coffee.

A quick check of my messages shows a missed text from Carol to remind me to get back to Frank Bancroft. *Right.* Interesting timing, that. I should've called him back on Sunday, but it being Sunday, I figured it could wait. Then yesterday was a total loss and now I'm left wondering what the hell he wanted. Why did he contact me before the Phoenix PD did the next day? How did he find me? As far as I know, Naomi never mentioned where she was to him. In fact, she was quite adamant in saying she didn't. I'll have to get back to him this morning, and find out what he wants before heading back into the office, awaiting the shit storm to inevitably hit me. I have a feeling things are about to go downhill fast. All the more reason to get clean with Naomi, no matter how tough a conversation it might be.

Coffee ready, I pour two cups and take them back into the bedroom, where Naomi is just rolling over and stretching, the covers sliding low leaving her glorious tits exposed. Fuck, but she's beautiful. One hundred percent real; not a fake or phony part to her. A pained groan escapes me as I will down the resurgence of my morning wood and she turns her gorgeous chocolate eyes to me.

"Morning," she smiles, making to draw up the sheets to cover herself.

"Wish you wouldn't 'cause I'm liking the view, but with this hot coffee around, maybe you should. Wouldn't want those beauties to get burned," I point out, putting the coffee on the nightstand.

"Smooth, Joe. Real smooth," she snickers.

"Hey. I speak only the truth," I say, sitting beside her in bed, my back against the headboard.

"Why so early?"

"Because unfortunately, we have some stuff to discuss before the day hits us."

She turns to me looking concerned and I palm her face and kiss her lightly. "Morning, Beautiful. Last night was exactly what I needed. What I'd wanted for a long time. But you were so tired and worn out physically and emotionally, I didn't have the heart to get into it then. Not for me and not for you."

"Okay, Joe, this is not making me feel better. If you're gonna walk away, just tell me please?"

"Not a chance in hell, honey. Not going anywhere," I say wrapping her in my arms. "I got a call from the Phoenix PD yesterday. First they grilled me because they weren't happy when they discovered I had the transcripts for James' last case delivered to me. I told you they'd already been pissed for me not being cooperative in telling them where to find you. Anyway, after some territorial bullshit, they dropped a bomb on me."

Her eyes are on me and I need to have her closer for this so I lift her to straddle my lap so I can hold her to me when I tell her.

"Four days ago, now five, they found a body just west of Phoenix on the banks of the Gila River. The coroner confirmed yesterday that the body is James."

I can feel her body go rigid in my arms and her face shows shock, before her eyes fill with tears and she starts shaking.

"He's dead? James? I don't understand—How?"

I pull her head into my chest and let her weep. I didn't know. Hadn't considered she might still have residual feelings for the man, but it doesn't stop me from hurting at the sound of her pain.

"I'm sorry, baby, so sorry..." I mumble in her hair as I stroke her back. "He was shot."

What I don't tell her is that the man had been worked over good before that. By the sounds of it the bullet would've likely come as a relief.

"Poor Fox. My... my baby's gonna be crushed," she hiccups, and I realize that her pain is for her son and I give myself a mental slap, before sitting her back and cupping her face.

"I'm here. Whatever you need, for you and for him."

"You already are, Joe. I don't want you putting so much on the line here. Don't want you getting into deep water over me."

"Not for you to worry about. Besides, we have bigger things to worry about. You've gotta check in with Emma and Arlene to see how things went with Katie and I have to put a call into the office. Then we go get Fox and bring him back here. You want me here when you tell him?"

She covers her face with her hands and rubs hard. "Oh God... yes. Yes, please. I can barely get my head around this. He might have questions I can't answer, and maybe you can. Do you mind?"

"I said anything, babe." And I mean it, even if the thought of Fox hurting hits me almost as hard as seeing Naomi in pain does.

With the coffee cold and forgotten on the nightstand, I lift her off me and grab her hand, leading her into the bathroom where I turn on the water and divest myself of my pants again. Under the hot water spray I quickly wash her hair and soap her body and mine, trying not to get turned on. Impossible feat, so I work hard at ignoring my body's almost involuntary response to her.

Naomi's fingers trace over the tattoo on my chest and the initials prominently displayed inside it.

"Someday, will you tell me about this?" she asks, almost tentatively.

"Absolutely," I give her, and see relief flit over her face.

Naomi calls Emma, who reports that other than having to wake Mattias up for his feeds, the night had been uneventful and mom was doing well. I put my own call in to Carol who had just walked in and told me it'd been a quiet night and that she'd keep me in the loop.

After I manage to get Naomi to eat a slice of toast with her coffee, we take off to pick up her son; who probably had one of the most exciting nights of his life, judging by his enthusiasm from last night, only for us to have to bring him the worst possible news. Parenthood fucking sucks.

CHAPTER FOURTEEN

"It was awesome, Mom. You wouldn't believe all the shit he has on his computers. I'm so going to study Computer Science."

My son is flying high after an exciting night for him and I'm not even gonna bother killing the buzz by harping on his language. His buzz is gonna crash soon enough. Fox is a little surprised to find me with Joe in his truck, looking between us, but after a shrug of his shoulders seems to take it in stride. I hadn't considered what it would be like for both of us to show up at the motel at such an early hour. Luckily Fox is still a typical kid in some ways and easily distracted. In this case, all I had to do was ask how his night was.

"Glad you had a good time, Bub, and fantastic you found something you think you'll like." I smile at him finding him staring at me slack-mouthed.

"Really?"

"What do you mean really? Of course. That's a great choice with amazing potential. I can totally see you do that. Why is that so hard to believe?" I turn all the way around in my seat to face him straight on.

"Dad always said you guys would want me to be a lawyer like him, so I could take over his part in the firm."

I can't help myself. The timing is completely off, but I snort and I do it loudly, causing Joe to take his eyes off the road and look at me, eyebrow raised and lips twisting.

"Nope. Wasn't my wish for you. Not ever. Not unless it was something you were really passionate about."

I reach for his hand and squeeze. "I'm sorry Dad made you think that, honey. I wish you'd have told me; I'd have set you straight. I don't care what you choose for yourself, as long as it is legal—" Fox rolls his eyes at this, "—makes you a living and is something you love doing. Could be anything."

"Cool." The smile that accompanies that answer makes it so much more meaningful than the single syllable.

Fuck, I hate that I'm about to wreck this good moment. I just want to wrap it up and keep it safe somewhere so I can look at it later. Joe's hand sneaks over and settles on my knee, giving it a little pressure. I have a feeling he gets it. He gets a lot. Surprising for a guy who doesn't have kids. He'd make a great dad.

I know I should probably be angry that he didn't tell me about James right as he found out, but I just can't find it in myself. What he gave me last night was a little pocket of goodness, of happiness. Some strength I can tap from when my stamina runs low again, which it undoubtedly will. I'm not as strong as I make myself look.

"Don't think too hard," I hear Joe's deep voice softly and I look over to find his clear blue eyes softly on me.

"Okay," I whisper back, and try not to think too much as we make our way home.

"Dead?"

"I'm so sorry, baby," I whisper as I run my hand over my son's back.

We're on the couch in the guesthouse with Joe across from us in the big club chair, where we sat down the moment we walked in announcing to Fox we had to talk. It's only eight thirty in the morning and already I've managed to yank my son off cloud nine into the brutal reality this day will bring. No matter what James was, or had done, my boy just found out he lost his father. Furthermore, my kid is smart. He suspects the timing is too coincidental to spell anything other than big trouble. His face is pale, but his eyes are sharp when they shoot up at Joe.

"Did he do this? That guy on the phone? The one Dad was representing? Did he kill him?"

Joe briefly looks at me before turning back to Fox.

"Can't say for sure, bud. No way of knowing at this point, but it looks like it was foul play. Your dad was shot."

I can feel Fox's body jerk under my hand and I want nothing more than to fold him in my arms and shield him, but the clench of his jaw and the rigid tension in his shoulders tell me that he is struggling to hold on. Trying to be a man, perhaps even for my sake, and it breaks my heart. Sudden anger surges through me, at James mostly, for a lifetime of skimming the boundaries of the law to safeguard his precious clients, yet creating a situation that endangered his family, his son. One that cost him his life.

"Where is he?" The question is asked in a small voice and is one I hadn't even thought of to ask Joe.

"He will be at the coroner's office for a while, most likely. It may be some time yet before they release his body."

Joe's answer has many different implications, none of which I want to think about or more importantly, want my son to have on his mind, so I ask one of my own.

"James has a sister in Boston. Do you think she's been contacted?" I'd met Ruth only twice throughout the entire duration of our marriage; once on the day of our wedding and then again when James' mother passed away about a year or so after Fox was born. Needless to say James and Ruth had never been close.

"They mentioned having been in touch with a family member but needing to speak to you."

Fox abruptly gets up off the couch. "I'm gonna go lie down. Didn't get much sleep." With that, he walks off into the bedroom before I have a chance to say anything. I get up to follow after him, to make sure he's ok, but Joe grabs my wrist when I pass.

"Let him be, babe. I watched him sit there, trying to be strong; holding it together like a man. Let him do his grieving in his own way."

"But he's my baby," I whisper, my voice cracking with the pain I feel for him.

With a tug Joe has me on his lap and tucked under his chin.

"I lost my parents young, Doc. It was a tough blow, but it was something I had to work out myself. My dad and I had never seen eye to eye growing up and once he was gone, there was no way to fix that. Ever. I'm thinking what's going through that boy's mind right now, may run along similar lines. Losing his dad, a dad who was too busy criticizing him to see the awesome kid he had? I'm thinking Fox is all kinds of conflicted right now with what he's feeling and it wouldn't be something that'd be that easy to express. Least of all to you."

I bristle at the last and open my mouth ready to launch into a defense when Joe simply puts his hand on my mouth, effectively silencing me.

"Beautiful, you think maybe he carries guilt? You and I both know he's got no reason to. But he knows you. He knows you won't hesitate in telling him that and he's not in a place where he can hear it yet. He'll get there. Give him some time."

While he's talking, Joe is stroking me as if to calm me and I'm irritated that it works.

"You annoy me," I tell him which only makes him chuckle.

"Why's that?"

"'Cause I don't like it when you make better sense of my son than I do. I'm his mom," I admit grudgingly.

"I'm a guy. He's a guy. It's that easy, babe," he says, the smile evident in his voice as his arms tighten around me.

The little pocket of peace in the comfy club chair lasts only minutes, when it's interrupted by Joe's phone. I slide off his lap so he can fish it out of his pocket and go to busy myself in the kitchen to give him some privacy.

"Morris." I watch Joe get up and start pacing, tension in his posture. "Right, have them wait in my office. I'll be there in twenty."

"Everything okay?" I can't stop myself from asking when he slides the phone back in his pocket and pushes a hand through his hair. Almost distractedly, he looks over to me.

"Yeah. No worries. Just have to go into the office for a bit. Think you'll be okay for a couple of hours? I'll be back as soon as

I can, just don't take off on your own. Call Gus or Neil if you have to go out."

I curb the urge to call him on his bossiness, because I don't like the bleak look I see in his eyes. That phone call was something. Instead I walk over and wrap my arms around his waist and lay my cheek on his chest. After a few seconds his arms come around me and I feel him breathe me in.

"I'll be here," I tell him, tilting my head back and he slides a hand up my neck to rest on my cheek.

"That'd be good."

An all too brief touch of his mouth to mine and he's gone, the house quiet but my mind loud with questions.

I'm tempted to go and check on Fox, but decide to give him a little more time to see if he'll come out of the room on his own. In the meantime I want to check in with Katie.

"Hey girl. How's the new momma this morning?"

"A little sore. The stitches are bugging me a little, but other than that we're doing fine. I've had food, I've managed to go pee normally, even though it burns like a son of a bitch and little peanut is as fascinated with my ever expanding boobage as his father. If I'd known I could go to a D-cup almost overnight, I might've done this baby thing sooner," she chuckles, making me laugh.

"Good to know Mattias is taking to the breast so well, but don't be discouraged if there are days when you have to struggle with him. It's still a learning process for both of you. As for Caleb's fascination? Not sure I needed to know that, thanks." I can't help but smile when I visualize Caleb's adoration for his wife, not something he does well at hiding. "And Katie? Peanut is hardly an appropriate nickname anymore for the little bruiser you popped out. I was tempted to fit him with shoes for crying out loud."

"Don't care how big he is, he'll always be our peanut. He'll just have to get used to it."

The temptation to bare my soul to my friend is great, but I'm not going to burden her with my issues right now so when she asks how I am doing, I dodge.

"I'm actually home for another day or two and am thinking of taking a second look at that old feed store. Maybe I'll call Clint and see what he thinks of the possibilities for what I have in mind."

"Ohhh, that would be so exciting! I would love for you to be closer by. I know for a fact you won't be lacking for patients and you fit in here perfectly. You'll love it—I promise." Katie's enthusiasm lifts my spirits a little.

"Is there anything you need from me right now? Because I'll come right away if you do, you know that. Otherwise, I'll check in again with you later. I'll be by at some point to check on you guys in person."

"We're fine. I promise I'll call."

Just then I hear a knock at the door of the guesthouse and quickly say goodbye to Katie.

On the doorstep are two men; one younger one who looked like he'd had a career in boxing at some point, his nose broken at least a few times, and the second an older, much slicker—slimier even—and well-dressed man, both holding out badges.

"Ms. Waters?" the slimy one asks.

"That's me."

"Detectives Warner and Libretti of the Phoenix PD, ma'am. We'd like to speak to your son Fox Miller. Is he home?"

"I'm sorry. What exactly is this about?" I know I'm being suspicious, but I clearly recall Joe saying that he had not revealed our whereabouts, arranging instead to have the detectives meet with us at his office tomorrow morning. So what they're doing on my doorstep wanting to talk to Fox about right now, I'm not quite sure, but I know I don't like it. Don't want to talk to them without the security of Joe here.

"Ma'am, if you could just get him, we have some questions for him." It's the older one again, Libretti he said his name was. The other one is trying to look over my shoulder into the guesthouse and I find myself pulling the door closed a little, hoping Fox will stay in the bedroom until I get this figured out. Something feels off.

"I'd be happy to as soon as you inform me what this is regarding, otherwise I'm sorry, I'll be forced to contact my lawyer. You're Phoenix PD, as you indicate, and as far as I understand we are about four hundred miles from your jurisdiction, so forgive me if I am a little cautious."

"Ma'am. Ms. Waters—" the young one, Warner, says trying for a soothing tone, which only serves to raise my hackles further. "Your son's name has come up in two murder cases that we believe he holds crucial information on, or at the very least, had some knowledge of."

At a loss for words, I sag against the door. Are they crazy? They think Fox had anything to do with that? Taking advantage of my shift in position, Libretti squeezes past me into the house before I realize what's happening.

"Hey wait! I haven't given you permission. What are you doing?"

I'm about to tear after him when I see him going into the hallway to the bedroom and bathrooms, but my arms are suddenly pulled behind me and I'm being pushed face first into the door.

"I'm charging you with obstruction of justice and the possible harboring of a fugitive, ma'am." Detective Warner's voice is close to my ear. Too close and shivers run down my spine, but my temper flares anyway.

"Are you out of your fucking mind? Do you think I'm an idiot? You have no right to charge me or anyone else in this town. Hell, in this state! If you lay one finger on my son, I will come after you with every damn resource I have, and you may not think I have any, but you'd be terribly wrong!"

I'm screaming at the top of my lungs when I see the older guy coming back into view... without Fox.

"Ma'am you'd better calm down and tell us where your son is."

Suddenly a new voice from behind me.

"If you don't have those handcuffs off her in the next few seconds, your mother won't recognize you by the time I'm done with you. And if you are thinking of trying to throw any so-called 'official business' in my face, let me tell you that my wife is currently on the phone with my good friend, Assistant Chief Wayne Carr of the Phoenix Police Department. Your boss. He was very interested in hearing that I saw one of his Chevy Tahoes pull up and what looked to be two detectives walk up to my guest's quarters. In Colorado, it's considered bad manners to barge in on a neighbor without prior warning, especially to the local law enforcement. Your Chief wasn't too impressed when I had to hand over the phone to my wife because I heard my guest screaming."

Gus's voice has a lazy and deceptively calm timbre, but the threat in the delivery of his words is unmistakable and once again, I'm so very grateful for the friends I've been blessed with. The click behind me and the release of the tight pinch around my wrists immediately following shows the young detective takes his words seriously as well. The next thought on my mind is Fox as I move past the other detective, down the hallway to the bedroom, only to find it empty. What the hell? I check the closet, thinking maybe he slipped in there when he heard the detective coming down the hallway, but it is also empty. Next the bathroom, where I find no Fox, but the small bathroom window above the tub seems to be off the lock and my shampoo and conditioner that sit on the edge underneath have been moved to the other side. Little bugger went out the window. A quick peek outside only shows the edge of the cornfield and beyond, but no sign of my son.

CHAPTER FIFTEEN

"Where is she?"

I know I'm being rude when I walk through Emma's kitchen, virtually ignoring her, after finding the guesthouse empty, but my day has gone from bad to awful.

I had been expecting a reprimand for not willingly giving up Naomi's whereabouts to my colleagues from Phoenix, especially after I'd already pissed them off by being too interested in James Miller's disappearance. What I didn't expect was to be put on suspension pending further investigation. Someone obviously has a hard-on for me.

Driving home, still reeling from the blow and needing some time to clear my head, I get a call from Emma telling me to get my ass over to Cedar Tree because Gus is facing off with two Phoenix detectives who have Naomi in cuffs. My own woes instantly forgotten, I turn my truck around and break every speed limit getting here, but the guesthouse is empty and neither Fox nor Naomi are anywhere to be found.

"They're out in the fields," Emma says from behind me as I stomp through her house into the GFI offices, hoping to find her there. "Gus and Naomi; they're out there looking for Fox."

I shake my head, not quite computing the information. "Sorry. I don't get it."

"Fox took off. Or at least they think he did. He was gone from the bedroom when one of the detectives went looking for him and later Naomi. She thinks he went through the bathroom window. The two from Phoenix were called off and are gone now, but he hasn't come back. He left his cell in the kitchen, so he doesn't have that with him and they were calling around the edge of the field for him, but no response yet." Emma looks at me with worry all over her face, so I grab hold of her hand and pull here into a brief hug.

"Sorry for barging in on you like that. I promise we'll find the boy. Let me go out there and look around."

"Okay, but just so you know, I called Neil and he's on his way over to help. Mal is out of town on that job Gus was supposed to go on, but I didn't call Caleb. Should I?"

"Leave Caleb for now. They have enough to worry about with the little one. If things change we can always call him in. Thanks Emma. Gus is a lucky man," I tell her with a quick kiss to her forehead before I head out the backdoor and start for the fields.

I've stayed in the immediate vicinity of the guesthouse, scouring the ground underneath the bathroom window—even though I'm sure that was likely the first thing Gus would've done—and checking anywhere for prints or signs of a possible struggle. I found an area right by the edge of the trees on the side of the cornfield, about ten feet in that looked like it had been recently stirred up. Right now Neil is going over it with a fine-tooth comb.

With Fox gone for over two and a half hours now and no sign of Naomi and Gus, other than his text a few minutes ago saying *'coming back,'* I don't really have a good feeling about this. Thank God Doc is on her way back here. I need to feel her in my arms. It won't take away the nagging worry about Fox, but it will at least take away the uneasy feeling I have when I'm not around her. This day could not get more fucked up.

Voices at the edge of the field alert me to their approach and the moment I see her shiny brown hair coming out of the cornstalks I stalk over, my eyes only for her. I just have time to register the fatigue around her eyes and the tightness of her mouth before I have her up off the ground, safely in my arms. Hers cling tightly around my neck, her head burrowing there too.

"So glad you're here," her voice breaks as she mumbles against my skin.

My eyes search for Gus, and aside from the slight shake of his head, our entire conversation is held in silence, conveyed only by our eyes. Years and years of friendship and working together will do that.

Neil, who must've heard their return as well, joins us, but as he is about to launch into a description of the spot we think we found, I cut him off with a look. My girl needs some attention and some food first and then we can discuss details. I'm not about to keep what we found from her, but first I need to get a little of the strain off her face. I'm still holding her, her legs are wrapped around my waist and she clings to me like a monkey, as we turn to head back in the direction of the house. Emma is in the door of her kitchen, looking at our procession, wiping at her eyes with her apron.

"I'm sure Emma has food for an army by now. Get yourselves cleaned up and come over. We'll plan then," Gus says, putting a hand on Naomi's back. "Got a smart kid, Doc, and a bunch of fucking smart men on your side. He doesn't come back, we'll find him. He can't come back on his own, we'll go get him. Either way, your boy's coming home."

A final nod at me and he's off with Neil on his heels.

I'm worried about the woman in my arms.

"Come on, honey. We're gonna grab a quick shower."

She doesn't even say anything when I carry her into the bathroom. Deja vu. The only difference being that this is her bathroom, not mine. Actually, she also doesn't seem quite as out of it as she was that first time. At least she's looking at me and stands straight as I strip her down. I quickly throw off my own clothes and step in with her under the warm spray. A quick soap and rinse, that's all.

"Do you think he has him?" Her voice is low and rough, as if she has to force the words out.

"Heffler? It's doubtful. He may still be off somewhere on his own, scared at what he may have overheard. Upset about his father's death."

"I thought that at first, but I don't believe for one minute he wouldn't leave word for me somehow. If he overheard what was going on, he would've been worried about me. He would've tried to go for help. He could've gone to Emma and Gus. Why didn't he? It makes no sense."

She's right of course. She voices everything I've been thinking already. There isn't a fucking thing I can say to her right now. I'd just be guessing at things, making up more possible scenarios when the ones I have going through my mind now are disturbing enough.

After making sure we are both rinsed off, I step out of the shower and grab a towel from the shelf, holding it open for her.

I'm trying not to notice the blush from the hot shower on her tempting curves, but my cock has other ideas. Her eyes briefly come to rest on my groin before quickly raising to meet mine. She immediately starts drying herself vigorously while I grab a towel for myself. Some of the tightness is gone around her mouth and at least she's communicating instead of falling apart. My girl is so much tougher than she gives herself credit for. It's been a hell of a day... for all of us.

"Beautiful, it's been a matter of hours at this point and I know that Gus is on the phone right now calling in every favor he can. As soon as we're dressed, I'm calling the Cortez Chief of Police who may not be a close friend necessarily, but he owes me a favor or two. The entire county will be on the lookout."

"Thank you," she says softly, the ghost of a small distracted smile on her lips.

"Don't thank me. I care for your boy and honey, you've gotta know how deep you are under my skin by now."

Who am I kidding? She's not just under my skin, she's in my heart. But this isn't the time for such declarations.

Once dressed, we head over to the main house. It's been only fifteen minutes, give or take, since I carried Naomi in the house, but with it being so late in the season, the sun goes down earlier each day and the temperature drops dramatically. Despite both of us wearing sweaters, the chill is noticeable. I put my arm around Naomi's shoulder and tuck her in against my body.

"He must be cold," she says, shivering slightly under my hand.

"He's bright. I'd like to think he's found shelter or is keeping warm somehow."

A single nod is my only response.

Emma's seen us coming 'cause she's at the door waving us in. Both Gus and Neil are sitting at the counter with bowls of some kind of soup and a big plate of sandwiches in front of them.

"Pull up a stool and I'll grab you some bowls. Fresh chicken noodle soup and a few sandwiches; I thought simple would do the trick. Y'all have to eat something. Can I get you a drink?" Emma directs her attention at Naomi, who hesitates at the door. With a little nudge at the small of her back I get her moving further into the kitchen.

"Just some water for me, Emma, thanks." Her voice is soft but steady.

"I'll have the same, unless you've got coffee on the go." I smile at Emma who has returned to the opposite side of the counter, her favorite spot in the house.

"Boys wanted coffee too, so I have some. Black—right, Joe?"

"Please."

Taking the stool next to Naomi has her wedged in between Gus and I, and when Emma slides a bowl of soup in front of her, and she tries to refuse, I see him lean over to her.

"Gotta eat, girl. Keep your strength up. It's light fare, so just try a few bites; maybe a couple of bites of a sandwich too. No one is served by you collapsing, right?"

Knowing Gus is just trying to look out for her, I'm curbing the urge to step in for her. Judging from the scathing look she throws him through slitted eyelids, she doesn't really need my help. My feisty Doc is present and accounted for. Thank God.

"Not a child, Gus. I'll eat, okay?" she bites out through tight lips before turning to her bowl of soup and demonstratively shoveling a spoonful in her mouth. Only to wave her hand in front of her face hissing and blowing. "Fuck me. That's hot."

"Could've blown on it first, maybe?" This from Neil who's chuckling on the other side of Gus.

"Thanks smartass. I'll take it under advisement for my next go around." Naomi gulps down her glass of water as I smile seeing her spunky side return.

Gus fills us in on the phone calls he's made, and Neil explains he's been able to find two distinctly different footprints just inside the tree line but aside from some evidence of a recent scuffle judging by the torn up soil and snapped and twisted branches, there wasn't much concrete information. He has made high-resolution images of the prints though, and plans to do some research on the type of shoes they may have come from.

"So it would seem that everyone is in agreement he appears to have been taken?" Naomi puts it out there, straightening her back as she does it.

"Looks like he may have left on his own accord but was picked up shortly after and not far from the house. What's most concerning is that not only was the Phoenix PD able to locate you without my input, but someone else was as well," I point out.

"Afraid I already might have the answer to the first one," Gus says with a brief look at me before turning his eyes to Naomi. "Had a brief call before we sat down, with my buddy in Phoenix. Just so you know, the two detectives who were here will be disciplined for their actions. They broke protocol on every level. He found out his guys went to Cortez Memorial and talked to the hospital administrator."

I feel sick to my stomach. My fucking mistake with Jenna was coming back to haunt me big time. That miserable bitch.

"I quit! That fucking hateful Barbie bitch! She's done nothing but make my life absolute hell since Joe's shown an interest. I'm so done with this." Already off her stool, Naomi goes straight for the backdoor. With her hand on the doorknob she turns to me. "Don't know what the hell you were thinking, Joe, getting with that mean-spirited piece of plastic. At my place of work and under my fucking nose!"

With that she storms out the door and only Gus's hand on my shoulder holds me back from taking off after her.

"Let Emma. Neil will keep an eye on them. Let her cool down buddy. This is all emotion coming out."

I stand there like a fucking idiot watching Emma and Neil follow Naomi to the guesthouse. What a colossal fuck up. I can't blame her; if not for my stupidity, her son wouldn't be missing. Simple as that. I chuckle bitterly when I think that a few hours ago I thought the day couldn't get any worse.

Gus slaps his arm around my shoulders and guides me down the hall to the GFI office where he pulls out a bottle of scotch. When I put up my hand in refusal, he shoves it aside.

"One shot to take the sting off, my friend. Then we put the bottle away and get Fox back."

It's frustrating when suddenly you have no jurisdiction, no power.

For the last half hour I managed to get a hold of the Cortez Chief of Police who promises to put as many men on the search as he can spare and put a BOLO out for all the patrols, but not without giving me a hard time about what he's picked up from the rumor mill. Fucking hell. Already? Haven't had a chance to drop that bomb on Naomi and frankly after what happened earlier, I'm not sure it'd be a good idea.

Of course the Cortez PD generally refers to the Sheriff's Office for anything outside of their city limits, but this time it squeezes by because of the possible connection to the attack on Michael Vincent. Personally I doubt it. I'd be more inclined to think Heffler would be a more likely candidate to be behind this, but I'm not gonna argue.

I also wanted to call and tear a strip off Jenna, but Gus says he'll take care of that. Probably. I can't promise that my vow never to hurt a woman is going to hold with this one.

Calling the Sheriff's Office is out of the question for me, that much was made clear to me this morning. I am not to have contact with my staff or have access to any of the files in my office or on my computer, so Gus ends up calling Carol and puts her on speakerphone. She sounds pretty pissed and even though she knows very well I am on the other side listening, she makes it a point to say loudly, "You tell my sheriff we'll get this shit cleared up in no time. You hear me, Gus? Damn place is going to hell in a hand basket when they suspend a man for protecting his own damn family. Bunch of paper pushers!" The last was said with such vehemence, as if it were the absolute worst insult you could bestow on a man, so much so that Gus and I both burst out laughing. A diamond, my Carol, and in her way, she lets us know clearly that she is being monitored... and not liking it one bit.

"I'll send Drew by and alert the other boys. No worries. You tell that woman we'll find her boy yet."

With all local law enforcement notified and from all appearances on board, we sit back to contemplate our next move, when the door to Gus's office slams open and Naomi storms in. She stops right in front of me, all five foot and spit of her, hands on her hips and fire shooting from her eyes.

"Are you ever gonna stop keeping shit from me?"

CHAPTER SIXTEEN

That jealous skank.

I'm fuming as I storm over to the guesthouse, contemplating all the ways I can take that bitch down. Anger has replaced most of the growing sense of despair and part of me is grateful for that. I'm angry at everyone right now; James, Jenna, the Phoenix PD and last but by no means least, Joe. My boy is out there somewhere in the fucking cold, and their combined shitty decisions and poor judgement have put him there.

I can hear the door opening and closing behind me, but I'm not interested to see if Joe is following me. Don't really care. I'm too worked up to face anyone right now. I barge into the guesthouse, not bothering to close the door. I know whoever is behind me will follow me in anyway. I head straight for the kitchen and open the fridge staring blankly at the shelves. What the fuck am I doing in here? It's not like I'm hungry, but the stressed and angry energy propelled me right to my biggest nemesis; the fridge. Back when I would lose myself in a cycle of depression and panic attacks, I would often self-medicate with food, which would lead to more verbal abuse from James, which in turn would bring on further depression. A vicious cycle I knew I was in and seemed incapable to bring to a halt. Until I walked away from my marriage. I've done too well the past four years, only to fall apart now. With a frustrated scream I slam the fridge door shut and swing around, only to find Emma standing behind me, regarding me with one eyebrow raised.

"Feel better now?" she asks me sharply, and I'm a little taken aback at her tone.

"Hardly," I mumble, a little embarrassed now at my tantrum. With a few words and one look she has me thinking about my behavior and—*oh shit*—my words, and as suddenly as it came up, the burst of angry energy deflates. Emma just looks at me as I slump down on a kitchen stool, putting my head to rest on my arms on the counter.

"You know you can't hold him responsible for that woman's behavior, right? I love you to bits, Naomi, and I only recently got to understand the full depth of your hurt, but I've seen a good friend try hard for years to try and make what was a fucked up situation right. You slammed the door in his face at every turn, girl. Nobody's happier than I am to see you both finally getting your heads out of your asses to give what should've happened a long time ago a chance, but if you insist on dragging up past history that Joe no longer has any control over, I don't see it lasting long."

Ouch. I flinch at the direct hit of her words. It fucking stings. Not that she's lying— no—everything she says is dead-on. I'm fighting not to dissolve into tears again. I've done so much crying recently, I'm sick of myself. Can't seem to hold back my natural instinct to defend myself just a little bit, though.

"My boss, Emma? Did he have to fuck my boss? A woman who hates me on the best of days? She took every opportunity to rub that fact that she was dating him in my face. I guess word must've gotten around that we'd had something years back because she was like a dog with a bone and the moment he dumped her ass and turned his attention back to me, I got the brunt of it."

God I even sound whiny to my own ears. Emma shakes her head slightly as looks at me with a mixture of reprimand and compassion.

"I'm sure he'll be the first to admit he fucked up, Naomi, and if my guess is right, he probably already has, one or two times. Let's clear something up too; he never 'dated' her, as much as she liked to spread around that she did. My guess is, she did that for your benefit alone, or perhaps she's just that delusional. Fact is, the only relationship that ever existed between them was in her head. And let's face it, that man's ego took a hefty beating at your hands. How long was he supposed to hold out waiting for you to let him in? I'm sure he made an easy target for the likes of Jenna at that point."

This is a good old-fashioned 'talking-to' and I can feel myself shrinking with every direct hit I take. Her voice softens as she continues, "You gotta at least own some of that, sweetie. And what about James? I know it's not easy being angry with a dead man, but Christ, if anyone deserves blame for whatever shit you guys are in, it would be him. Better yet, that douche he was defending... plenty of others to shoulder the blame, girl. All I'm sayin' is, shouldn't be putting it all on the shoulders of the man who went so far as to risk his job to protect you."

Okay, now I'm crying again. I'm officially as emotionally unbalanced as a pre-teen on the rag who's about to meet Justin Bieber. Well. The thought of that snot-nose punk just shriveled up my emotions on the spot.

"I never asked him to," I snivel pathetically as Emma pulls me into a hug.

"I know that, honey, but it doesn't change the fact that he risked and lost for you."

My entire body seizes up.

"Lost? What do you mean 'risked and *lost*?'" I pin Emma with my glare and I dread the answer when I see her eyes doing everything to avoid mine.

"Shit," she mumbles, "Me and my big mouth."

"Never mind. I need answers, Emma. Please."

"I don't think he wanted you to know, honey. Probably didn't want to add to your worries," she pleads with me.

"Emma..."

"Fine. He was suspended indefinitely. They took his badge pending investigation or some such horseshit. Gus is working on it. Was actually sorting things out with the Phoenix Assistant Chief when those yoyos pulled up."

A sick feeling settles in my stomach and I inadvertently wrap my arms around my midsection.

"I don't get it. He's the sheriff! How does that happen?" I'm trying to make sense of this as the implications are slowly starting to sink in. "Oh my God, Emma. I was horrible to him, and all while, he just had to hand in his badge? Over me?"

With my hand over my mouth, I just make it to the bathroom where I throw up what little I had managed to get down earlier. Emotional wreck, that's what I am. But while I'm berating myself over being so insensitive, I also become angry once again. This time for being left in the dark… again. Had I known, I wouldn't have made an ass of myself. He must've had a suspicion when he left this morning but never said a word.

I rinse my mouth and quickly wipe my face before moving in front of Emma who is standing in the doorway.

"You okay?" she asks, wiping a strand of hair off my cheek and tucking it behind my ear.

"I love you for giving it to me straight, but the truth is, I'm pissed again. I'm like a friggin' ping-pong ball. Don't try to keep up with me." I give her a kiss on the cheek and march past her out of the guesthouse.

"Never willingly tried to keep anything from you, Doc."

Joe sits up straighter in the chair he's occupying across from Gus's desk. "What did I do this time?" I wince slightly at the bitter edge to his tone, but I can't blame him for that. Doesn't mean I should back down.

"Think maybe you could've given me a heads' up on the mess you had gotten yourself into on my account?" From the corner of my eye I see Gus sneaking out of the room, leaving just the two of us behind. Mighty gracious of him, seeing as it's his office. "Before you lost your job— hell, your career—over me? I asked you specifically not to put yourself on the line!"

"No," he says, as calmly as can be as he slowly erects himself from the chair to stand in front of me. "For exactly this reason. I did what I had to do… for me." He punctuates the last part by leaning in so his face is only inches from mine. "You are not taking this on. It's not your responsibility or your fault. Besides, I didn't lose my job, I got suspended indefinitely until they can sort out what those pricks in Phoenix are complaining about. Although I'm sure after today's fuck up by Phoenix' finest at your door, the suspension may not last that long. As it stands, I couldn't be happier to be able to focus my time on getting Fox back." He slips his hand around my neck and pulls me into him, and after a futile minute of resistance, I wrap my arms around his waist and press my cheek to his chest. I feel and hear the deep relieved sigh Joe expels.

"We okay now?" he rumbles into my hair.

"So sorry I threw that out at you. I was upset and made it sound like I blamed you for everything. You know that's not the case, right?" I lean back and look into his tired eyes and he tries to smile, tucking me back under his chin.

"Yeah, I know babe."

"I really am gonna quit though. Not going back there, I can't. I'd lay her out the first opportunity I got."

Joe doesn't say anything, but when I feel his chest shaking, I look up again to find him struggling to keep a straight face.

"What?"

"Lay her out?" Joe bursts out laughing, trying to stop me from punching him by wrapping me tightly in his arms. "God, you're something else. I love it when you get all fierce and feisty, and the thought of you getting into a bitch fight with Jenna Stanley... I've gotta admit, that's kind of hot."

"Please! That's like a fight between Barbie and Betty Boop," I complain hiding the smile that's threatening to appear.

"Exactly! Betty Boop is fucking hot."

"Joe. Your phone on?" Gus is in the doorway looking at me and I automatically release one of my arms from around Naomi and slide it in my pocket to check.

"Yup. Why?"

I'm not happy that Naomi is pulling out of my arms. I like having her there. But I can tell she senses something is up too as she turns around to face Gus with her arms now crossed.

"Neil picked up on some chatter over the police scanner. Units are being called in to that old auto shop on Alamosa, just north of town? Shots were fired. Sounds like some kinda hostage situation. The description of the hostage rang a bell with Neil." He cautiously looks over at Naomi, who is still standing with her arms crossed, but her lips are drawn in a tight line and her fists are clenched.   I inadvertently edge closer when Gus continues. "Neil thinks it might be Fox."

The burst of air that leaves her is audible and I go to reach for her, expecting her to fall apart, while trying to puzzle the information together in my head. But Naomi surprises me once again when she starts running out of the office. I'm barely able to catch her before she reaches the front door.

"Hold up, Doc. Don't go off half-cocked."

I'm having a hard time hanging on to her as she struggles to get free. Just then my phone rings.

Shifting Naomi to the side, I manage to position myself in front of the door and use one hand to answer.

"Morris."

"Sheriff, it's Carol. Couldn't call sooner. Those idiots are breathing down my neck, but I heard about your boy missing. Got a general call for assistance not too long ago. A hostage situation at the old mechanic shop at Alamosa and Lebanon. Shots already fired and it sounds like the kid may be in the thick of it. The descriptions of two that match the suspects in the Michael Vincent case and another of a kid with a cast on his arm. Drew is out there, but you might wanna head over and look out for him because those idiots from Phoenix are floating around too."

God I love Carol. As much as she has her nose up in everyone's business, she's still loyal to a fault.

"Owe you, Carol."

"I'll add it to your tab, Sheriff," she deadpans before hanging up.

"What? What was that?" Naomi is hanging on to my shirt now and I cup her face in my hands.

"We are not running out there like idiots, Naomi. Just hold on."

I look up to find Gus tucking away his gun and nodding to the door. I had to turn in my service gun, but have a license to carry my own. It's in the glove compartment of my truck.

"I need you to stay here with Neil and Emma, Naomi," Gus says, "Joe and I will take care of this. If Fox is there, we'll bring him home."

I sense more than I see Naomi stiffen before she turns around and lets loose with both barrels.

"Gus, I respect you and you're a good friend... but are you out of your fucking mind? My boy is out there. I'm coming! I don't fucking care what *you* need—I'm all about what *he* needs and what *I* need right now. So if we can cut the goddamn chitchat and get going? That'd be good!"

Even drawn up to her full length, Naomi barely makes it to Gus's shoulder, but that doesn't stop her from poking her finger in his chest for emphasis as she shouts the last words in his face. From the kitchen I hear Emma, "You tell him, girl!" costing her a sharp glance from her husband.

I make my position clear when I grab Naomi's hand and open the door, throwing a look over my shoulder at the somewhat startled Gus.

"One thing, Doc," I say to her in a low voice, "once there, you do as I say; no questions asked. Okay? As much as I'm not gonna stick my hands into one of your surgical patients for fear of fucking it up, you're gonna have to give me that same trust back. You get me?"

I can see the struggle to reign herself in play out over her face and her hands are in fists by her side.

"Okay." She manages, her jaw clenched on the word of compliance. But I can't afford having her endanger herself or Fox by running into a situation we don't seem to have any control over yet.

It takes us a little less than fifteen minutes to get to Lebanon Road. Naomi has been quiet in the seat beside me the entire time and Gus is driving his Yukon behind me. In the distance, I can see a large congregation of emergency vehicles already gathered, right at the intersection with Alamosa. Pulling over to the side of the street, I slide down my window and motion Gus alongside.

"What are you thinking?" he wants to know.

"Don't want to go through that. That's for sure. We turn around, back to North Broadway, we can try cutting in the back way on Alamosa. Maybe pull into Bane's Packaging?" I suggest.

"Sounds good to me."

Gus pulls ahead before making a U-turn and passing the other way. I follow suit, behind him now. All this time, Naomi's stayed quiet. I take one of her tightly clenched fists in my hand.

"You okay?" A curt nod is my only answer. "You're a rock. You know that, right? We're gonna go get our boy out of there."

"Okay."

I look over to see a small smile edging out some of the tension on her face. So much stronger than she thinks she is, my girl.

Only two patrol cars on this side of the intersection and by the looks of it, one is Drew. He is beside it talking to a uniformed officer of the Cortez PD. A small stroke of luck. As I pull in behind them, Drew turns around, spots me and comes walking toward me, holding up his hand to the officer to hold him back.

"Stay here for a minute," I tell Naomi as I hop out of the truck.

"Carol called?" Drew guesses.

"Right on one. Don't wanna get in your way, but if our boy is in there, we need to be here."

"Your boy?" he asks me, one eyebrow raised and I meet his challenge straight on.

"My woman, her son, therefore our boy. Yes. There a problem with that?"

Drew's response is a smirk. "No problem, Sheriff. Just glad to see that shit sorted."

If his response surprises me, I'm determined not to let it show. Looks like Drew is coming out of his shell a little and already knowing he's a great deputy, the added bite is only going to be an improvement. He nods over my shoulder at Gus, who's walked up behind me.

"Here's what I know; Cortez PD received a call from the night watchman at the packaging plant. When he came on shift earlier, he had seen a couple of youths struggling in the parking lot of the abandoned building next door. Not sure if it was a friendly tussle or something else, he pulled up his car a little further and looked back just when he saw one hit another over the head with what looked to be a gun. Both he and a third guy dragged him into the old shop. He immediately called the police. The one whose bell got rung had a cast on his arm."

A sharp intake of breath alerts me to Naomi, who's managed to slide over to the driver's side and listen through the open window. My mistake. Seeing her pale face, I open the door.

"Might as well come out," I say as gently as I can, helping her down. I pull her in front of me and fold her inside my arms.

"Go on," my girl says to Drew, her voice cracking but still managing to hold her shit together.

"When the first units arrived and tried to approach the building, some shots were fired. From what we're told, all of them were from the inside to the outside." The last part, he directs at Naomi, making sure she understands all of them appeared to have been directed away from Fox.

"Any idea who they are? Holding the kid, I mean?" Gus is all business and I'm glad to have him at my back. Right now I'm even glad not to be sporting my badge, 'cause I wouldn't be able to maintain a professional distance. My heart is fucking buried in this shaking woman I'm holding and her son whose life is in danger.

"Spoke to Detective Dooley earlier over the radio. Description for one of them seems to match the one you gave for the two thugs in the Vincent assault. The one we have on file for Felipe Rivas. The witness didn't get a clear look at the other one."

"The drug dealer? I don't get it," I wonder out loud, "I mean, we know he broke into Doc's house and left the message—at least he was there—but what does he stand to gain by kidnapping Fox? And who the hell is the other kid?"

"Dunno what to tell you, Sheriff. That's all I know, except that Dooley is trying to make contact with Rivas while the Chief is conferring with the K-9 unit and the two detectives from the Phoenix PD on how to try and get in. Not easy with the building being exposed on all sides."

"Those bozos are here?" Gus barks out, voicing my thoughts exactly. What the fuck are they hoping to gain by showing up here?

Just then, we hear a volley of shots from down the road.

CHAPTER SEVENTEEN

Fear, hope and adrenaline have carried me through the last half hour or so since Gus interrupted Joe and I in his office. Aside from my blow-up at Gus, I've held myself as still as possible, knowing full well either or both of them can prevent me from tagging along if they really want to. I almost blow it when I hear Joe talk about Fox, calling him *our boy*, but I tamp down the emotions that those words bring to the surface because frankly, right now there is no room for them.

The moment I hear the shots fired, however, all control is gone and I pull out of Joe's arms and am running at full speed down the road in the direction of the sound, driven by pure fear and adrenaline. The hope is waning with every step.

"Naomi! Fuck!" I can hear Joe behind me, but there is nothing, no one, who'd be able to stop me now. I ignore the various yells of caution, focusing only on the sound of my feet slapping against the asphalt and the sparsely lit building in the distance where more and more emergency vehicles are pulling up.

When I am almost to the intersection, I'm suddenly jerked back into a familiar hard chest with an arm around my waist. Joe's heavy panting in my ear.

"Damn, babe, you can fucking move. Hold up. We're going together, but with caution. I don't want anyone shooting at the crazy woman hauling ass into their scene, okay?"

I notice he hasn't stopped moving but has only slowed us down to a walking pace. Seeing several law enforcement officers crouching behind their vehicles for cover, it dawns on me that I might've run into an active situation. *Jesus.* My boy is in there.

Joe is whispering in my ear and I barely register what he is saying; something about staying behind the patrol cars. The Sheriff's deputy Joe had been talking to drives past us and pulls up beside the other cars in the parking lot of the abandoned building. Joe grabs my hand and tells me to crouch as he pulls me toward the deputy's patrol unit. Ducking behind the trunk, he tugs me down and close to him.

"We've gotta wait here. Gus is going to get the lay of the land."

The next few minutes feel like hours, with very little sound other than the occasional rustle of the parking lot gravel as someone shifts. Occasional radio crackle flares and each time my ears perk up hoping to hear something— anything—but very little is decipherable. I'm about to burst out of my skin when finally I see Gus approach on a crouch from a Cortez PD car a little further down.

"A few officers went around the back quietly and were supposed to use the element of surprise to take control of the suspects without shots fired, but—" Gus's eyes shoot up when something behind us distracts him. "What the fuck?"

I turn to see the younger of the two Phoenix officers walk out holding up a half-dazed Fox, and almost take off running toward him, when both Joe and Gus hold me back this time.

"Wait," Joe hisses in my ear, "Let's make sure all is clear first."

I watch helplessly as my son is being lead to a patrol car and placed in the back. I am beside myself.

"He needs to be seen by a doctor, Joe. He looks dazed and if he was hit over the head like that guy said, he may very well have a concussion. Jesus, he could have a bleed. He needs to go to the ER."

I'm confused. There is an ambulance waiting right in the intersection. I spotted it as we were standing by the truck and we walked right by it. Why aren't they looking after him?

"I'll go check. You guys stay here for now." Gus carefully moves in the direction of the patrol car.

Just then a call comes over the radios and one of the officers starts waving the ambulance over. It backs between two of the patrol cars, all the way up to the shop entrance. EMTs jump out, open the loading bay and pull out the gurney to take it inside the building.

When I look back to where Gus has gone to check on Fox, I see him motioning us over, and around us everyone appears to be out in the open. Joe must've spotted Gus too, 'cause he grabs me by my elbow and steers me in his direction.

"Second ambulance is on its way. One of the suspects got shot, as did the second officer. Fox will be taken with a patrol car," Gus says with a serious face.

"We'll take him," I say. "I can make sure he's ok. It can be dangerous after a blow to the head. He needs to be monitored." I lean down to look in the window and try the door handle, but it won't budge.

"Why is he locked in here?" My eyes seek out Warner, the detective who stepped to the side, when Joe and I walked up. His eyes are shifting around, not quite settling on mine.

"Bringing him in for questioning, ma'am. Can't have him running off again like last time."

I'm about to tear into this snot-nosed idiot, when I hear Joe inhale sharply behind me; feel his arm wrap around my waist and lift me aside before he steps up in Warner's face. Like... *right* up in there.

"Open this fucking door, now! This kid received a blow to the head, which was witnessed and reported, and he was obviously unstable when you brought him out here. He needs immediate medical attention. I swear I will fucking rip you apart if anything happens to him. Do you understand me?" I've never seen Joe this irate. Never seen him anything other than perhaps grumpy, but his face is bright red and the veins in his neck are bulging out. I grab onto his arm, afraid he's gonna let one of those tightly clenched fists fly. Gus steps up beside him on the other side, ready to intervene.

"Problem, gentlemen?" A man with a badge clipped to his jacket who I don't recognize walks up, eyeing the situation suspiciously.

"Dooley," Joe bites off, "Can you tell this idiot to unlock the door so the boy's mother, who happens to be a physician, can make sure he's ok?"

"The fuck? Warner, are you trying to get your ass in trouble? Your partner's already been shackled to the Chief's side because he's been identified as a loose cannon. We thought you were the smart one."

"But—" The protest falls on deaf ears as the officer Joe identified as Dooley snatches the keys from his hand and unlocks the backdoor. I immediately dive in, ignoring the continued argument, and find my son slumped in the backseat with tears streaming down his face.

"Oh baby..." I put my arms around him as best I can and the poor kid buries his face in my neck. Deep sobs wrack his body. I try to soothe him by rocking back and forth gently while stroking his back. With half an ear, I can hear Gus's deep rumble.

"Did you not get the message this morning? I'm thinking another call to your boss is in order, since you bozos apparently are still not clear on how to follow the rules."

When Joe gets fired up again, Gus cuts him off. "Go see to your family. Dooley and I have this."

Next thing I know, the door on the other side of Fox opens and Joe slides in, closing it behind him, and finding my eyes over Fox's head.

"Hey Bud. It's gonna be ok."

The moment he puts his hand on my boy's shoulder, Fox lifts his head and turns to Joe.

"They gonna arrest me?"

"Fuck no, kid. Over my dead body."

I don't even think to mentioned language; I'm too moved by the interaction between these two guys. My two guys. Pushing down the tears for later, my inner doctor bubbles up and I gingerly touch Fox's head, where I encounter a sticky mess.

"I've gotta take him in to the ER, Joe. He's been cut. I want a scan done to check for bleeding. Baby," I turn his face to me. "Were you unconscious at any time?"

"Uhh... I think I may have blacked out. Can't remember too well."

One look at Joe is enough to see he gets the significance and he immediately calls out my open door for Dooley to drive us to the hospital. Gus says he'll make sure to get Joe's truck

there, and with flashing lights and sirens, we're off.

Naomi has gone with Fox for a scan and I'm in the waiting room with Gus, who's been on the phone since he got here just minutes after us. The only thing he's mentioned is that the Chief was getting in touch with his counterpart in Phoenix to file an official complaint regarding the conduct of his two detectives. Movement by the door draws my attention and I lift my head from my hands, hoping to see Naomi with some news. Instead Jenna leans against the doorway, a nervous little smile on her face.

"Hi," she says, her voice thick with what I assume to be an attempt at seduction. It only turns my stomach and boils my blood. Obviously missing the fact that I'm not alone in the room, she saunters over to stand in front of me, her hand on her hip. "I've missed you."

And my control snaps.

I'm up out of my seat, grabbing her by the shoulders and backing her into the wall in an instant, my face inches from hers.

"Are you out of your fucking mind? Do you have any idea what you've started? You stupid bitch!"

"Easy my friend." Gus's voice penetrates the loud rushing of blood filling my ears as his hand carefully peels away my fingers from her neck. Only now do I notice how her eyes have turned fearful and her face is beet red. I remove my hand but stay in her space.

"Stay away from Naomi or me, and don't you ever mess with what is mine again, or so help me God..."

I turn away trying to reel in my anger.

"I'm sorry... I was just trying to help. I thought..." she stammers, but I'm not buying her manipulative bullshit for one second.

"Joe?"

I turn around to see Naomi walking in and I don't hesitate, I walk right up and wrap her up in my arms, but she pulls out and turns to Jenna, her back ramrod straight.

"I have a shitload of vacation time saved up. Consider that my official notice. I'm done working for a petty, mean-spirited, unprofessional little bitch. I quit! Find yourself another ER physician to abuse at and another sheriff to harass. We're done with you." Turning to me she smiles big. "Fox wants to see you. Let's go, love." And with her head held high and my hand in hers, she walks us straight past an open-mouthed Jenna, leaving a chuckling Gus behind.

Fuck me, she can get me from murderous to horny as a three-balled tomcat in seconds. My girl's got talents. Walking down the empty hallway, we pass a unisex washroom with the door slightly ajar and I can't resist; with a tug on her hand, I pull Naomi inside with me and shut the door.

"What the he—" The rest of whatever she was about to say disappears down my throat, since my mouth is on hers, drinking in a much-needed taste of this woman who can rev me up, turn me inside out and flip me on like a switch. I don't just need her…no, she's become as essential to me as food and water —as air.

"You were missing from me. I needed to remind myself," I tell her when I finally pull back.

"Joe..." she whispers with her hands still clenched in my shirt.

"You called me love...before."

"Hmmm. I did do that," she admits, but won't look at me.

"Alright," I chuckle at her unwillingness to meet my eyes. "We'll get back to that later. For now, there's a boy waiting for us I believe."

With a quick glance down the hallway, we slip out of the washroom as unnoticed as when we entered. Outside his room she pulls me aside and quickly fills me in on the results of the scan. No fractures to the skull but there appears to be a small bleed and some swelling, so he will be admitted. I don't know what I was expecting, but the almost detached and clinical way Naomi seems to handle this development is not it.

She leads the way into the room, where a uniformed officer is standing guard just inside the door. A precaution I'd expected. The lobby is full of officers, uniformed and plain-clothed, since both shooting victims have been transported here as well, their injuries apparently non-life threatening. Gus managed to glean that information before the two of us had retreated to the small waiting room for some privacy.

Fox is lying in bed. The kid looks to be asleep, a small portion of his hair shaved on the side of his head where I guess they stitched his cut. Damn. He looks like death warmed over.

"Hey Bub," Naomi says softly as she approaches the bed, and his eyes blink open. They shift from her to me and then land on the police officer still standing by the doorway, before sliding back and looking straight at me. It takes me just a second to register what he is trying to tell me.

"Excuse me, Officer? Is it possible to give us a little family time?" Although I've seen the guy around town and would normally not think twice to send him out of a room, I force myself to stay in my role as a mere citizen. Thank God he doesn't do more than nod once and step outside, closing the door behind him.

"Thanks," Fox's voice croaks from the bed.

"No problem, buddy. Anybody come and talk to you already?"

"Somebody came in just after Mom left to get you but I pretended to be asleep. I wanted you to be here too."

"Not going anywhere, kid."

"He had a gun. I heard the detectives at the house this morning and got scared so I climbed out the bathroom window. I was planning just to hide in the tree line on the side of the cornfield until they left, but when I got there, this guy stepped out from behind a tree with a gun. I tried to run but he tackled me and said he'd shoot me in the back if I tried again. He duct-taped my hands behind my back. Then we walked for maybe twenty minutes alongside the corn, I don't really know. I heard you yelling my name at some point." His eyes turn to his mom and he swallows hard before continuing. "There was a car waiting on the far side of the field on one of those farmer access trails? The kid who was at the dig that night was in the driver's seat. They put me in the trunk and started driving. Seemed like forever and every time we stopped, I thought for sure they'd get me out, but then the car would start up again. At some point I could hear the one guy yelling but I couldn't hear the other voice so I thought maybe he was on the phone. When we finally stopped, the guy with the gun opened the trunk. We were at this empty gas station or auto shop or something, but I heard a car engine and thought we might be close to a public road. I tried to get away, but the bastard cold-cocked me with the gun. Don't remember much after that, until I heard some shots and found myself tied to a car lift. The driver was sitting with his back against a wall while the dude with the gun was acting all crazy, running from one bay door to the next, peeking out those little windows, waving his gun around. When he noticed I had my eyes open he pointed it at me and I thought for sure that was it. I asked him what he wanted with me. He said I was gonna make him rich. Would shoot him from small time, right into the 'big leagues.' Something about Max making sure of it?"

The fear on his face is unmistakable, as I'm sure the shock on mine is.

"He said 'Max?'"

Fox just nods and I see Naomi covering her mouth with her hand. Fucking hell. My mind is already starting to re-sort and re-file all the little bits and pieces of information I have and the scenario I come up with is chilling. It reaches back further in time than I'd been aware of. And that scares the fuck out of me.

I lean over the bed and put my mouth close to the kid's ear. "I promise you, I will keep you and your mom safe. If it's the last thing I do."

Then I turn to Naomi who still stands almost frozen beside the bed and take her in my arms, pressing her head against my chest.

"Beautiful, you with me?" I feel the nod of her head and pull back so I can look in her eyes. "Everything I care about is in this room, you hear me? I will do anything to protect it. Anything."

"Joe...I..." I cut her off with a hard kiss, not caring that her son is right there. He's not stupid and he better get used to me all over his mother. Gonna happen a lot.

"Later. You and I? We talk later about us." With that I turn to the door and pull it open.

"Dooley! Gus! Better get your butts in here!"

CHAPTER EIGHTEEN

"Anything happens, it'll take us all of five minutes to get back."

I'm pissed. Joe's basically kidnapped me from the hospital to get some sleep at his place despite my protests. Unfortunately I have very little steam left...if any.

Having to listen to Fox recount the story again for Gus and Detective Dooley to hear didn't only tucker him right out, but me as well. I swear my eyes were blinking in sync with my poor kid's. I was about to curl up on the chair when Gus came back in with Neil and decreed that he'd stay the night and I was to get some sleep. Somehow, somewhere he and Joe had worked this little arrangement out—without bothering to include me in their planning session. So I'm pissed, but also very, very tired.

I startle when I'm lifted out of the truck. Damn, must've dozed off. Just as easily I snuggle into Joe's chest, closing my eyes again.

When I wake up next, I can't breathe. I'm in a dark room, alone and I can't breathe. I try...my mouth is open and I try so hard to pull the air in, but there's nothing. Just a vacuum. I drop myself from the bed and crawl into a corner. Tears start squeezing from my eyes as I look around for something— anything—to help me. Jesus. The beating of my heart is so hard, I can feel it against the wall of my chest, swelling...bursting. My hands are clawing and scratching, grabbing for something to hold onto...grab onto. I can't breathe...no air...no...

"Fuck!" I can hear Joe. I can even sense his hands on me—lifting me off the floor—but I can't see anything through the film of tears. I feel detached and cold. Still in the dark.

"Hey, baby. I'm here...not leaving you. It's alright, you're alright—" His deep rumbling words are like a soothing life-line; an anchor for me to hold onto, preventing me from disappearing completely. My body starts shivering with cold air, hitting exposed skin, as I try to focus on the continuous litany of softly spoken words, while his hands strip me naked. I finally gasp a breath full of blessed air when I'm submersed into a bath of warm water, held tightly by strong arms against familiar skin. After the first breath, the next comes easier, and the next...and the next. A full shudder runs down the length of my spine, taking the remainder of the shivers with it and now I can feel the rapid rise and fall of Joe's chest—hear his fast heartbeat—and I lift my hand over top so I can feel its solid rumble under my palm. Connection.

"I'm here," I manage.

"Thank God. That freaked the fuck out of me, beautiful."

I can feel his arms tightening around me and a deep breath clearing his lungs.

We stay in the bath for a while, not saying anything, just holding on. Settling down. Suddenly, the reality of the past day comes barreling at me and I surge up, splashing water everywhere.

"Fox! I need to call and see how he's doing. Need to go back."

"Settle. I'd just left the bed to call when I heard you drop out of the bed. He's fine. Talked to Neil who says he's been sleeping aside from his forced wake-up calls every couple of hours. He likes Neil a lot. It's fine, baby. It's only four o'clock in the morning. Let's try and catch a couple more hours before heading back, okay?"

I know he's right. I know if I don't try and sleep at least some of this stupid panic attack off, I'll be a zombie again the rest of today and Lord knows I'll need my strength. So I give in.

With the water only lukewarm now, I get out and grab us some towels off the shelf. Still a bit wobbly, but determined to stand on my own two feet, I gently but firmly push Joe's hands away when he tries to take over drying me off. Neither of us bother putting clothes back on before we crawl into bed. When Joe curls his body around my back, tucking me close, he presses his face in my neck and mumbles, "Tomorrow we're gonna sit down and do some planning. It may be temporary, it may be permanent, but either way, we're gonna do something constructive. I think we both need something positive to work on. What do you say? Ready to make some plans?"

"I want to call a realtor."

My life is unravelling around me and my carefully constructed stability has evaporated. I feel suspended and need to start taking control where I can. Joe's right. I'm selling my house and want to look buying the old feed store. Step one.

"I'm good with that, beautiful. Now sleep."

Soft lips trailing from my sternum down to my belly button, taking a slow dip of a tongue, only to take their journey further south, wake me up to the crisp light of morning. My hand inadvertently reaches down to find the messy waves of Joe's hair and a moan from my mouth alerts him to my arousal. It only takes a second before his tongue and fingers find the evidence slipping from my pussy. I lift my knees and drop my legs open, and Joe settles his shoulders between. When I look down, I see his bright blue eyes dark with lust focused on me.

"Morning, honey," I breathe. "Best way to wake up is with your mouth on me."

"Can't do that, beautiful." Joe pulls himself up and over me, lines his cock up with his hand and slides inside me right up to the hilt in one hard move, taking my breath away.

"You start talking while I'm trying to pace myself and it ain't gonna work. You'll have me finish before even starting," he growls, pulling his hips back before slamming back home as deep as he can, slapping his balls against my ass and grinding himself on my clit. The tone of his voice, the words, the intensity of his eyes and the sensations he creates in my body all conspire to have me tumbling toward climax blindly with only a few strokes of his cock.

"Holy fuck—Joe! I'm coming..." And just like that I convulse around him, a seemingly endless pulsing of my inner walls around the substantial size of him. Pulling, pushing, massaging, until his breathing halts and the veins in his neck bulge. I watch in wonder as his mouth drops open, his head falls back and with uncontrolled jerks, Joe comes apart between my legs. Beautiful.

"Beautiful," I whisper to him, stroking my hand over his face. His eyes find mine and I swear I see his heart right there.

"You give that to me," he says before tucking his head in my neck and staying there until our breathing returns to normal and he slips softly from my body

"Gotta get my girl fed. Much as I don't want to move, we should get going." Joe rolls off me and out of the bed. The sudden cold air sends a shiver over my skin. "Come on, hop in a warm shower. I'm getting the coffee started." With a quick kiss on my lips he turns to walk out of the room and I take a minute to enjoy the flex of his tight ass, before the chill forces me into the bathroom. Once up, a sense of urgency to get back to the hospital and Fox hit me, and I'm in and out of the shower in a matter of minutes. Joe walks in with a steaming mug just as I wrap a towel around myself.

"Here. Some wake-up juice. Some bread ready to go downstairs in the toaster. Have at it while I take a quick rinse, okay? I know you're eager to go see our boy."

"I like it," I say softly, my voice a little rough.

"What, beautiful?" he asks, standing behind me, finding my eyes in the mirror.

"The way you say 'our boy'...I like it. Makes me feel like I'm not alone in fighting for him."

His hands slide around my waist from behind and he rests his chin on my shoulder, never looking away.

"Grown to care about your son, Naomi. He had a dick for a father who fucked with his mind and his self-esteem. No kid deserves that. He's a good kid, he just needs to know it. Besides, I've grown to care about his mom a great deal too."

The feeling bubbling up in my chest is so intense, it borders on painful, like something is ready to burst through, but all I say is, "Yeah?".

"Yeah," he whispers, kissing my shoulder.

"Well, I like that too."

"Nice signal, you fucking asshole!"

The green Toyota that's been stuck in front of us ever since leaving my street, going slower than a geriatric with ankle weights, finally decides to turn into a parking lot without any indication. I have to slam on the brakes and my arm inadvertently shoots out to hold Naomi back in her seat.

"Sorry, babe. You ok?" I look over to where she is holding up the two travel mugs of coffee we took with us, eager to get to the hospital.

"Fine. Good thing I was holding these, or they'd be all over the floor. What an idiot."

"You can say that again. Changing lanes in front of me every time I'd try to pass. Normally I would've had the number down already, but I never even thought of it until just now. Head's just not in the game." I'm actually pissed at myself, because this is supposed to come naturally to me as the fucking sheriff of this county, but it seems my vision has narrowed in a huge way these last few weeks. Definitely off my game and not quite sure what that says.

I can feel Naomi's eyes on me when I turn to her with a little reassuring smile.

When we walk into Fox's room, he is sitting up in bed, looking only a little worse for wear. Neil is lounging on the La-Z-Boy by the window.

"Did you bring me a coffee?" he asks, checking out the travel mugs in our hands.

"Sorry, Neil. I'll buy you a cafeteria breakfast though?" I walk up to the bed and ruffle Fox's hair, who is wrapped tight in his mother's arms. Might not be a bad idea to give them a little alone time.

"You gonna be okay here, Doc? While I take Neil for a quick bite? Dooley has a uniform posted outside the door still. I can bring you something back?"

"Yeah, go right ahead. The toast was enough for me for now. I don't need anything else. We'll be fine."

I bend down to kiss her before winking to Fox who looks on with an eyebrow raised, and turn to follow Neil out the door.

"Serious between you then?" Neil nudges my shoulder as we make our way down the hall to the caf.

"Not that it's any of your business, but yes, I think so."

"God. I swear every time someone steps foot inside Cedar Tree city-limits, another one of our team goes down. Next thing I know, I catch them going at it like bunnies. Just you wait and see—you're next—it's like a curse." The semi-disgusted look on his face has me laughing out loud. I like Neil. He's like a big kid with an even bigger brain, and from what I can tell, he has a set of balls to match.

"Your turn will come, kid. Your turn will come."

"Fat chance of that, old man," he deadpans, before pushing open the door to the smell of bacon.

With plates piled with food, we find a spot by the window.

"How did last night go?"

"Kid slept most of it, except when the nurses would wake him to check his vitals. Dooley checked in at about six this morning on his way to the station, wanting to know if there were any issues overnight. He's a pretty good guy. Seems to like you all right. He was pissed as hell you got suspended. Sorry about that by the way. Bureaucracy at its best," Neil shakes his head while wrestling an entire piece of toast in his mouth.

"Yeah well, it is what it is. Right now I'm pretty happy to be able to stick close and make sure Doc and Fox stay safe. Did Dooley say anything about the investigation? About Rivas?"

"He was hoping to question him today. Apparently they removed a bullet from his shoulder yesterday. They've kept him here under guard overnight, but today he'll be released straight to jail. Seems the officer wasn't quite as lucky and ended up in surgery trying to fix his gut. The second kid turns out to be a new transplant to Cortez. His dad's in business with Les Vincent and apparently the parents have been putting pressure on the kids to hang out. Joey Gruber hails from Grand Junction as well and knew Rivas; had apparently bought drugs off him from time to time. He'd been surprised when Rivas approached him in Cortez a while back, offering him money to get close to the other high school kids. The game was supposed to be that Joey would introduce a little meth that Rivas would give him and give the kids a taste. As far as the kid knew, Rivas was setting up shop in

Cortez and he was going in at ground level. Joey managed to invite himself along with Michael Vincent to a bonfire and passed around meth to the kids. But when Fox and Michael got picked up, Rivas insisted they had to be 'taken care of,' and the two of them went after them. Michael was first. Joey claims he tried to back off after he saw Rivas stab Michael, but was afraid of him. Looks like Rivas is gonna have a much longer rap sheet than petty drugs now. Dooley wouldn't give me the guy's cell number, but I managed to dig it up anyway. Did a bit of 'sleuthing' while the kid was still sleeping and found some interesting stuff on his account. Sent it all through to Gus already. He's following up on it with his connections in Phoenix. Looks like there may have been some intense contact between Rivas and someone with a Phoenix number."

"Maxim fucking Heffler I bet. Jesus...how far is that guy's reach? And he's still blowing in the wind, right?"

"The phone number may help trace him. Leave it with Gus. He mentioned something about calling Malachi back as well."

I'm itching to go out and work the case myself, but if there is anyone I trust as much as I trust myself, it's Gus. Well aware of my shifting priorities, I walk back into Fox's room after sending Neil off, telling him to get some well-deserved rest.

The rest of the morning, I spend going back and forth between the lobby and the kid's room, checking in with Carol at the office, talking to Gus and setting up an appointment for Clint to meet us at the feed store at five o'clock this afternoon. Clint is a contractor who has done work on Arlene's Diner and recently finished the renovations on Katie and Caleb's barn. He's an honest guy and is fast becoming a permanent fixture in Cedar Tree and at Arlene's Diner, although I have a sneaky suspicion that may not just be because of the good food. Naomi talked with the real estate agent who sold her the house here in Cortez, and he is drawing up some papers to get that on the market as soon as we can get it cleaned out. She is dead serious about not wanting to set foot in there again. Arlene walked in a little while ago with Emma to visit Fox with a care package from the diner—putting the first big smile on his face. She was able to get the realtor for the feed store to promise to open up the place for us this afternoon. That woman has connections up the wazoo, and anyone with a lick of sense knows not to stand in her way when she has her mind set on something. It's clear Arlene has her mind set on setting Naomi up in a clinic for Cedar Tree.

When I get back in the room, Fox is licking the crumbs that remain from his care package and the girls are sitting around chatting.

"That the bitch who ratted you out?" Arlene says, looking past Naomi into the hallway where Jenna can be seen talking to one of the doctors with her eyes firmly fixed on this door.

"I already quit last night, Arlene. And gave her a piece of my mind, so just drop it."

"Yeah, but your piece of mind and my piece of mind likely have a distinctly different flavor to it, honey," she says with a smirk.

Oh boy. I see someone is out for blood. Before Arlene can barrel out the door, I manage to catch her.

"Hold up there, you amazon. Love you wanting to go to battle for my girl, and I can't say it wouldn't be entertaining to see her cut down a few, Arlene-style, but the kid is gonna have to be here—in *her* hospital—for who knows how much longer. So let's try to hold off until he's in the clear, shall we?"

"You're a fucking party-pooper, you know that Sheriff?" she says leveling me with a pointed glare and settling a hand on her hip. "I even had my nails sharpened this morning in hopes I'd get a chance to have a go at her, and now Seb's gonna complain I'm ripping his back to shreds. Again," she finishes with a pout as she returns to sit down beside Naomi who is fighting not to laugh.

"Good lawd, Arlene! TMI already. *And* language. We have an impressionable young man here who doesn't need to hear about your bloodthirsty bedroom antics, or listen to your potty mouth," Emma scolds her friend who throws her head back and cackles loudly.

"You shitting me? You have the mouth of a long-haul trucker, woman. And as for bedroom antics, who keeps getting caught on the kitchen counter with her clothes off?"

Naomi's loud snort sets everyone off. When I look over at Fox his eyes are huge in his head before he starts laughing along and I can't hold back either. These two are fucking nuts, but they make everyone around them always feel a shitload better.

CHAPTER NINETEEN

"Well this is a surprise, isn't it?"

Clint looks around the large living room of what I now know to be the old Parker property. The feed store.

It is quite surprising. From the road, all you can really see is the wide, old brick storefront with the ample parking lot, both of which reveal rather obvious years of neglect. Around the back, however, is a sizable, older family home, hidden somewhat by the store that sits in front of it, and the trees on the side. And in the back, is an open view over a decent yard, bordering on some farmer's fields, and Ute Mountain in the distance. A porch runs along the side and back of the house and looks to be in need of repair, but once inside, the house looks to be in decent condition at first glance. Big too. Much bigger than it appears from the outside.

The realtor is waiting outside, at Joe's request, giving us a chance to do a walk through with Clint by ourselves. Not exactly pleased from the look of him, but apparently smart enough to realize that when people showed up with a contractor, they were likely interested, he retreated to his fancy car to wait.

I can hear Clint stomping around, opening and closing doors and cupboards while I'm still taking in the space. This is pretty nice. Scratch that; this is fucking amazing. What looks to be a large mudroom with laundry hook-ups connects the building in front to the house and opens into a foyer of sorts. One that has the front door to the house on one side, a powder room and a stairway going up and one going down on the other. A big opening in the separating wall leads into the living space with a large eat-in kitchen to the left. Somebody has done at least some work on this place at some point, because the kitchen is an open concept and the big room almost wraps around it in an L-shape. Against the back wall, the living or dining room—whatever it is—becomes the full width of the house. The only thing missing is some large windows or a sliding door. My mind is already working up visions of what the right window placement would do in here because, I bet with a few changes, it would be bright as day in here.

"What are you smiling about," Joe mumbles in my hair, as I feel his arms slide around me from behind. I swing around and loop my arms around his neck, smiling into his eyes.

"The place feels right. It feels good. What do you think?" I watch him closely as his eyes scan the space and linger on the view out the window.

"I like it. It suits you and also… killer view," he says as he turns back to me with a smile. "But then again, with you around, I always have a killer view."

"Oh please… save the lines. Not like you need them on me. Thought it was obvious I'm pretty easy for you." I punch him lightly on the arm.

"*Easy?* Never. But so fucking worth it."

The kiss he plants on me has me reach up on my toes to get a little bit more. When he breaks away, I can't help the little whimper that escapes. A self-satisfied smirk appears on his face and I roll my eyes.

"Oh please, like I'm the only one affected here." And to prove my point I grab his now solid, hard cock through his jeans, causing him to hiss sharply.

"Uh… Sorry to interrupt," Clint's amused voice comes from the doorway to the foyer, "but I thought you guys might want to come upstairs for a look?"

I plant my face in Joe's chest where I can feel the rumble of his chuckles.

"Let's go see the rest of your new place, beautiful."

Upstairs the hallway runs the length of the house with a window at the end and has doors on both sides. I'm surprised to find two bathrooms side-by-side, until I see that one of them is the ensuite to the master bedroom. The other two bedrooms are across the hall. The en-suite is in decent condition and must have been added later, but the family bathroom desperately needs some work done; it dates back to the fifties at least.

With the wood floors throughout the house in good condition, there really isn't a whole lot I can see to raise flags, until Clint tells us to come to the basement and I'm envisioning carpenter ants or something equally devastating. When we start descending the second set of stairs, though, I'm surprised how clean everything looks. Pretty unusual for a basement. Joe lets out a slow whistle.

"Holy shit. This place is the bomb!"

I walk around him into a big newly finished carpeted space where someone has left behind a massive pool table. In the far corner, we find a built-in bar. A set of small windows allow plenty of light to flood the space.

"What am I supposed to do with a man-cave?" I point out, causing both Clint and Joe to turn to me with incredulous looks on their faces.

"Babe? You serious? Look at this. This place is perfect and this pool table is incredible. It's huge!"

"You know you sound about sixteen now right?" I chuckle at the excitement on his face as he walks around and admires the bar and the pool table.

"I know exactly where the big screen TV should go," he says to Clint as they start scanning the wall for outlets. Before they lose themselves in a discussion over the best furniture to put in *my* basement, I point out the doors on the side.

"Hey. What's in there?"

Clint looks over his shoulder and shrugs. "Oh, that's the extra bedroom and bathroom. I think the furthest one is storage of some sort. They must've just done this. The walls hardly have any scuff on them."

I peek into door number one, and sure enough, there is a narrow space with basic shelving units on either side. It's a bit chilly. Cold cellar? Judging from the rubber stripping on the edges of the door, I would think so. Next is a three-piece bath, and the last door opens into a huge bedroom, where one wall is almost completely taken up by a closet with mirrored sliding doors. *Shit. Maybe I'll sleep down here.* I know that's not going to fly. If I buy this house, I know damn well who's going to be down here. In fact, I'd be lucky to ever see him again.

The thought of Fox gets me moving. We left him earlier in Neil's great care again, who had caught up on his sleep. Something Fox doesn't seem to mind at all. Despite the age difference, the two have more in common with those games of theirs than you'd think. I still don't want to be away from him all night. I want to at least be close by. He was getting irritated a little with me hovering over him all day and I can't blame him, but for my own peace of mind, given the danger that is still out there, I've gotta be nearby.

"Doc?" Joe sticks his head in the bedroom. "Wow, if you weren't already interested, I'd buy this place. I'd move down here and never come up for air. Fox is gonna fucking love this, you know that right?"

"I know, but we came here to see if this was feasible, not to fall in love with a pool table," I point out a little sharply.

"Naomi." Joe takes my face in his hands. "You know there is no room left in my heart for a damn pool table, but if Clint says this house is sound? Buy the house. The place has been on the market for a long time and I suspect the feed store at the front is what has kept it from selling. Lucky for you, it's exactly what you're looking for. You can put in any reasonable offer and I bet you'd get it."

His words stir a host of feelings in me and I almost blurt out what has been at the forefront of my mind for the past few days. I love the way he talks to me like I'm the most important person to him. I love that he voices support for anything I might decide. Fuck. I love him. But instead of telling him that, I reach up for a kiss and turn to go find my contractor.

After a short discussion with Clint, during which he tells us that aside from the pretty obvious renovations needed on the storefront to turn it into a working clinic, the house itself is sound, we head out the meet the realtor. The plumbing is working as is the electricity, which the realtor had turned on when I'd shown interest last week. Most of the work needing to be done is cosmetic and not urgent. In short, other than needing some new appliances and a good cleaning, there is no reason it couldn't be lived in. Music to my ears.

I tell the real estate agent I'll have my guy get in touch with him as soon as I get a call in and take one last look over my shoulder.

"Happy?" Joe asks, as we drive toward the diner for a quick bite with Clint before heading back to Cortez to see Fox.

"Yes. Yes I think I am, even though I would've like for Kendra to have a look at it first. But I love that it's my money, my house, my decision. Yeah, I feel good about it. What do you think?" I turn to him.

"Place suits you, and I think Fox will like it too. Especially when he gets a look at the basement," Joe winks at me.

Arlene's isn't that busy. When we walk in, Clint is already there at a table by the window having what looks to be a heated discussion with Beth. I'll never figure out what it is with those two. They can't seem to keep their eyes off each other when one thinks the others doesn't notice, but they do nothing but bicker when they're together. Actually...now that I think about it, it is a little familiar to what Naomi and I had going for a few years. Naomi elbows me in the ribs and tilts her head in their direction. She's noticed too. I just shrug. To give them some time to sort out whatever it is they have going on, I grab Naomi's hand and pull her toward the kitchen with me to go say hi to Seb.

"You guys attached at the hip now?" Arlene pops her head out of her office when we walk around the counter into the kitchen.

"Pretty much," I respond, pulling Naomi to my side and getting an eye roll in response.

"So?" Arlene pins Naomi with her glare. "How'd it go?"

"I'm gonna go for it. Already put a call in to my real estate agent on the way over here," she smiles.

"Fuckin' A! You'll get the place. I have a good feeling about it. Seb, you hearing this?"

"Picked up on it, Spot; seeing as you're louder than a foghorn. I'm sure half the diner knows now too." Seb walks over from the grill and throws his arm around a grumbling Arlene. "Congrats, Doc. That's awesome news," he smiles at Naomi.

We catch up for a few minutes, filling them in on Fox's condition, when Beth comes storming through the kitchen, passing by us without a word and goes right out the backdoor to have it slam shut behind her. Close on her tail is Clint who doesn't say a thing either, giving us a distracted chin lift before following outside right behind her.

"Again?" Seb asks Arlene, who just smiles and shrugs. "Jesus. Those two need to fuck and get it over with already. This has been going on for months. I thought you were a hard one to tame, love, but Beth? Holy shit. Never thought I'd say this, but I think the woman's got you beat."

I can feel Naomi's shoulders shake with laughter and I'm having a hard time holding it in myself, especially when Arlene elbows Seb in the gut hard enough to double the man over with a "Fuck, woman," growl.

"Serves you right. Let's get this clear, I tamed *you* and not the other way around. As for those two? I hope they figure it out at some point, there seems to be enough fire flying, but Beth's been burned way too many times before and you've gotta admit that Clint is about as subtle and sensitive as a rhinoceros during mating season. Every time that man opens his mouth, something inappropriate flies out. He can't seem to help himself." With a wistful last look at the backdoor Arlene turns back to us. "Since we seem to have temporarily misplaced a waitress, I'd better get my ass in there. Why don't you two give your order to Seb and I'll find you a spot."

"Actually," I tell her, "we were meeting Clint here, so where he was sitting is fine. We're gonna talk about the Parker place some over a bite before heading back to Cortez."

"Suit yourselves. I've gotta feeling he might not be the best dinner companion though," Arlene points out when the backdoor opens and Clint walks back in—sans Beth—frustration clear on his face.

A few quick burgers, a rough outline of a plan for the clinic and a promise to stay in touch later, we leave Clint in the diner's parking lot looking a bit forlorn. Beth had avoided our table like the plague, letting Arlene serve us. I feel bad for the guy. I remember all too well that feeling when everything that comes out of your mouth seems to be the wrong thing, and he has a severe case.

"That was Dooley, by the way. The call I got during dinner?"

"Yeah, I was gonna ask you. Anything new?"

"He'd been able to interview Rivas who was released in his custody from the hospital earlier this afternoon. Sounds like he may be getting somewhere. The guy was clammed up at first, but after confronting him with all the charges he is facing, I guess he came to the conclusion it might be best to admit he was working for someone else. As we suspected; Maxim Heffler. He had been sent to try and pull Fox in with drugs at first, ordered to stick close, but when I interrupted them at the dig that night, I guess plans changed. Rivas was told to 'take care' of Michael Vincent, the other kid who was picked up, then he was to warn your boy. The message on your wall was Maxim's message, put there by Felipe."

"I don't get it, though," Naomi pipes up, "wasn't Felipe from Grand Junction? How do those two connect anyway?"

"Apparently Felipe's older brother has been working for one of Maxim's clubs in Phoenix."

I want to hold back on the one piece of information I know will be devastating, especially for Fox if he ever finds out, but Naomi goes and asks the question I've been worried about.

"Okay, but I still can't figure out how they knew where to find us. How did he know?"

I look over at her, tightening my hold on her hand.

"James. Rivas said Maxim mentioned when he gave Fox's name and address, that it should be current, since he just got it off Fox's father."

All color drains from her face and her jaw clenches as she turns her eyes forward to stare straight ahead through the windshield.

"Miserable, low-life, son of a bitch, bastard," she hisses between gritted teeth, before turning back to me, tears brimming in her eyes. "Fox can never know. It would hurt so much."

"I know," I tell her softly, brushing a stray tear from under her eye.

"One more thing you need to know, something I didn't want to have to tell you, but it's important now; James was killed by a gunshot like I said, but it appears he was beaten severely and there was evidence of prolonged torture before he was finally shot. I don't think he gave up the information easily."

When she pulls her hand from mine, I know she's pissed. *Fuck.* She turns in her seat, her back to me now and I give her some time to process.

By the time I pull into a spot at Cortez Memorial, her silence is starting to worry me and I quickly unbuckle and pull her in my lap, meeting no resistance.

"Babe, talk to me please," I plead, wiping her hair back from her pale face, half expecting a panic attack, but finding a pair of clear chocolate brown eyes looking at me.

"Thank you," comes out of her mouth and totally takes me by surprise. What the hell? I thought for sure I'd at least get it with both barrels.

"Gonna have to clarify for me, beautiful."

She puts a small cool hand on my face and leans her forehead against mine.

"I get it. I got mad. I thought about it, but I get now. Thank you for trying to keep that from me. I was gonna yell at you for lying, or at least omitting information I think had a right to know, but I can see it came from a caring place. I haven't exactly been a pillar of strength. But Joe? I don't expect you to share the details of everything when it comes to your work. Just like I can't always share things with you, but if it relates to either of us or Fox, the other has a right to know everything. You don't get to decide what I can and cannot handle, just like I don't have a right to make that call for you. Those clean lines of communication you want? They require trust and I see I have some work left in earning yours."

Surprised by her words, I reel back in my seat causing her hand to drop from my face. *What the fuck?* She thinks I don't trust her?

"Here's the deal, keeping the graphic details of James' death from you had nothing to do with trusting you, but everything with my need to protect you. You're a doctor, I know you can handle more than most. Babe, you've gotta understand, I'll always try to shield you from the ugly side of life—from danger. Not because I don't think you can't handle it, but because I don't want you to have to."

The soft look on her face and the way she snuggles against my chest tells me she's getting it, but I have more to say.

"I want those clean lines more than anything, but since we've finally gotten our act together, we've barely had a chance to do anything the normal way. Haven't even been on a proper date. I haven't had a chance to get to know all the things that make you who you are. I want that. I want to know all about you so that when I tell you the words that have been in my heart and on my mind, you'll have no doubt I mean every single one of them."

CHAPTER TWENTY

"Mom! Where'd my Coyotes ball cap go??"

I can hear Fox holler from the bedroom where I told him to start packing up his shit.

He's been home—well, at Gus and Emma's guesthouse—from the hospital for a week now and has milked his concussion for the entire time, driving me up the wall. He was released last Thursday, with strict instructions to stay away from any alcoholic beverages—to which he rolled his eyes, the brat—as long as he was taking the blood thinners. We were driven home by a veritable army of men. Joe with Fox and I in his truck, Gus with Neil in his Yukon behind us and behind that was Malachi, who Gus had called back from his assignment. Ridiculous if you ask me, but Joe said it was a necessary show of force to whomever was watching, so they'd know we were well protected.

Maxim Heffler has still not been caught, even though law enforcement nationwide is on the lookout for him. I've made a choice not to be paralyzed by this situation, even though my instincts have me cowering in a corner. I've tried to focus all my energy on planning for the clinic, although I've had to do most all of it online. Neither Joe nor Gus will let me go anywhere alone. In fact, I couldn't even tell you right now where my car is. Joe even drove me to check in on Katie the other day and hovered around while I checked on Mattias' progress and Katie's healing. Both were doing extremely well and that little boy with his shock of black hair is already displaying signs of being about as even-keeled as his father is in terms of temperament. For a woman who a year ago wasn't considering anything further than perhaps walking again, let alone a future that included motherhood, Katie is turning out to be an absolute natural. And she's more laid back now than I've ever known her to be. I feel a small pang of envy at my friend's blissful existence, but catch myself quickly, remembering the hell she's had to live through to get to this place. Perhaps there is hope for me too.

Everything is so chaotic with Fox and I now sharing the bedroom; Fox on a cot on the floor, and Joe spending most nights on the couch, refusing to leave our side during the night. Soon that's gonna change. I was able to negotiate a temporary rental agreement for the Parker place until my place in Cortez sells. There have been a few nibbles but until we can get our furniture and the rest of our things out, it won't show at its best. It's also just been a week. Thank goodness for the cleaning service that managed to clear and then clean the place so it was at least in some shape for viewing. Joe and I had needed to spend quite a few hours there first to sort through the mess before they could even come in, but by Sunday the first viewings had already been scheduled.

Fox is scheduled to stay with Neil at the motel tonight for an evening of gaming. The kid's been going stir crazy being cooped up inside, and frankly, I could do without the constant sound of gun battles in the background for a night. I've secretly been hoping for the damn Xbox to give out, but that would probably create an even bigger headache. No. This is good. Although I did tell him to get his crap off the floor and pack a decent bag before I'd let him go.

A quick peek at the clock tells me Neil should be here shortly. I'd expected Joe back by now too. He'd gone off early this morning to pick up a few clean clothes and run some errands and other than a quick text midday asking if I needed anything from town, I haven't heard a thing from him.

"Mom! Have you washed my Drake shirt?"

Good lord! Grabbing the pile of laundry I've been folding, I walk into the bedroom where if anything, it looks like an even bigger mess than when he started.

"Holy shitballs, Fox! You're supposed to be picking stuff up, not spreading it around."

"Yeah, but I can't find any of my stuff. I need space. I can normally find everything just fine on my floor, but with you cramping my style, everything is a disaster." For dramatic effect he runs his free hand through his hair and gives it a good yank. That coupled with the pained expression on his face makes me burst out laughing.

"Oscar-worthy performance, Bub. High marks for angst and torture, but you're talking to your mother. You forget nothing much impresses me."

A little tilt to his mouth and the sparkle in his eyes lets me know he hasn't lost all of his good humor yet. Well...and he's probably excited to be spending another night with Neil staring at a screen. Whatever.

"Your Drake shirt is in this stack and—" I have to intervene and rescue the perfectly folded laundry he almost flung to the floor in his haste to get to his precious shirt. "And did you find your cap yet?"

"What cap?"

"The one you were hollering at me for just five minutes ago? Coyotes?"

"I was? I think I may have left it in Joe's truck. Doesn't matter, as long as I have my Drake shirt."

Oy vey. The attention-span of an ant when it comes to anything but gaming. Putting away the folded clothes, I turn to my son who seems to be staring at his peach fuzz in the mirror. "Hey, pick up this stuff and put it away...again, before you leave this room, okay?" When I get no response, I prompt, "Fox, you hear me?"

"Yeah whatever. Do you think I should let my beard grow?" He leans in even closer to the mirror picking at the sparse hairs sprouting from his chin and I'm struggling not to snort.

"Maybe wait a year or two, Bub. Give it a chance to fill in a bit?"

"Ya think? I just hate shaving and beards are in now."

I have to leave the room, I can't take it anymore. If the kid shaves once every two weeks it's a lot. I mean he's in the shower night and day, but the rest of his grooming leaves much to be desired. A beard though? On his baby face? I snicker to myself as I sit down at the dining table to do some more online shopping, when Joe comes in. He walks right over and kisses me full on my still smiling mouth.

"What's funny?"

"Fox wants to grow a beard," I enlighten Joe, making him chuckle

"I have some fertilizer left from last year. He's gonna need it with that spotty shit he's got on his chin."

"Hush, don't let him hear you," I giggle cuddling into his neck. "What've you been up to?"

"For me to know and you to find out. And you will soon, Neil is right behind me to pick up the boy."

"Is my Coyotes cap in your truck?" Fox walks in and immediately makes his opinion of our PDA clear by rolling his eyes dramatically.

"Hello to you too and no. Haven't seen it and I cleaned the truck this morning. Where did you last have it?" Joe straightens up but keeps his hand on the back of my neck.

"I was sure it was in your truck. I was wearing it when we came home from the hospital. Wasn't I? Maybe I left it there. Damn, I—" A knock on the door has him swing around on his heels and leap for the door. "Neil! Awesome! I'm ready; I just gotta get my bag. Let's go."

Ball cap forgotten, Fox disappears into the bedroom leaving Neil at the front door with his hand still half raised.

"Come in Neil. Never mind him. He's a bit cabin-fevered and can't wait to 'get out of jail,' by the look of things."

"S'okay," Neil chuckles, "I was gonna see if he wanted to go grab a bite at the diner, but seeing as he's probably eager to get down to playing, maybe we'll just run into Cortez for some fast-food instead."

"Fuckin' A!" Fox appears with his bag and pillow in hand and a big smile on his face on hearing the words fast-food.

"Language, Bub. Watch your mouth. Did you finish cleaning like I asked you?" Another eye roll, this one aimed at gaining sympathy from his 'buddy' Neil.

"Yes, Mother. All done."

Little snot.

"You dare 'Mother' me and I might just start pinching your cheeks in public. Better watch that smart mouth of yours, mister." I try to look all stern, but it's difficult when I can feel Joe's restrained chuckle against my back and see Neil staring at the ceiling to hide his amusement. Thanks guys.

"Sorry, Mom," he mumbles, coming over to give me a quick hug and kiss on the cheek.

"Neil," Joe's deep voice says from behind me, "Make sure to stay alert."

"Drive-thru, Joe. Just the drive-thru." A message passes between the two of them that I can't decipher but can guess at, before Neil says to Fox, "No time to sit down, got a game waiting, don't we?" And with a fist bump and a final goodbye, those two are out the door.

I lean my head back against Joe's stomach and close my eyes.

"You think Neil's gonna be able to look after him all right?"

"Neil may not look the part, but he's one of the very few men I would trust with that boy's safety, Doc."

"Okay," I sigh.

"That's it? Okay?" he chuckles, leaning down to kiss my neck, "You're not going to fret all night? Worry about him? Call him every two minutes?"

"Hush. No I'm not, not every two minutes. Besides I trust you, and if you say it's safe, then it's safe."

Coming around the front of the chair, Joe pulls me up and into his arms.

"So compliant. I like it." The low rumble of his voice makes my insides do a little jerk. It's been a good week since we've anything but kissed and I am craving his hands on me and from the feel of the hard length of him rubbing against my lower belly, he's craving something too.

"We've got the place all to ourselves..." I raise one eyebrow and bite my lip suggestively, making him groan.

"Don't, babe. I made plans for us. I'm following through on something I said to you last week, so you're just gonna have to be patient." Stepping back from me, he quickly adjusts himself with a grimace. "And I'll have to keep my hands off for a little longer, or that'll be the end of my honorable intent."

"Watch it! Fucking moron."

A car comes flying out a side street cutting right in front of us, and I almost end up in oncoming traffic. Straightening out the truck, I try to have a better look at the car speeding off in the distance.

"Was that a green Toyota?"

"Don't know, didn't really pay attention to that," Naomi says beside me. "Where are we going anyway?"

It took everything I had to step away from Naomi earlier. Sleeping on the couch every night while knowing she was just a hallway away curled up in bed almost did me in a few times, but Fox served amazingly well as cock-blocker. I wanted nothing more than to pick her up, throw her on the bed and sink myself balls deep into her warm, tight pussy, but I'd fucked up before because of my eagerness to get what I want before doing things in the right order. I might be a little slow off the mark on this, but I'm determined to show her how much more she means to me before I tell her.

"Joe? Are we going to the Parker place?"

Fuck I'm glad we're almost there.

"Bear with me okay, beautiful?"

Not easy to organize a surprise in a town this damn small. Everybody is sticking their nose in everyone else's business making it impossible to keep a damn thing hidden. Not only had Arlene already called Emma after I went to the diner to pick up dinner, but Emma was waiting by the kitchen door when I walked past on my way to the guesthouse half an hour later. I'd just dropped everything I needed off and was planning to simply pick up Naomi and go, when Emma called me in for a minute while she put the finishing touches on a load of cupcakes. That woman is forever feeding people. Finally, fifteen minutes later, with twelve iced and boxed up cupcakes tucked in the back of the truck on the floor, I'm finally picking up my girl.

When we pull around the feed store—it *is* where we were headed—I hear Naomi's gasp beside me. While Neil was working on installing the high-end alarm system today, I put up a few strands of Christmas lights around the porch. Too early yet, but at least it gave the place a bit of a homey feel. I'd managed to get the key off the realtor a day early and Gus and Caleb helped me move in some of Naomi's furniture this morning. It looked semi-liveable.

"So pretty...when did you do this? Wait. Did you get into the house? How?"

I turn the ignition off, turn in my seat and cup her face.

"Stop asking questions," I tell her with a smile. "The house is yours. It's safe and dinner is getting cold. Let's go." I can't let her go without bending down to have a thorough taste of her mouth. Mistake. My relief deprived cock is back. And so fucking hard I want to unsnap my jeans right here and now to let the poor bastard out.

"Mmmm..." she moans in my mouth and I tear myself away forcefully.

"Inside. Food first."

With a high flush on her face Naomi blows out air through her pursed lips.

"I'm thinking maybe a cold shower."

"Babe, no talk of showers, please. I'm trying to behave. Showers equal nudity. You and showers equals me coming in my jeans like a pimple-faced teenager any minute now. Have mercy."

The soft giggle as she slides out of the truck does little to relieve my situation, and I forcefully adjust myself getting out.

"You should've waited. I would've gotten the door for you."

"I know," she says, slipping her arm around my waist, "but I wanted to give you a chance to...calm the beast?"

"This is why you were gone all day." Naomi walks around the large living space touching the few pieces of her furniture the boys and I moved over here earlier.

"I didn't know where you would want everything so I just guessed, but it can be easily moved around if you like. We only brought over some basic stuff for now. The rest we'll do this weekend or whenever you want." I start rambling a bit when I see a deep frown appear on her forehead. Hadn't really considered she could get pissed. I'd been so focussed on getting her out on a date to a place she would love, but where I could make sure she was safe at the same time. Her new place seemed the perfect solution.

"I'm sorry if I—" I'm cut off when she suddenly turns and throws her arms around my neck.

"It's perfect," comes her mumbled voice from my neck.

I snake my arms around her waist. "Yeah?"

The furious nodding against my chin is my answer and I let out a sigh of relief. Thank fuck I didn't screw that up. I was worried there for a minute.

"Come. I have food." I try to step away before my body gets too distracted with hers again, but this time she holds on, her face tilted back; dark eyes full of emotion.

"Joe, I lo—"

I swallow her words, with my mouth on hers. Not gonna let her live the rest of our lives thinking maybe I gave her those words because I felt I had to. No fucking way. She'll hear it from me first and the right way. I pull back tentatively, replacing my lips with my fingers and when I see the hurt in her eyes, I know I have to be fast or this is going to hell in a hand basket.

"Beautiful, please… let me? Trust me?" I hold her chin when she tries to look away, trying to show it all in the way I look at her. Slowly I see the sting disappear from her eyes and the warmth returning. With a crisp nod, she concedes.

"Let's eat," I say leading her to the bar in the kitchen where I laid out two place settings earlier when I dropped off the insulated bag with the food from the diner. Appliances were not coming until this Saturday, otherwise I would've cooked something. Waiting till then wasn't an option.

"Pretty." Naomi smiles when I light the candles I set up around the room. I'm a long way out of my comfort zone here, but I want to make her feel special.

During dinner I tell her a little about my parents, about losing them when I was still fairly young and about my strained relationship with my dad. One I never really had a chance to resolve. Give a bit of background on my friendship with Gus and then I ask her about her past. Though hesitant at first, she tells me she too was an only child and had a great childhood, but lost her parents in an accident shortly after Fox was born. She's happy they never knew how bad her marriage had been. We give some insight and tell stories back and forth, sharing anecdotes and memories and slowly get to see a more complete picture of the other. This is what I wanted tonight to be about. Well, that and getting in some skin to skin time. Well hell, I am a guy.

"Leave that. Come sit with me."

I'm lounging on the couch watching Naomi put shit away in the kitchen.

"Just a sec."

"Doc," I say firmly, "Quit stalling and get over here."

With an eye roll, but a small smile at the corner of her mouth, Naomi wipes her hands and slowly walks over to where

I'm sitting and grabs the hand I'm holding out. When she goes to sit next to me, I give her a little jerk so she lands on my lap. Right where I want her. I push her back so her head leans against the armrest and I can look down into her eyes and touch her face. I trace the lines and edges of her face with my fingers.

"Do you even know how beautiful you are?"

She scrunches her face up at that and gives a small shrug. "I'm just average, Joe."

"Quiet. You're always beautiful. After pulling a twelve-hour shift you look just as beautiful as when you started it. When you first wake up in the morning, you're as stunning as when you are dressed to go out. It doesn't matter under what circumstances I see you, you're always knock-out gorgeous. But you know when you take my breath away the most? When you make my heart skip in my chest? It's when you're smiling. Happy. That's when the high beams go on. When all of you comes shining out all at once and it's damn near blinding. I want to be responsible for putting that smile on your face. I want to be the one who gets to make you happy. I love you, beautiful. So much it makes me crazy. Can't tell you when it started, but I know it feels like the most natural thing in the world."

Her mouth is half open and the eyes looking up at me are large and a liquid brown.

"You're gonna catch flies." With a finger under her chin I gently close her mouth and smile as she swallows and blinks. Leaning down I touch my mouth to hers, tracing her lips with my tongue before I slide my fingers into her hair and tilt her head for better access. When I start kissing along her jaw and down her neck, I'm interrupted by the buzzing of my phone.

"Fuck." All too aware this could be important, I kiss Naomi on the nose before sitting up and fishing out my phone to look at the screen. Not quite believing what I'm seeing, I tap my finger on the screen to get a closer look.

"Is this some kind of joke?"

CHAPTER TWENTY-ONE

I'm a puddle.

The lights, the date, the food; all of it, so thoughtful and ridiculously sweet. I almost lose it when he stops me from spilling my heart all over him. Almost run for the door then, but when he asks me to trust him, there is nothing but warmth and tenderness in his eyes and fighting down the urge to take off and hide somewhere, I stay. Fuck am I glad I stayed. Talking about our childhood, our life before we met is a little awkward at first, but nice...so nice. He doesn't run off when I tell him about my bouts of depression after the death of my parents, nor does he seem to make a big fuss about it. Same as with the panic attacks, he appears to take everything in stride. And I've been so worried that a man like that, one who had been marked once before by someone with mental health issues, would be at the very least sceptical or suspicious. Not Joe. He simply asks how I would deal with things or what some of my triggers could be and leaves it at that. Huh.

Now he gives me these words; the truth of his feelings visible in his eyes and spilling from his lips. Beautiful sentiments about me. His full attention so focused on my face, as I'm laying back on his lap. These things he sees in me, make my chest swell like a bubble about to burst. When he says 'I love you,' it fills me to the brim. I want to tell him...it's been on my lips so many times before, but just when I'm about to, we are interrupted by his phone.

"What's wrong? What is that?" I try to get a peek at the picture he is looking at on his screen, but I don't see much more than a blur. Before I get a chance to take a better look, he is dialing with one hand and grabbing my hand with the other.

"Neil. Good. Everything okay there?"

I raise my eyebrows in question and struggle to sit upright. Joe helps me up before pulling me against his chest, his arm wrapped firmly around me.

"Nothing then? No disturbances? Okay good. I'm forwarding a text from an unknown number I just received. Check the image and carefully ask Fox if that is his ball cap. If you have to obscure part of the picture, do it. I'm calling Gus next."

When he disconnects, I immediately try to grab the phone from him.

"What the hell, Joe? Show me."

"I will. I'm sorry, I needed to make sure first." When he pulls up the text, I can barely see. The image is so small, but then he clicks on it. A Coyotes' cap. Covered in blood with a bullet hole right in the center. My hand goes up to my mouth, whether to stifle a scream or hold back the vomit that's threatening to come up, I don't know, but Joe grabs my shoulders firmly and gives me a little shake.

"He's fine. That's why I needed to call first. Fox is just fine. Now let me quickly send this off and then I'm going to call Gus to give him a head's up. Are you holding it together?"

I am. I am holding it together dammit, so I nod my head in the affirmative. Half listening to Joe's conversation with Gus, I hear Gus is coming here and catch that Malachi will head over to the motel to keep an eye out as well. That's good, but I still want to pick my baby up right away. So when Joe hangs up, I try to get up, but he holds me back.

"What? Let's go."

"Naomi, think for a minute. Why would someone send a picture like that when there is an easy way to check he's safe? What would be their objective?" He looks at me intently, and I'm struggling to sort through the possible reasons, when suddenly it hits me and I tense as my eyes wander to the window.

"We're safe right here, babe. Let Gus and Caleb do the rounds outside and find out what they can. Neil is with your son and Mal is keeping an eye on the motel, but I honestly think Fox is safer where he is right now."

"What kind of sick joke is this?" I manage, my emotions swinging between anger and panic. Such a different place from where I was just minutes ago when I was ready to lay my heart on the table for the man whose large hands are currently trying to soothe me. Somehow it spurs me toward anger. I don't cower. Not anymore. Been there, done that and I think I've had my fill, so I push off Joe's lap and get up holding my hand out.

"What?"

"I need your phone." With a pensive look on his face, he hands it to me and I immediately dial Fox's number. I don't care how many people tell me my kid is fine, I need to hear it for myself. After ensuring he is okay—he almost sounds charged with the evening's excitement—I disconnect and start scrolling through Joe's messages. I want to find the picture of the ball cap for a closer look, but I can't help notice the substantial number of messages in the last few days. Messages that catch my eye because of their very *friendly* tone. Joe must see something in my face, 'cause he holds out his hand for the phone right away.

"Something else come in? I didn't hear it. Let me see?"

I drop the phone in his hand and start moving toward the hallway. I need a minute to collect my thoughts. I don't want to overreact, but some of what I picked up from the messages is enough to rattle me. I mean *'can still feel your mouth on my cunt'* is pretty explicit, right? Could be anyone, though. A sick prank. Except *'lick my initials on your chest'* sounds pretty specific. And disturbingly accurate. I shouldn't have looked. I hear Joe say my name but I need just a minute.

I'm not quite sure what happened. One minute I have her in my lap and the next she's backing away from me and making a beeline for the washroom in the hallway. When I look down at the phone she dropped in my hand and look at the messages that were pulled up on the screen, realization hits me. *Fuck.* My ex and her occasional, delusional trips down memory lane popped right up. Every couple of months Brenda gets a hankering to see if she still affects me with her tawdry messages. I suspect when she was feeling particularly low, or lonely. I never respond, other than an occasional *'Stop'* in return when she won't let up after a few. Two days ago she started up again. God only knows why this time, and I hadn't thought much about it. It's par for the course for me, but I can only imagine what it looks like to Naomi. *Christ.*

"Naomi!" I try calling after her before the bathroom door closes but it's no use.

Should've blocked Brenda's ass a long time ago, but a sense of responsibility always nagged at me. Idiot. "Naomi, please," I try again, knocking on the bathroom door, just as there's a knock on the front door.

From the dark hallway, I can see the outline of a dark figure in the narrow windowpane beside the door. I cautiously approach, leaving Naomi safely in the bathroom for now, when I hear another rap and Gus's voice.

"It's me. Open up. Now."

I open the door to find Gus and Caleb standing just off the porch a few steps back.

"I think we've got a problem," he says, pushing me back into the house toward the basement door, Caleb pushing close behind.

Looking over his shoulder, I notice a glow coming from outside, but before I can act, a large explosion propels the three of us down the basement steps, landing at the bottom in a tangle of limbs. Dust, debris and smoke stir around me as I scramble to get up.

"NAOMI!!"

Blind and deaf to the sounds and impressions around me, I surge up the stairs I just flew down to find my way blocked by the basement door, now wedged the wrong way in the doorway. I claw and kick, trying to get it out of my way, but it isn't until I see another pair of hands coming up from behind me that we're able to create an opening large enough for me to slip through.

The devastation in the hallway is terrifying, the blast having blown out the front windows and the door right off its hinges and flung it toward the stairwell in the back, where it has partially pierced and pushed in the washroom door. Where my girl is.

"Naomi, babe, can you hear me?"

Nothing. I fucking hear dick-all. My heart is in my throat and I force myself not to give in to the panic I'm feeling.

"Help me try and get this door," I snarl at Caleb who comes up behind me and starts yanking on the front door with me.

"Hold up. Let me climb to the other side." Gus, who has blood running down his face, sets his boot on the handle of the door and clutters over. "Step back, gonna try and move it from this side. Same direction it got wedged in."

Caleb and I take a step back, and Gus hauls out with his boot, kicking the door right where it's caught on the wall. Again he slams into the door, and this time it shifts. Two more massive kicks and Caleb and I grab hold of the bottom of the door and manage to pull it back into the hallway, cracking it loose from the washroom door. Leaving the guys to deal with the door, I slip through the opening and find my heart bleeding on the floor behind the toilet.

Please God.

"Joe. How is she?"

Caleb's question stirs me into action, and my hands start moving to clear her body, covered in dust and shards, and a deep moan leaves my chest when I feel the flutter of breath under my hands.

"Baby? Can you hear me?"

A soft whimpering comes from her pale lips as her body starts to shiver.

"She's going into shock. I have to get her out of here." The moment I lift her up into my arms, I realize my mistake, but it's too late to do anything about it. All I can do now is get her to help. I can feel hands helping me climb over the scattered rubble in the hallway and leading me outside where I find burning chunks of what may have been my truck scattered around. Emergency vehicles start pulling around the feed store and I start walking toward the ambulance as soon as it stops. The EMT opens the bay doors and I climb in, but when I try to put Naomi down, her body suddenly comes to life and clings to me so hard her nails are digging into my skin.

"Sir, you need to put her down so we can examine her." The young EMT gestures to the gurney.

"She's not letting go. Fuck it, *I'm* not letting go," I tell him, sitting down on the gurney myself with Naomi still in my arms. "You'll have to examine her like this."

The kid tries to object, but one look has him changing his mind. Smart move. This is one battle he wouldn't have won.

"Joe…"

I wake up to a hand shaking my shoulder. I'm a little disoriented finding myself squeezed into a hospital bed with Naomi still attached to me; Dooley standing over me. In a flash it all comes back, the message, the explosion. *Jesus*. Naomi hadn't let go of me the entire way to Cortez and even here at the hospital, she fought every time they tried to lift her away from me. Finally they administered some kind of sedative after I told them she was prone to panic attacks and I was able to put her down so they could tend to her injuries. Thank fuck those turned out to be relatively minor. She has cuts on the back of her head and back, a few of which needed some stitches. Other than that, only bumps and bruises that were starting to pop up all over her body, but will fade with time. I have a few of those myself, but nothing that needs looking at. I crawled into bed with Naomi right after the doctor left, saying they'd keep an eye on her for a few hours; at least until the sedatives wear off, to make sure she's okay.

"You got anything?" I ask Dooley, slowly sliding my arm from underneath Naomi and slipping off the bed.

"Not much, I'm afraid. For the last four hours we've come up with some possible tire tracks, but given that that parking lot is used for making U-turns all the time on that stretch of road, I'm not holding my breath on it. Phoenix PD is stepping up on their end, pulling in Felipe Rivas' older brother to see what he knows. They owe me one since sending those two yo-yos down here, throwing their weight around. For your information, they're both being investigated by IA. The pair was tightly wrapped into the Heffler murder case too. The older one? Libretti? He's turned up on a lot of cases where Bancroft, Leeds, Miller and Associates were representing the defendant."

"No shit? Naomi's douchebag ex's firm?" And suddenly I remember the call I never returned. An out of the blue call from someone who for all intents and purposes shouldn't know who I am. *Fucking hell.*

"Frank fucking Bancroft," I say, remembering how odd Naomi said he had been on the phone with her when she was still trying to find out where her ex had gone. How surprised I'd been he'd even know to call me, wondering where he would've gotten the intel to come looking in Cortez of all places when Naomi hadn't said a word.

"Dammit Dooley, he's the key. It's been out there the whole fucking time, and I've been too blind to see it."

I tell him what I know about Bancroft from Doc, about the phone call I never returned, and how things went to shit in a hand basket right after. I'd thought it had been coincidence, that he'd somehow found out about the request for the Heffler trial transcripts and was calling about that, but that never really made much sense. I'm thinking very differently now.

"Check him out. I bet you he's neck-deep in this. See if there are connections to be found between him and Heffler; we've been staring blind on the connection between Miller and Heffler, and never considered looking deeper into Miller's associates."

A rustle from the bed has me look over from the far side of the room where we've moved not to disturb Naomi, but she seems to be waking up.

"Joe?"

"Right here, babe."

I walk over to the bed and find her eyes trained on me before flicking to the doorway, taking in Dooley.

"Detective," she says, trying to sit up in the bed. "Can anybody tell me what happened?"

"Sure thing, Doc," Dooley answers, moving into the room and taking a seat against the wall. "Looks like someone rigged Joe's truck to blow. Now whether it was intended to go off right when it did, I don't know, but when Gus and Caleb went around to check, Caleb noticed the seatbelt on the driver's side stuck in the door. When he opened the door to slip it back in place he could smell the distinct odor of motor oil. It made him suspicious and when he checked the chassis, he found a brick of C-4 explosive stuck behind the rear axle with a timer already counting down. That's when he warned Gus and they took off for the house. We're thinking the opening of the door somehow triggered the timing device. There was less than a minute left, not enough time to try and dismantle the bomb. The good news is that although the truck is toast," he throws me a regretful look, "the house is still standing minus a bunch of windows, some busted doors and a bit of fire damage on the outside, but other than that, there is no structural damage."

"Is everyone alright? No one hurt?" She looks at me, the concern all over her face.

"Other than you? I think Gus may have had a cut somewhere. I noticed blood on him, but no one was down."

"He was checked out by the EMT's on scene. He was gonna stay until some contractor showed up to help him board the place up. The alarms were going off all over the house too. Sounded like someone breached the White House." Dooley face scrunches up at the memory.

Go figure. I hadn't even noticed it. Mind you, my ears were still ringing from the impact of the explosion. Good to know something worked. Neil was going to have to fix some of that.

Dooley gets up and wipes his hands on his pants. "Well, I'm gonna head back to the station. Have some leads to work on, but I'll leave a uniform here for now. Let me know where you'll be going when you leave here. We'll coordinate with GFI to make sure things stay buttoned up." He turns to leave but stops at the door. "Oh, and Joe? I'm thinking I'll be calling the feds from the office, just so you know."

"Sounds like a plan to me." I give him a chin lift.

"FBI?"

"Slide over, beautiful," I tell her, crawling back in beside her. "Couple of things are popping up that might indicate this case is a bit too entangled for simple interdepartmental cooperation.

There's a state line running right through this investigation and it is becoming a bit difficult to be sure on where everyone stands. Safer to let the feds take charge."

Her head is on my shoulder and her hand is laying over my heart. She feels fucking perfect there.

"Okay. I'm gonna need more when my head is clearer, because you're not gonna brush me off with an obvious evasion like that, but for now I'm happy to let you take charge."

I chuckle at her words, glad to have her 'bite' back.

"Only because I have to apologize first," she continues.

"The fuck? Apologize for what?" I roll over so Naomi is on her back and I'm leaning over her. "Explain."

"Holy shit, Joe. Calm your tits," she says her hands bracing against my chest.

"Did you just tell me to calm my tits?" I can't believe that just came out of her mouth and my voice drops a few octaves. Just to prove a point. Apparently this is amusing, 'cause suddenly Naomi is limp with giggles underneath me.

"Should've seen your face," she hiccups. I try, but the snort will not be held back any longer.

"You're crazy, you know that?" I snuggle in her neck and feel her body still.

"I know...and that's what I'm so sorry about," suddenly serious, her voice is quiet. Too quiet. "The messages upset me, I just needed to process it. I know you wouldn't do anything...you know? But what she sent is so intimate; it took my breath for a minute. I mean—you do seem to have a penchant for crazy chicks, you know? Your ex, then Jenna and now me."

I'm not liking where this is heading. "Do not compare yourself to those two. You shouldn't even be mentioned in the same sentence. Jenna was nothing but a fucking mistake from the get-go, she was never anything else. In fact, that's the last time I want to waste words on her. Those messages from Brenda came in just the other day. I barely pay them any attention. She does this every so often when she feels low or has some kind of setback. They make me sick. I've thought about blocking her ass so many times, but part of me feels responsible. Not because of any feelings I have—whatever I may felt at one time has died a thousand deaths—but because she has no siblings or living relatives and is sick. I don't like the idea of completely cutting her off. Don't like what it says about me. And finally, most importantly, you suffer from panic attacks. What's the big fucking deal? You think that even dings on my radar when it comes to you? With everything that you are? Now *that* is nuts. Yes, I want to make sure you feel safe and secure and not stressed to the gills, so that you won't get them all the time, but that's for your sake. If taking pills is gonna help you—great. If talking to a therapist is gonna do something—wonderful. But don't fucking do it for my sake. Do it for you. I love you with or without...makes no difference to me. I just want you to feel good, to be happy and show me that beauty all day, every day."

"Okay," she smiles, her eyes moist but no tears. Not this time.

"Okay?" I smile back.

"Yeah. Joe?"

"Mmmm"

"Love you too."

"I know, beautiful. I'm a lucky bastard."

CHAPTER TWENTY-TWO

"What time is it?"

I can see sunlight filtering through the blinds in the bedroom of the guesthouse. Gus drove us back here from the hospital last night—or I should say early this morning—after I was finally discharged at about two o'clock. Thank God I had a solid sleep, even if it looks like it may just have been a couple of hours. After last night's events, it wouldn't have surprised me at all to have woken up to another panic attack, but instead I slept like a baby. I'm sure it helped that Joe insisted on carrying me right from the car all the way to the guesthouse and into the bedroom, where he stripped me completely naked before tucking me in bed.

"Just saying goodnight to Gus, babe. Be right back."

And the next thing I knew I felt his arms come around me from behind and pull me tight against his naked chest. It was lights out after that. Everywhere.

This morning when I crack my first eye, squinting against the light of day, I find myself draped over him, my cheek on his chest with a small wet spot at the corner of my mouth. Lovely. I'm literally drooling all over him. I lift my head and notice the tattoo on his chest. The one Brenda mentioned licking. An involuntary shiver runs down my spine as I wonder why he still has her initials so prominently displayed on his chest.

"What are you doing?" his voice rumbles from his chest, as I surreptitiously try to wipe his skin and my mouth with a corner of the sheet. Hoping for distraction, I wipe while pushing myself up at the same time.

"Gonna make some coffee," I announce, but he tugs my arm and I tumble back down on top of him.

"Did you just drool on me?" he chuckles.

"Who? Me? Nah. Just let me go. Need to pee." Again I start pushing off, when he uses one finger to wipe at my chin.

"Missed a spot," he winks and finally lets me go. Before I have a chance to get up from the side of the bed, he grabs me by the waist, leans over and plants the sweetest kiss in the middle of my back.

"It's not her," he says quietly from behind me freezing me in place.

"What do you mean?"

"The tat. The initials. They aren't her. I had it done after I found out she'd gotten rid of our baby. Never even got a chance to grow, but I didn't want to forget, so I had the baby tattooed on me. She may have been able to rid herself of it easily, but I never would."

I sit quietly, taking in the deep-rooted pain he just shared with me. B M; baby Morris. I turn my body so I can stroke his face, trailing my fingers down to his chest where I trace the letters. Leaning down, I kiss the center of his chest before getting up.

"You coming back?"

"I might," I tease, intending to get some coffee going first. I really need my hit in the morning and I need a minute to gather myself.

After I do my business in the bathroom, I slip down the hall to the kitchen and get my coffee fix going.

Waiting for my brew to stop sputtering, I lean on the sink and look out over the fields in the back. Most of the remainder of corn has come down in the past week and the view goes on forever now. The coffeepot lets out a few last burps and I can already start inhaling the first hints of caffeine when a very warm and solid body braces me against the sink from behind.

"You're taking too long," Joe says softly in my ear. "Although I much appreciate the naked-in-the-kitchen look. I'm thinking we should make it a daily rule."

A shiver runs down my spine at the warm breath dancing over my skin. Never really considered being naked. Somewhere along the line, I appear to have lost all inhibitions around this man. Or maybe...maybe this is exactly what I had hoped.

I can feel myself already wet in anticipation as Joe's hands start skimming the skin of my shoulders and down my arms, never moving his body back from mine. We're plastered together and I can feel the ridge of his hard cock against my ass. When his hands slide to the front, rubbing his palms over my protruding nipples, the sensation shoots right down to my core and I drop my head back against his shoulder on a moan. My own hands reach back and find his strong thighs keeping me captured against the edge of the counter. The coarse bristle of the hair under my fingers getting sparse as I slide my hands up to find the hard clenched muscles of his ass. I can't help myself—I squeeze, causing Joe to hiss in my ear. "I need my breakfast." Before turning me around to face him, his hands on my waist.

"Up you go, beautiful," he says, trying to lift me on the counter, but I stop him; a smile on my face.

"First dibs." I sink on my knees in front of him closing my hand around his glorious cock, eyes trained on his. "After all, I made the coffee," I say right before I slip the tip in my mouth, taking in the taste of him. My tongue teases the crown, running the tip along the small slit and around the flanged rim. When I reach the underside, I press up with the flat of my tongue and suck hard.

"Jesus, babe..."

Those clear blue eyes on me are on fire, his hands tangle in my hair and I love that I can have this effect on him. With one hand guiding his cock in my mouth and the other clasping his ass, I can feel the flexing of his muscles underneath my hand. Fucking amazing. Joe is intoxicating. The combination of his taste, his scent, his response to me and the lust in his eyes is setting me on fire and I moan around his length, shifting my hand from his ass to tug lightly on his balls. I want to make him lose all control, I want him to lose it all in me. Working his cock deep I can feel him struggle to keep from fucking my mouth, when suddenly he pulls back from between my lips with a pop.

"You owe me breakfast, baby, but I need in your pussy. Right now," he growls

Hauling me up, he turns me around and has me facing the kitchen window again, except this time he lifts one of my legs and rests it with my knee on the counter so I'm standing on one leg, spread wide open.

"Fucking gorgeous. Stay like that. Don't move."

I try to look over my shoulder and just see him dip down on his knees behind me, holding my ass in his hands. Then I feel his mouth on me. *Holy motherfucking hell.* The slow, deep, firm stroke of his tongue catches me from my clit to the base of my spine, causing every synapse to stand up and cheer in its wake. Again he laps at me, before sucking my clit hard into his mouth, making my one standing knee buckle.

"Holy crap, Joe..." I barely breathe out, overwhelmed by sensation.

"Was hungry," he chuckles as I can feel him get up behind me, lining his cock up with my drenched opening teasing the head along my super sensitive clit.

"Please honey," I moan.

"You want this?"

"Fuck yes!"

In one hard stroke he fills me completely, the sensation unlike anything I've experienced, with the way I'm spread out. His body bends over mine, his teeth are in my shoulder, grunts filling my ears, and his hips are fucking me with fierce thrusts, balls slapping against my detonation button. And I'm close to detonating.

"Coming... Joe, please, I..."

All it takes is the lightest touch of his finger over my clit and I'm bursting apart in an eruption of pleasure that temporarily blinds me, taking my breath. My body is still convulsing around him in climax when I feel Joe go rigid behind me and bury himself so deep inside, he lifts me completely off the ground, moaning my name.

"Mercy," he whispers against the skin of my back, making me giggle. Mercy indeed.

"Mom? When can I get this thing off?"

Fox is standing by the counter in Emma's kitchen where we find him and Neil scarfing down breakfast. Naomi walks over and ruffles his hair, ignoring the cast he is waving in her face.

"Your appointment with Dean isn't until next week some time. I have it written somewhere, I think it's on Thursday. No guarantee it'll come off though. It all depends on how it's healed and you better remember there's a good chance those metal plates and screws are gonna have to come out at some point."

"But he's not gonna do that right away, right?"

"Not likely. He'll want the bone to grow stronger first, which is why you shouldn't be in such a hurry to get that cast off in the first place," she looks at him sternly but all she gets in return is a roll of his eyes. Fox turns and walks down the hallway to the washroom, but before he goes in he looks over his shoulder at Naomi with a mischievous smirk on his face.

"Can't wait to use both hands take a piss, Mom. The load's getting too heavy to carry with one." With a big grin he pulls the door shut behind him, leaving Naomi slack-jawed. The rest of us burst out laughing.

"Fox Miller!"

"Erm, Doc," Neil's amused voice stops her. "I'm thinking he just got you back for having to stand on the front step of the guesthouse, listening to his mother go at it in what sounded to be the kitchen."

Naomi's hands fly to her mouth and her face turns beat red as her eyes find mine. All I can do is shrug. I mean really, I'm not going to apologize for what happened. Not cool that the kid had to hear it, but I'd be lying if I said that memory doesn't stir me right back up again. Emma and Gus just chuckle along with Neil, until he slams the palm of his hand on the counter startling all of us.

"And can someone tell me what the fuck the deal is with kitchen counters??"

It's kind of funny to watch Naomi try to talk to Fox about what he almost walked in on. He keeps walking away with his hands in the air, warding her off.

"Ma, I don't wanna hear. Please can you just drop it so I can attempt to erase it from my memory completely?"

Dejectedly she finally leaves him sitting on the couch, walks up to where I'm sitting on a stool and leans her head on my chest.

"I fucked my kid up, Joe. I've scarred him for life. I'm a horrible parent."

I pull her between my legs and rest my cheek on her head.

"A bit more X-rated than necessary, sure. But you figure maybe with all the nightmares he's been through lately, getting the message that life and love go on regardless, is a good thing. As for parenting, I don't claim to know much about it, never had the chance, but I'd say you show him what it means to survive, sustain and stand strong just about every day. Today you showed him how to savor, and trust me." I drop my voice even lower. "That particular talent of yours, I won't forget easily either."

"Joe." She turns around in my arms and slings her arms around my neck, standing up on tiptoes to kiss my mouth sweetly.

"Enough already," comes from the peanut gallery on the couch.

Leaving Fox in front of the TV and Naomi chatting with Emma over coffee in the kitchen, I follow Gus into his office, Neil right behind us.

"What've you got?" I ask Gus as soon as the door closes behind us.

"Bancroft was picked up early this morning. They're working on getting a search warrant for his office and house right now, but the feds are right on top of this thing. Neil tried to work with that message you sent through. The message itself came from a pay as you go number. Burner phone most likely. But the perp wasn't so smart when it came to the image. It was shot on a camera phone, but not the same phone the message came from. He took the picture with one phone, attached it to a message and sent it to the burner phone, downloaded the image onto that phone and sent it as an attachment to yours. Probably thought he'd have eliminated all links, forgetting the original information would be embedded in the image. It links back to an account in the name of a Guy Rush. Neil's putting a trace on it now. Digging some more."

"Did you talk to Dooley?"

"He's the one who told me about Bancroft, but I didn't get a chance yet to pass on the information on Guy Rush. Doing that as soon as we're done here. You know Clint's going to be at the Parker place at nine thirty this morning, right?"

"Yeah, you told me last night. I'll go over and take Naomi and Fox with me; see if we can do a bit of clean up inside while they put the doors back in place. Windows coming later this morning you mentioned?"

Gus nods and indicates toward Neil, who's already been typing away at the computer on the conference table. "Once windows and doors are in, Neil can come back and make sure the alarm is hooked back up and working. Mal is tackling motels, hotels, boarding houses; pounding the pavement already trying to see if we can get any information to float up. I'm gonna try and trace the C-4, but I'm afraid the relatively small amount will likely make it impossible to pin down the source. Still, won't hurt to try."

"Okay, well I'm off then. Don't forget to call Dooley and I'll check in later."

Naomi's new place looks pretty beat up on the outside. Police tape is still wrapped around the porch and big sheets of plywood cover what's left of the windows and the front door. Some of the siding is scorched as is the porch, and there is still some debris left from my truck. The big pieces have been hauled off to the Cortez PD shop, where the feds are going over it with a fine toothcomb. Luckily Naomi's truck was still at Gus and Emma's, so between the two of us we have wheels. Gonna have to pick up something else to drive this afternoon when I have a chance.

"Holy shitballs," Fox exclaims. "That's better than Grand Theft Auto."

"Bub! It wasn't that much fun being inside when that thing exploded, you know." Naomi throws a stern glance over her shoulder and Fox is wise enough to zip it with a grimace. "Besides, I hate that damn game. I can't believe you snuck that back in from Phoenix. You know I didn't want it in my house."

I have to back my chuckle, because I know Fox is trying to disappear into the upholstery right now, wishing he never would've brought it up. I decide to help him out by distracting Naomi.

"Let's grab the gear Emma loaded us up with and do this thing, guys. Clint should be here soon."

Ripping the yellow tape down, I use the crowbar I tossed in the back of the Denali to loosen the board closing off the entrance.

"Grab the other side, Bud, so it doesn't come back down on me when I pull it back."

With Fox on the other end, we manage to pull the sheet away from the doorway and carry it down the porch. In the hallway, Naomi stands and surveys the damage.

"Lucky I didn't have anything hanging on the walls yet," she deadpans, looking at the huge gauge in the wall between the mudroom and the hallway where the front door had been wedged.

"First let's just pull out whatever loose material we can find and be careful of glass. Emma put some heavy gloves in those buckets." The doctor is in the house, and I'm more than happy to let her take charge. I'd been worried coming back here might have triggered something for her, but that was apparently for nothing, because she just ploughs right in as if I didn't find her bloodied and curled in a ball behind the toilet last night. The memory of that vision will haunt me for a long time to come.

After Fox and I drag out the mangled front door and toss it over the side of the porch, I grab a bucket and head into the living area, where the remnants of our dinner still sit on the kitchen counter. Glass first. The window closest to where my truck had been parked had literally been blown to smithereens. Doc's gonna need a new couch. Aside from being torn up by the bigger shards, this one is full of slivers and there's no way I'll ever sit my ass down on it again.

"Fox! Wanna give me a hand hauling this couch out? It's a total loss." Against Naomi's protestations and with a bit of nifty manoeuvring we manage to slide it through the hole where the window used to be. Outside, we lob it over the porch railing onto the parking and are about to pull it out of the way to the back of the house, when Clint's truck pulls in. He's got just one other guy with him and waves as they start pulling tools out of the bed of the truck, taking them inside.

I'm about to walk inside behind Fox when my phone rings.

"Joe, it's Caleb. I can't get hold of Naomi. She with you?" There's an edge to his voice I haven't heard before.

"Yeah. We're cleaning up at the Parker house. Hang on, let me get her. Everything ok?" I ask, walking over to where Naomi is shaking hands with Clint and his helper.

"Not sure. Mattias is sick."

I put my hand on Naomi's shoulder and hold out the phone. "Baby's sick. It's Caleb for you."

Clint and the other guy have moved into the living room to take stock of the damage there. Doesn't look nearly as bad with all the debris gone.

"Did you check for fever?" I hear Naomi ask. "So how long has it been since he's kept anything down? Okay. I'll be right over, but you tell Katie for me that if that boy is in danger of dehydration, I'll be the one calling the ambulance myself. Okay. Soon." She turns to hand me my phone back.

"So sorry, but I've got to pop over to check on Mattias. Don't want to take a risk with a little baby and Katie would rather not take him to the hospital if it isn't serious for risk of infection there. Caleb doesn't agree," she chuckles, "I'm afraid I have to side with Katie on this one. We should only bring him in if it's serious. People get sick in hospitals. Can I have the keys? I won't be long."

Like hell.

"I'll drive you."

"But what about Fox? He just slipped downstairs, probably to play some games in his 'man cave,' as he calls it."

I walk to the basement door and holler downstairs. "Hey Bud? Your mom's gotta go check on the baby real quick, let's go!"

"I'll just stay here. Clint's here right? Not like I'll be alone," he yells back.

I turn to look at Naomi who shrugs her shoulders. "Okay fine, they're barely five minutes away, but I'll drop you off and am coming straight back here. You can call when you're ready or have Caleb drop you off."

Ducking my head in the living room, I give Clint a head's up and ask if he can keep an eye on Fox.

"Yeah. No problem. We'll be fine." With a wave of his hand he turns back to scraping the remaining shards off the window frame.

I hop out and pull Naomi's bag out of the back for her when we arrive at Caleb's just under five minutes later. She's about to run inside when I grab her by the arm and spin her around.

"One second," I mumble against her lips before taking her mouth deep, swiping my tongue along hers and tasting her thoroughly. When I let her go, she smiles and takes a step back.

"What was that?"

"Don't know. I just needed it. Don't like the idea of leaving you here, but I don't like leaving Fox alone either. Now I can take your taste with me."

A soft smile settles on her face as she steps up to me again, reaching out to swipe her thumb over my lips.

"Sometimes you surprise me. I love you, Joe."

"Ditto, beautiful."

I watch her go inside before getting back in the car. Just then my phone goes off in my pocket. A quick glance at the screen identifies Gus.

"Talk to me."

"Where are you?"

"Just dropped off Naomi to check on Mattias. On my way back to the Parker house now, why?"

"Thank God. Mal found a short-term furnished rental just on the far side of Cortez in the name of Guy Rush. Paid cash for a month, couple of weeks ago. Talked to the neighbors who say he got picked up a few times by a work truck in the mornings. One of them remembers seeing the name Mason Brothers on the side. Whatever you do, don't go back to the house. Clint's not answering. We're on our way."

My blood freezes in my veins and my foot slams down on the accelerator as I bite out, "Like fucking hell! Fox is at the house!"

CHAPTER TWENTY-THREE

"Hey little man. What are you doing spitting up all over the place? You've got your daddy worried sick."

I've just finished unwrapping little Mattias who looks a little flushed, but barely spikes a fever. He does seem a little lethargic though and when I palpate his stomach he scrunches up his little face and starts screaming loudly. Katie is calm enough sitting on the bed beside me, but Caleb is a wreck pacing back and forth across the upstairs landing of their home.

"Tummy ache, huh? Let's figure this out." I undo his diaper and notice a urine stain. Should be clear as water if he was drinking properly. Nothing else seems to be amiss. When I put my pinkie finger in his mouth though, he starts up his wailing again and a little light-bulb goes off.

"How has he been feeding?" I ask Katie.

"Not well the last twenty-four hours or so. I thought it was a phase and every time he would latch on enthusiastically enough, but as soon as he starts sucking he pops off and screams. I don't think he's managed to get a whole lot in. We even tried pumping and giving him the bottle, thinking it might be easier for him, but it doesn't seem to make a whole lot of difference."

I pick up the little guy and walk over to the large picture window where I gently widen his already open, screaming, little mouth to the daylight. Sure enough, the inside of his mouth and side of his little tongue is coated with small milky white patches. Cradling the unhappy baby against my shoulder, I turn to his parents. Katie sits quietly waiting on the bed and Caleb leans against the doorway, concern etching his face.

"Thrush. This little guy has thrush and Katie, babe, you probably do too. It's a fairly common yeast infection that can flare up in breast fed babies and is transferrable from mom to baby and vice versa. Have your nipples been sore? I mean getting worse instead of better?" I correct after seeing the slight wince on Katie's face.

"I thought I might be getting cracked nipples but I couldn't find anything other than that they seemed a little redder and more sensitive. So what? We need antibiotics or something?" She asks and I feel baby Mattias settle down a little at the sound of her voice.

"Actually no. No antibiotics, but what I'd like you to try is Gentian Violet. It's a topical treatment, perhaps a bit old-fashioned but it does the trick nine out of ten times. You should be able to pick it up over the counter at Walgreens and use a sterile gauze to wipe the inside of Mattias' mouth as well as your nipples. I'll write down instructions because I don't want you to use too much. It's gonna be messy enough as it is; I suggest you get latex gloves," I chuckle, remembering the time Fox had thrush and I had bluish purple fingers for days after getting too much of the stuff on the gauze. "You should sterilize everything he's had in his mouth, though; bottle nipples, soothers, toys—anything that might re-infect him. And run all your nursing bras through a hot cycle before wearing them again."

"Does she have to stop nursing?" Caleb wants to know.

"Absolutely not. Keep trying and keep pumping a little, 'cause the bottle might still be a little less painful at first than the bottle, but don't start with the bottle, always breast first. That reminds me, any leftover breast milk has to be tossed, and don't forget to sterilize the pump."

I hand Katie over a now quieted Mattias, and he snuggles right into her neck with a little satisfied grunt before closing his eyes tightly, while I start writing down detailed instructions for the Gentian Violet. When I tear the prescription note off the pad and hand it to Katie, Caleb takes it from my hand and walks toward the door.

"Okay, let's go." Caleb stands in the doorway motioning me to come when Katie throws him a scathing look.

"Caleb! What in the blazes is wrong with you? That's rude. Let me have a visit first."

"Little One, our boy is sick and I need to get to Walgreens to get this stuff. I'm gonna pass by Naomi's place on the way so I can drop her off. I'm just being sensible."

Katie rolls her eyes and opens her mouth to object but I beat her to it.

"Actually, that works well for me, honey," I tell her, "A lot of shit's going on, as you know, and I know Joe's back there already, but I'd still feel better if I were close to Fox right now."

Understanding settles on Katie's face. "Gotcha. I was being totally selfish."

"No way. We're gonna have some quality time when all this settles down. I have much to discuss with you." I smile at her.

"I bet, I wanna hear all the deets."

"As long as I can be out of the house when that happens," Caleb pipes up, still waiting in the doorway.

With a quick kiss for little Mattias and my best girl, I grab my bag and jog down the stairs after him.

Fox

This basement is da bomb. The only thing missing is a separate entrance, that would be perfect, but I doubt Mom would let me put one in. Still, it's way cooler than my room in the other house.

Instead of playing my game, I decide to hone my pool skills. Not that I really have any to begin with, but Dad had a table—smaller than this eight foot beauty—and I played a little. Wouldn't mind playing a game or two with Joe. He doesn't seem like such a bad guy once you get over the sheriff part. He did let me off the hook pretty easy. He's also been a decent guy to my mom. I didn't know if I was gonna like it at first, but I like seeing her happy. And despite this fucked up situation, he does seem to make her happy. I think. What the fuck do I know?

I rack up the balls again and wind back to break them when I stop to listen. Thought I heard the basement door and I look up at the stairs. Nothing else though—must've come from upstairs. I focus back on my shot and break the balls. Not bad, two stripes in opposite corner pockets. Stripes it is. Walking around the table I try to pick the easiest next shot, which is on the far corner. An easy shot, that is, if I can keep it in a clean line; something I've not been particularly good at with this cast on, bouncing my cue ball of the sides and other balls. It's a matter of hitting it in just the right spot.

I'm concentrating so hard, I don't hear anything until I feel the press of cold hard steel against the base of my skull. I know what that is—I've felt it before. Laying the pool cue down on the table I slowly straighten up dragging my hands over the surface of the table when I feel the smooth surface of a ball against my thumb. Shifting my body, I hope to distract whoever is behind me, while I slip the ball inside the sleeve of my hoodie and grab the end of the sleeve to keep it from sliding out again. When I finally stand, I try to turn around but a vaguely familiar voice stops me.

"Don't turn around. Got a phone? Pull it out. Carefully," he hisses, as I reach for my pocket. "Call your mother and tell her your contractor got hurt and they need to come back. Now."

I'm fighting hard not to piss my pants. I try dialing Mom's number but nothing happens. No ring tone. Nothing. I try again, but the call doesn't even connect. When I check my screen, I see I barely have a single bar.

"Call your fucking mother, you little useless dickwad!"

"I'm not getting reception down here," I manage to get out quickly when he yanks back on my hair, the gun now wedged under my chin.

His hand holding me by the hair and the gun back behind my ear, he swings me around to the stairs, moving me forward. I let him push me up the steps, the ball still hidden against my cast. I'm not quite sure how it's going to help me yet, but I feel better for its weight in my sleeve.

When I stick my head through the doorway at the top of the stairway, movement to the left catches my eye. But before I can help it, the hitch in my movement must've alerted the asshole behind me, because with a final shove, he pushes me up the stairs and out in the hallway, where I land on hands and knees. Turning my head, I finally see Clint's sidekick standing over me, the gun still aimed at my head, but his eyes are focussed down the hallway.

There are three stop signs between Caleb's and the Parker place and I run them all. Luckily at the first two, I encounter no traffic, but at the third I have to swerve to avoid hitting a mini-van. No time to check, I blow through the intersection leaving the blaring of an angry horn behind me.

My instinct is to drive right the fuck up to the doorway, and jump out with guns blazing, but I catch myself just as I'm about to pull around the feed store. I take a minute to let my years of training override the fear and adrenaline that's fueled my movements thus far, and then I slip out of the Denali, leaving it on this side of the store, careful not to close the door. Even though I have the keys to the place in my pocket, I can't remember for the life of me if the connecting door between the store and the mudroom is unlocked or not and I'm not about to waste precious time on the chance of finding it locked from the inside, so the front door seems my only option.

Instead of coming along the driveway however, I decide to circle around the back way, so I end up on the far side of the porch, by the back windows of the house first. It might give me a chance to see what I'm up against before anyone knows I'm here.

Coming around the back, I can't see much from the first rear window, no movement anyway, but when I move to the second one, I can see work boots sticking out from behind the kitchen counter. No fucking idea whose they are. Slipping around the side, I sneak a peek inside the first hole left by the blast and get a better look at whose feet are in those boots. Clint is lying face down and unmoving. Cold fear grabs hold of my heart as I think of what that motherfucker has done to Fox. In a few strides, I'm stepping through the door opening into the hallway. Muted sounds are coming from the basement, even though the door seems to be almost closed. Is Fox still down there? But when I make a move in that direction, I see the door crack open and the kid's head appears. I can pinpoint the exact moment he registers my presence, because there's a falter in his movement. Whoever is behind him notices too, because suddenly Fox comes flying through the door and lands on the ground, and the son of a bitch I saw earlier, getting out of the truck with Clint steps out of the basement behind him, holding a gun trained on his head. His eyes, though—his eyes are fixed on me. Creepy fucker.

"Maxim Heffler, I presume? You're gonna want to let the kid go."

The asshole only grins wider, putting a foot in the middle of Fox's back and pushing him further to the ground.

"Not gonna happen. I'm gonna need the missus in here. Where'd you leave her?"

"She's not here. I left her with a friend."

I've kept my gun hand by my side and he either doesn't care or doesn't seem too impressed. Either way, he hasn't commented on it yet so I'm not about to draw any attention to it. Not yet anyway.

"Not falling for that bullshit. Get that bitch in here, or I'm gonna start shooting parts off her boy." He looks down at Fox, lifting his boot back on the floor beside the kid. "I'll be kind. Start with the hand that looks to be fucked up already."

A quick glance down shows me Fox has turned his face sideways and is looking at me with fear in his eyes, but there's something more there. Something calculating. Hoping to hell he's not gonna be trying anything, I attempt to send that message with my eyes. A quick blink from him makes me think he may have gotten the idea.

"I'm dead serious. She's on the other side of Cedar Tree checking up on her friend's baby. Won't be back anytime soon."

"Too bad," the bastard says, taking aim at the kid's hand. "Her old man told me he left some *insurance* behind with his family; thought it would save his life. Shoulda seen the surprise on his face when I pulled the trigger. Dumb fucking waste of space. But I am gonna need those files, and she's gonna help me find them."

My mind's going a mile a minute. Insurance? The fuck is he talking about?

A sound from the living room draws Heffler's eyes away from mine, and in that moment of distraction, I lift my gun. Heffler spots the movement and instinctively swings his gun my way at the same time as Fox turns around with a ball clutched in his hand. Shots are fired along with a litany of screams I hear from somewhere behind me.

"You're sure he'll be ok?" Caleb asks me for the third time since we got into the car. It makes me chuckle; this huge and highly dangerous man from what I've been told, is terrified of a little thrush.

"He's gonna be fine and so is Katie. It's possible it might come back at some point, but that's pretty rare and now you know what to look for, so you'll be able to catch it before it becomes a big problem."

"He's just so damn little and he can't tell me what's wrong. Drives me fucking nuts," he grumbles and my heart melts a little.

"From the mother of a teenage boy I can tell you, won't be long before you'll wish he'd stop complaining about everything. Try to enjoy him while he's this cuddly and sweet, okay? He's a boy. Trust me, it won't last long."

We turn onto the front parking lot and Caleb slams on the breaks.

"Something's wrong," he says.

"Why are the cars parked here? What do you mean?"

"Like you just said; both you and Gus' trucks are parked over here for a reason. Something is up."

Caleb pulls in beside Gus's truck and turns off the engine before turning to me.

"Need you to stay here while I go check things out, Naomi."

Bristling at being ordered to stay put like a good little girl once again, I whip my head around to face him. "Like hell I will. My boy is in there, Caleb—and my Joe." With that I push the door open and slide out, leaving Caleb to mumble expletives under his breath as he comes around the back of the truck and grabs my arm.

"Now you listen to me, anything happens to you and by some miracle your man lets me live, you think my wife will? Fuck no, Naomi. Dead man walking here, one way or another. Goddammit all to hell. Get behind me, you stubborn thing, and not a peep."

Leading the way, he keeps my wrist in his hand, carrying a gun that appeared from somewhere in his other. As we round the side of the feed store, Caleb stops me. When I sneak a peek around him, I can see someone climbing in one of the blown out windows off the living room. Caleb leans back and whispers over his shoulder, "That's Neil. They must've come round back. Stick close."

My eyes are drawn to the left where I can just see the back of Joe's shirt. He's standing still just inside the entrance and I can hear talking, but not what's being said. We are still partially shielded by the back wall of the store so I can't see much more than that, but I figure talking is good. Caleb isn't moving though and I'm eager to see my boy.

"Here's what were gonna—"

Shots ring out, almost simultaneously and when I look over, I can just see Joe crumple to the floor. I open my mouth and scream.

Caleb's already off and running, yelling at me to stay. When he's almost to the porch, my legs finally get the message to move, because there is no way in hell I'm waiting here. Caleb is in the doorway, blocking my view. With the adrenaline coursing through my body, I manage to push him to the side and step into the hallway, where Joe is lying at my feet and further down, Gus is just pulling the guy who was working with Clint earlier off the prone and bloodied body of my son. My breath sticks in my lungs not moving; just sitting there painfully filling my chest until I feel my heart will stop from the pressure. A hand grabs my leg and a voice filters through the void I'm caught in.

"Beautiful..."

A sob bursts free releasing all the air that was trapped as I look down at my feet to find Joe's eyes on me, his hand loosely circling my ankle, which has started to shake along with the rest of my body.

"He's all right, baby—Look."

"Mom?"

CHAPTER TWENTY-FOUR

"Two regular coffees please. To go"

I'm getting so sick of this cafeteria. Actually, I'm pretty sick of this whole hospital. I've spent at least as much time here after quitting as I did before.

Paying the tired-looking older lady with a nametag displaying her name, *Elaine,* the cash after being handed my coffees, I'm about to walk into the hall when I bump into Dean; Fox's orthopedic surgeon.

"Here you are. Was looking for you. The new cast is on and he is miserable now that I've told him it will be at least another four weeks before I'll take it off. It's your turn now. Better go try and cheer him up." Dean leaves in the other direction with a smirk on his face. Bastard. First I have a coffee delivery to make.

I'm wearing the scrubs Stacy provided me with when we first arrived. I looked a mess. After hearing Fox call out to me and looking up to find him standing across the hall, I had him wrapped in my arms in a nanosecond. He was in one piece. The blood he was covered in belonged to Heffler who hadn't faired so well. He had collapsed on top of Fox after being shot. Twice. My boy just hurt his injured arm when he flung a ball at Heffler who was about to shoot Joe. Caught enough of Heffler's arm to save Joe from a full on hit. The bullet took a chunk out of Joe's thigh, but it could've been so much worse. Heffler himself was hit by two bullets, one in his shoulder and the other a headshot. That one is likely the one that killed him.

Both Neil and Gus had been hiding in the living room and I don't know, nor do I care, who actually fired their weapon. Detective Dooley gets to sort that out. He arrived within minutes, with first response vehicles in tow. Joe was transported by ambulance, with Fox and I in Caleb's car right behind them. I struggled with that; wanting to stay with Joe, but not ready to let go of Fox just yet. Until Joe called me over, pulled me down to him for a sweet kiss and told me to take care of 'our' boy.

So I did.

I know it's all kinds of wrong as a physician to feel any kind of gratification at the death of a human being, but Maxim Heffler has left so much destruction in his wake, I can't help but feel his death is justified. The mayhem he caused didn't just affect Fox and I, but so many other people who got caught in the cross-fire. Especially poor Clint who got hit over the head with a sledgehammer. His own fucking sledgehammer. The impact apparently left a substantial tear in his scalp and knocked him unconscious. With his vitals stable he's been taken by ambulance to Durango; the hospital there is better equipped to deal with complex head trauma.

I'm itching to find out how he's doing, but for now I'll just bring my impatient man a cup of coffee. He's still waiting to be stitched up, while I found Dean on his way out the door and got him in to see Fox right away. As a result, while Fox was being looked at, I snuck out for some much needed caffeine.

I don't know what it is that sets the hair on the back of my neck up, but walking down the hallways back toward the ER, I get an uncomfortable feeling I'm not alone. The hallways are relatively quiet, but still there's some traffic. I don't get it. I don't see anything when I look around and behind me. Must be jitters.

I'm actually surprised I haven't been hit with a panic attack yet. You'd think with the stress and emotional upheaval of the past few hours, I'd be whimpering in a corner somewhere. Huh.

My jitters are fast forgotten when I push the door to Joe's room open gently with my shoulder, hands full of coffee. Don't want to wake him if he's sleeping. Well hell. Through the crack I can see a half-naked Jenna leaning over the bed. I battle the rush of panic that sweeps through me and force myself to take in the scene before me. Not gonna run. I know this is not what it looks like. I *know* it, despite what my body tries to tell me. I swallow when I see Joe's hand come up off the bed and reach up to grab her hair and my heart almost pounds out of my chest.

"The FUCK?" His deep voice bellows out a string of expletives as he pulls her body away from him by the hair, which is my cue to enter.

"Are you totally out of your mind? Coming in here, mauling me when I'm asleep. You're fucking sick!"

Jenna looks shocked...or does she? She keeps glancing over, having spotted me quite easily, which makes me wonder if she knew I was there all along. When footsteps can be heard running down the hallway and a security guard and a nurse burst into the room, probably alerted by Joe's yelling, the smug look on Jenna's face disappears. Grabbing her blouse off the bed where she must've dropped it, she turns her back and starts covering herself.

"What's going on in here?" Security approaches Joe in the bed.

I can see the cogs turning in that vile bitch's head when she speaks up.

"I want to press assault charges," she has the gall to say, working hard to make a few tears appear.

Oh hell no. That is not going to happen. There is no way in hell I'm gonna let her pull a fast one on Joe.

"Really? You want to tell me you didn't come in here, undress yourself, while my man was sleeping in the bed and tried to force yourself on *him?* Because that's sure what it looked like from here. All Joe did was pull your mouth, which probably tastes like pond scum, away from his when he woke up. You're a repulsive human being, Jenna, and a very sore loser. You really think that little show you put on was gonna fool me? Or win him over? I know your mind is too small to comprehend, but Joe loves me. I love him, and some power crazy, surgically enhanced crotch muncher isn't gonna change that!"

GOD that feels good. Joe is smiling at me from the bed. No. He's actually grinning like this is the funniest fucking thing ever when I'm still energized with indignant rage, so I throw him what I hope is a scathing look. Only seems to make him grin wider. I hadn't noticed the increase in audience since I started my little tirade, but it appears the room has filled with onlookers. Oops. A quick look at Jenna tells me she isn't too happy with me. Go figure. If looks could kill? Yeah. Code blue.

"Ms. Stanley? I need a word with you in my office please."

Stare down interrupted, I turn around to find Gordon Pinchette, our Medical Chief of Staff standing in the doorway. The portly grey-haired head honcho is not one of my favorite people in the hospital, too politically colored and utterly intimidating on most days, but today I think I could kiss him. Jenna visibly blanches under his dark glare, but then straightens her shoulders and walks with her chin high through the throng of people now gathered around the doorway. Dr. Pinchette lets her pass before glancing around the room. "Show's over folks, back to work. Sheriff, Dr. Waters, my apologies for this unfortunate incident. I'll be in touch." With that he too turns on his heels and stalks off after Jenna in the direction of his office. *Oh my.*

When the security guard and the nursing staff along with a few nosy passers-by have dispersed, only Fox—who apparently heard enough to come see—Joe and I are left.

"Crotch muncher, Mom? And you tell me to watch my language."

Of course my son would hear that, *and* feel the need to repeat it, to Joe's apparent great hilarity.

"It slipped," I defend myself rather pitifully, but then Fox turns to Joe.

"And you actually went there?" The look he throws Joe is one tinged with disappointment. It's obvious Joe is affected by the way he flinches at the words and scrutiny from my protective son. Part of me wants to jump in and defend him, but I decide to let them figure this one out. After all, they had a pretty good thing going and if Joe wants to be in our lives, he's gonna have to deal with the brutal honesty he can get from a teenager. So I keep my mouth shut and go to set the coffee cups I've been clenching in my hands this whole time, on the bedside table.

"I messed up with your mom the first time, years ago, Bud. In hindsight that may not have been a bad thing. I needed time to sort stuff out before I was really ready for her." He throws me a regretful glance, before turning his attention back to Fox. "My last big mistake was when I was feeling sorry for myself and finally acted on a standing invitation from Ms. Stanley." A derisive snort from Fox has Joe raise his hands. "Not making excuses here; I effed up royally and regretted it almost instantly. Even then, I'm pretty sure I was already in love with your mother and still I went there. I'm responsible for a lot of the shit she's been putting your mother through and there's nothing I can change about that now. "

One look at Fox shows me the earlier anger in his body is already waning. His attention is completely focused on Joe's words.

"Trust me. If I could go back and make a different decision I would, but that's not the way things work. You mess up, you work hard to deal with the consequences — 'cause, Bud, there's always gonna be consequences—hoping you can set things right, and then you move past it. You hear me?"

I've snuck in closer to Joe's side and grabbed hold of his hand, whether to show Joe my support or Fox a united front. Either way works for me.

"I hear you." Fox's mumbled response is barely audible and knowing my kid, he's likely processing some of what Joe said. Recognizing some of that speech could just as easily be applied to his own situation. Joe's not stupid. He comes clean with him, but at the same time, tries to teach him a valuable lesson; one that Fox will hopefully tuck away somewhere safe. Joe's apparently not done, because he continues, "You know I'm proud of you though, Bud. You kept your cool and had my ass back there. If not for your dead aim with that bum arm of yours, I might not have been here. That right there is one decision I hope you will never come to regret, just like I'll never regret drawing on and shooting the man, 'cause you're still in one piece. Tucking that ball away was a dangerous move, but a smart one and don't be afraid to tell everything you know to the detective and the FBI when they ask you later. These are the good decisions we sometimes make—and even those come with consequences that have to be dealt with, those are also not always pleasant, but at least you can hold your head high. You saved my life."

"Why don't you give Gus a call to pick you up?"

"What? And have him drive out here again to pick you up later? I'll wait. Neil's already come to get Fox and the impression I got from Detective Dooley when he was questioning Fox earlier, the feds still want to talk to us both. Dooley's waiting for a phone call. Just sit tight. I'm sure we'll be out of here soon."

I finally got cleaned up and stitched by some pimple-faced doctor, who looked to be barely older than Fox. Naomi swears he is good, but I was watching him like a hawk anyway. Didn't like the way he got *friendly* with Doc. He said he was sending someone back with a sheet of information, some antibiotics, and painkillers, which I refused. All that was over an hour ago. In the meantime my phone's been ringing off the hook. Carol called having put out the original call. Drew did as well, even though I'd seen him briefly at the house and then there was the brass; they're on my case because I discharged a weapon while under suspension. Never mind that it was my personal weapon or that I was trying to save a life. No, they're more concerned about which bullet actually killed Heffler, and my apparent 'inappropriate conduct' as they called it. Fuck this. I just want to get out of here.

Just as I'm about to use the nurse call bell for the third time, the door swings open and Stacy comes in.

"Hey girl!" Naomi is on her feet hugging the nurse in a second. "Did you just come on shift? How've you been?"

Stacy bursts out laughing. "You serious? How have I been? My life is same old, same old. But from what I hear, yours is more exciting than an episode of 'Bones.' I'm surviving without you—barely—although this afternoon's little incident in the parking lot, when I was just getting out of my car, gives me renewed hope there is a God," she says snickering and looks at Naomi who has her eyebrows raised in question. "I spotted a certain bedraggled looking hospital administrator being led to her car by security with a big ole box in her arms."

"No shit. About fucking time too. The woman is a menace."

Both women look at me and Naomi smiles before turning to Stacy. "Here's the deal. You get Joe out of here in the next five minutes and I'll give you all the dirt."

Without hesitation, Stacy walks over to the bed and throws the covers back.

"Out." This to me, before she turns to Doc and says, "Now spill."

"Where to?" Gus asks when he finally picks us up an hour and twenty minutes later.

"Your guesthouse, if you don't mind, Gus," Naomi answers and I'm too tired to object.

Of course the minute Stacy has me ready to go, Dooley and Special Agent Marks walk in. *Christ.* Almost made it. Both Naomi and I go over the events as we remember them from this morning. Details of the brief conversation start floating back and I mention what Heffler said about James leaving 'insurance.'

"Fox said something about that in his interview with us too, but he can't think of anything his father gave him before he left.

Nothing that would contain files of any kind. I know I asked earlier, but have you come up with any ideas Dr. Waters?" SA Marks directs his attention to Naomi who just shakes her head.

"Nothing. Really, I can't think of anything. He hasn't sent anything by email or mail in the longest time and even then it had to do with Fox one way or another. School or health or something. I wouldn't even know what I'd be looking for, to be honest."

"Well if anything comes to mind, at any time, please let us know right away. Heffler may no longer be a problem, but we know he has a large network behind him. Until we can start tying things together, I'd still suggest you remain cautious. Phoenix PD has had to release Bancroft. Apparently they managed to get a search warrant for his home, but that didn't produce anything. Judge wouldn't allow one for the office though. He said evidence to warrant a search was too thin to justify compromising the confidentiality of all the firm's clients. We're keep close tabs on him, so that the moment he moves, we'll be on him. For now he seems to be doing his normal routines. Just stay alert."

Fucking great.

Things are wrapped up pretty quickly after that and I make it a point to get both of them to promise to contact me directly should anything change. Right now, I'm tired and just want to sleep with my woman in my arms.

"Come on, big guy. Let's get you to bed."

I must've dozed off, because when I open my eyes we're parked in front of Gus and Emma's place.

"Slept enough for now," I mumble, trying to battle through the lingering brain fog. My leg stings like a son of a bitch, instantly reminding me of the day's events. It's gotta be eight o'clock or even later, 'cause the sun is almost down.

"What do you want to do then? Come in for a quick bite—Emma's kept something warm for ya—or do you wanna go straight back?" Gus asks as he's helping me get out of his Yukon. The hospital provided me with a pair of scrubs since my jeans were toast, and there is a stiff breeze I can feel on my legs through the thin material. Damn. Already winter is close.

"Food I guess. Okay with you, Doc?" Naomi is just coming around the back of the truck.

"Yeah, sure. I'm good with that. After that, you're going to lay back down though. You can play the tough guy tomorrow again."

I suddenly realize the kid isn't there. "Where's Fox? Shouldn't he be here?"

"He and Neil came here, had a bit to eat and I told him it was okay for him to tag along with Neil to his room. Wasn't sure what time you guys were gonna be done and I figured after today the kid could use some distraction."

Naomi walks up to Gus and reaches up to give him a kiss on the cheek. "Thanks for looking after him," she smiles.

I can't help it. I don't like seeing those lips anywhere near another guy; even if it's my best friend who is happily married at that.

After allowing Emma to fuss over us with food and attention for a bit, I'm finally where I want to be; in bed with Naomi cuddled up beside me. God I love that woman.

First thing she did when we got here was lead me to the bedroom, sit me down on the edge after getting rid of my scrubs and giving me the best sponge bath imaginable. Stuff fucking dreams are made of and I didn't even move. The sight of dark hair spread out over my thighs and feel of her mouth around my cock was enough to have me come within a couple minutes. Wouldn't allow me to return the favor either. Now her breathing is deep against my shoulder and I'm still wide awake. Exhausted and sore, but awake and thinking about my future.

Our future.

CHAPTER TWENTY-FIVE

"Mom—I can't find my deodorant!"

"Bub, Jesus! There are spares in the second drawer in the bathroom. Will you hurry up? You're gonna be late for school."

I'm still lying in bed, having had a late night last night going over some loose ends with Gus and his crew. Naomi woke me up with a coffee this morning, only to tell me she'd be back after dropping Fox off for school and that if I catch some extra sleep I *might* be ready for her when she comes back. My girl's got plans for me. It's been a bit of a challenge, us all cramming into the guesthouse, with Fox now taking residence on the couch, but every time I suggest going back to my place, Naomi argues that I'm not quite a hundred percent yet. Bullshit, and she knows it, but who am I to argue. I like going to sleep with my woman in my arms, even if we have done little more than snuggle and pet with Fox constantly around. Things are about to change though, cause the day after the shooting, her realtor called to let her know she had a serious bid on her house in Cortez and the people were looking for a quick possession. That meant that Naomi was able to turn around and get the lawyer to start finalizing the purchase of the Parker place and by Wednesday the ink was on the paper. With a bit of luck she'll be able to move in after the weekend. I have already lined up a few surprises for her.

Today is the first day Fox is back in a normal school routine, something he's not too happy about. It's time though. He's missed enough school already and despite the fact that he's had work emailed to him at home, the return to a regular routine and doing it in their new place will be good for everyone. Including me, since it looks like Naomi plans to reap the full benefits of Fox's return to class.

I got no problem with that.

My hands behind my head, I'm just laying here enjoying the early morning quiet after Fox yells "Later!" before slamming the door on his way out. Letting my mind drift back to last night, I replay what was discussed in Gus's conference room. There apparently still was nothing concrete that could connect Frank Bancroft to Heffler, and so they haven't been able to get that search warrant yet. Although we all came to the same conclusion last night; whatever there might have been in that office at one time, has surely disappeared by now. Hopes had been pinned on finding something—anything—in Fox's stuff, but after carefully examining everything he owns, including the seams of all his clothes and his backpack, we still came up empty. Frustrating as hell. Dooley's been in touch a few times but has nothing new to offer from his side either. The Feds have up and left, since Heffler is no longer an issue and Brancroft seems to stay where he's supposed to. No reason for them to hang around.

Then yesterday I was called into the Sheriff's office only to find out when I got there that all they needed was for me to sign off on some statements. No fucking progress yet made on the investigation and no, they didn't have a handle on when the suspension might be lifted. Bunch of bureaucrats; I feel like a fucking yoyo. I left furious and just shy of telling them to stuff their job, before I realized I'd better talk to Gus first. See what other options are out there before I start burning bridges. So after we were done picking apart Heffler and Bancroft situation, and I told them what happened in Cortez, Gus came through with an interesting proposal. One that I want to discuss with Naomi first because it has possible implications for both of us.

Soft sounds come from the living room, and just as I'm about to go investigate, the bedroom door creaks open and Naomi's face peeks through.

"Oh hey. I didn't want to wake you. Did you sleep at all?" she asks, sitting next to me on the bed, running her fingers through my hair.

"Nope. Was just musing over some of the stuff that came up last night."

"Well do you want to talk first or do you want my proper good morning?" A hint of mischief shines in her eyes. Instead of answering, I scissor up and pull her over my body to the other side, rolling with her so I land on top.

"I'm thinking I owe you a turn," I mumble against her skin, already peeling back the layers she put on to ward off the cold morning.

"Mmmm. I'm not adverse to that idea," she says, pushing her body up into mine.

Pushing up, I pull off her jeans and underwear at once and take her in. Legs splayed open and pussy already glistening with her arousal, I have to fight the urge to bury myself to the hilt inside her slick, welcoming body. Nothing but the sweet encouraging sounds coming from her lips, I push her knees back spreading her even wider and bend down to satisfy my hunger. Teasing her with my lips, tongue and teeth, it doesn't take long before I have her shaking on the brink of orgasm. Rather than letting her come with my mouth, I want to feel the ripples of her climax around my cock, and in one move, I cover her body with mine, stretch her arms over her head and sink myself deep inside her. Her inner walls immediately clamp down on my shaft as she flies off the edge and spurs me on to move in fast hard strokes. Each time I bottom out inside her I grind down on her clit, prolonging her orgasm. After a long week of abstinence, a handful of strokes is all I need to feel the tingling at the base of my spine and the tightening of my balls, before I spill myself inside her.

No words—just the erratic breathing of repletion breaks the silence and without disconnecting we both doze off.

"Good Lord. This looks fantastic!"

After waking up from our little morning nap, Joe and I took what was supposed to be a quick shower but turned into round two of the morning lovefest we had started earlier. We've just walked into the Parker house where Clint's brother, Jed, has taken over for him. Knowing very little about Clint's personal life, I was surprised to learn he had family close by, but when Beth called earlier in the week, she had mentioned that she managed to get in touch with his family. Apparently the brothers had a falling out at some point and hadn't been on speaking terms, but with Clint still unconscious in the hospital in Durango, Beth had taken it upon herself to track down his brother. Jed contacted me the next day and wanted to meet up to discuss the work Mason Brothers was contracted to do. He promised to honor whatever agreements I had made with Clint, stating that it was the least he could do. I asked him if he was sure—that I could find another contractor if he'd rather spend time with his brother, but he assured us this is exactly what Clint would want.

I haven't been back there while he's been working at the house, because I've been busy helping out in the diner while Beth is glued to Clint's bedside, but Joe's checked in a few times.

This is the first time I'm seeing it and what hits me right away when we drive up is the fabulous looking new porch. No sign of the scorch marks and damage to the siding left behind by the explosion. How he managed to do that in barely five days, I have no idea. Joe mentioned he had a large crew with him every time he went over there.

A brand new front door is in its hinges and all the windows appear to have been replaced.

The biggest impact is on the inside, where they not only fixed any damage done to the walls, the basement and bathroom door, but a fresh coat of paint in a buttery yellow makes the entire hallway feel like the sun is shining inside.

"I love this color. Who picked it?"

With just a slight nudge of his head Jed indicates to Joe, who is chatting with some of the crew. He gives me a curious look when I walk up, slide my arms around his waist and kiss his chest.

"What's that for?" he wants to know.

"Brightening my hallway and my day," I reply smiling up at him.

"If that's my reward for the color in the hallway, I can't wait until you see the master bath."

"Bathroom? But we haven't even gone over the details for the house yet? The clinic was going to come first."

Confusion must've shown on my face because he chuckles. "Go have a look. You seem to enjoy the bathroom at the guesthouse so much, I thought this might go a long way toward making this feel a bit more like home to you. Besides, you'll be so busy with people trampling down those clinic doors when it opens, you should have at least one place where you can relax."

With a squeal I let go of him and sprint up the stairs. First door I open is the master bedroom, where a massive canopy bed, with simple lines and straight corner spindles that reach almost to the ceiling, takes center stage. A matching dresser with eight large drawers stands against the opposite wall and in the little alcove by the window sits a big comfortable looking club chair with fat armrests and a footstool. Perfect place to look out on the gorgeous views and read a book.

"But...I don't understand? When? How?" I stammer, not quite believing my eyes and looking for answers to Joe, who has followed me into the room.

"Do you like?"

"I love it! It's absolutely gorgeous, but this'll seriously blow my budget."

"Not your worry, it's my housewarming gift." He holds up his hand to silence me when he recognizes the argument I'm about to give him. "A gift to myself as well, beautiful, since I plan on spending as many nights as I'm welcome to, right here in that big ass bed with you."

He's right. When he puts it that way, I have no room to argue. Who am I to challenge a man who couldn't be making it clearer that he plans on taking up a substantial space in my life, especially when I so desperately want him there?

"Have I told you how much I love you?"

"You don't have to. I know. But only because I love you just as much," he chuckles planting a kiss on my forehead. "Now go check out your bathroom."

I have to admit, I'm not really surprised to find a fully decked out oversized bathtub replacing the old cracked one that was here before. Nor does it really shock me that the shower that's been newly installed is big enough to fit two people comfortably, with a large number of showerheads of different shapes and sizes for the *full experience*. Fact I've come to understand is that these men—Gus and Caleb being prime examples—all have a thing about their showers; they like them big and shared with their women. The boys love to play in water.

"I'm leaving now. I should be there in five. Do you want me to pick something up?" I ask Katie, when I'm heading out to check up on little Mattias, who appears to have survived his bout with thrush just fine, to his daddy's great relief.

"No need. Emma came by yesterday and dropped off enough muffins and sweetbreads to last me the month," is her response.

"See you in a few then."

I pull out of the Parker place—I really have to stop calling it that, since it's technically *my* place now—and turn toward town. Joe mentioned he was hoping we could meet up at the diner for lunch after, since he has something he needs to talk over with me. Thank God Joe was able to rent his own wheels until he's able to sort things out with his insurance company. They're being assholes since I guess they don't deal with intentional explosions that often. A bit concerning that they don't have that whole thing tied off with a neat little bow yet, but it looks like Heffler may have covered his tracks really well. There hasn't been any way to tie the C-4 explosives to him. Anyway, Joe having his own ride means we can get so much more stuff done, although I have to admit, I kinda miss having him join wherever I have to go and vice versa.

My mind is going over a checklist list of things I want to get for the house and this afternoon's scheduled visit from Kendra to discuss all things clinic when a car almost ploughs in to me at the first intersection in town. I'm sure I have the right of way, since I was just pulling up from the stop sign. Seems the other car never even slowed down approaching the intersection and ploughs right through. I have to swerve and slam on my brakes to avoid it. A pang of unease shoots through me when the green Toyota barrels through even after almost hitting me. I recognize the car from a few other near run-ins over the past few weeks. Other than a quick glimpse of what looked to be a woman behind the wheel, I don't register much else. The rear license plate is illegible with only 'BM' showing as part of the number. I consider calling Joe right away, but decide to wait until I get to Katie's.

The excitement of seeing Katie already waiting by the door with a happy little baby in her arms is enough to make my need to call Joe slip to the back of my mind. It isn't until after I've examined and declared Mattias healthy and the thrush gone, that I remember to give him a call, but by that time I'm almost ready to leave and meet up with him at the diner anyway, so I decide to wait and tell him face to face.

Walking into the diner is starting to feel like coming home, especially since I've spent so much time here this past week.

Some of the regulars wave when I come in and Arlene comes out from behind the counter giving me a big hug.

"Hey chicky. I don't do it much, so mark this down to warm you over those cold winter days coming up, and don't repeat it to anyone cause I'll only deny it, but thank you for your help this week. It made things much better with that extra pair of hands," she says in a low voice and immediately releases me, stepping back behind the protection of the counter.

"Aww, thanks Arlene but it's been my pleasure. I was starting to get bored not doing anything productive and picking up a little slack for Beth was the perfect distraction. How's Clint by the way?"

"Still out. I swear the man does it on purpose, knowing Beth is sitting next to his bed waiting to tear into him like she always does, keeping his eyes tightly closed hoping for her to leave him in peace."

After Arlene's own initial rocky start with Clint, she appears to have grown quite fond of the big lug. Has to be said though, the man does have a way of getting off on the wrong foot with just about every female he encounters. Once people realize the words out of his mouth aren't intended to be as offensive to the recipient as they might initially sound when they leave his mouth—being the true tender-heart that he is—it's easy to recognize the good man underneath. Well. For everyone except Beth, around who he seems to get so rattled, the holes he digs himself with his 'Southern charm' just keep getting deeper and deeper. Curious that she'd be the one sitting by his bedside, holding his hand and almost willing him to pull through this.

"Your man is already in the kitchen having a chat with Seb if you want to go in. I'll just clean off that booth by the window and you guys can sit when you're done."

I find the guys chatting by the big industrial stove where Seb is cooking something that smells absolutely amazing.

"What'ya making?" I ask leaning over his shoulder to peek in the pan. Seb turns around to give me a hug and kiss, and shakes his head with a chuckle when a low growl can be heard from Joe's direction.

"Jambalaya, with freshly ground spices, mango, chicken and spicy sausage. No shrimp in this one," he responds grabbing a tasting spoon from the drawer in his work-station, scoops some up and holds it out for me to try. "Here, have a taste."

The flavors burst out over my tongue; a sharp bite of the sausage and what I'm sure is hot pepper, the juicy morsels of chicken, the tang of the mango and the fragrance of the cumin and cloves I can detect, have me ordering a big bowl for lunch. Delicious. Joe follows suit and we find our booth, each carrying our own food to the table.

"What did you need to talk to me about?" I ask Joe, when both of us sit back with an after-lunch coffee.

"Gus offered me a place with GFI last night. I won't say this hasn't crossed my mind before, or is an idea that is entirely new, but with this suspension and the way the brass is dragging their heels to get it resolved, I'm getting tired of the political manoeuvring. Pissed that I'd have to be worried about placing my family's safety before everything else, knowing it could come back to bite me. It's no way to build a future. Be putting a serious kink in the pleasure I used to take in working. The thought of being able to continue in the law-enforcement field, with a company I know will always have not only my, but my family's back, is very appealing. I'm thinking about it, but didn't want to make any decisions without you." With a creased brow and pensive eyes he looks at me, as if to gage my reaction. So I grab his hand over the table and hold on while I seriously consider my words.

"I hate the thought that I may have been cause for the problems they've been giving you, but—" I hold up my hand when he opens his mouth to protest, "I realize it isn't much different from what I've just done with the hospital myself. I think you'll love working with Gus and the boys and though I'm sure you'll miss certain parts of the job you'd leave behind, you'll get so much more in return. You need to know that I've never felt safer, even with everything we've just been through, with you by my side. I'm so grateful for the promise of a future full of that security."

Joe reaches over with his free hand to wipe at the tears that have started trickling down my face.

"Happy tears then?" he asks smiling, cocking his head to the side.

"Extremely," I tell him.

After a productive meeting with Kendra in the afternoon, where we manage to create a long list of needs, wants and dreams for the future in terms of the clinic, I roll into bed that night wrapped around Joe's large protective frame, exhausted but excited by all the upcoming changes.

Around two in the morning though, I wake up screaming from a nightmare featuring a green Toyota.

CHAPTER TWENTY-SIX

"It's okay, beautiful. I've got you."

I wake up with Naomi screaming and thrashing in the bed beside me, but before I can grab hold of her, she bolts out of the bed and climbs in the bathtub where she sits curled up and shaking, looking at me like I'm the boogeyman. Fox comes flying in from the living room, his hair all askew from sleep.

"What's wrong? Why's Mom screaming?"

"Bad dream, Bud. Go back to bed. We have a big moving day tomorrow and we're getting up early. I'll take care of your mom. Don't worry."

I watch him shuffle back to the couch before closing the door and stepping into the bathtub to gather Naomi up and wrap myself around her. The whimpers from her lips gut me. She hasn't had an attack in weeks and I'm not sure where this one comes from. Out of the blue.

It's not that long before her breathing returns to normal and her eyes become clearer, and she lifts her face to me for a kiss.

"What happened, babe? One minute you're in the middle of what looked like a nightmare, and the next, you're in a full-fledged attack."

"I remember only bits and pieces of the dream, but I think I know what triggered it. With all the distractions yesterday, I forgot to mention the green Toyota."

"What green Toyota? Like the one that cut us off a while back?" I'm a little surprised something like that would be cause for a nightmare, but her next words send a cold chill through me.

"Looked like the same one. I actually had an incident with one just like it at the first intersection in town. It just blew through the stop sign and I barely managed to avoid being broadsided."

I grab hold of her shoulders and sit her back so I can look at her. "Why didn't you call?"

"I was going to as soon as I got to Katie's but then she was waiting with Mattias and I got busy examining him. It slipped my mind until I was on my way to the diner and meant to tell you then, but we got to talking about other things and it disappeared into the background."

"Naomi," I growl, angry at her for not contacting me immediately. "Something like this happens, you stop and call right away. Understood?"

"Whatever," she says turning away and making moves to get out of the tub, but I hold her pulling her back against my front.

"Not whatever, Doc. I mean it. The thought of something happening to you is enough to give me a heart attack. My job's to look after you and I can't do that if you don't let me know. I could've done more at that moment than I'll be able to do now."

"Fine, Joe. I get your point already. It wasn't intentional and it obviously was enough to worm its way into my subconscious and set off a panic attack. No need to treat me like a child." She is still stiff in my arms, so I get up out of the tub and carry her to the bed where I lay her down.

"Trust me, beautiful. Last thing I see you as is a child, but give me a break. Seeing you go through one of these attacks is hard enough when there is nothing I can do to make it better, but at least I'm here to hold you. Knowing that something might've happened when I wasn't around or even aware? That's the cherry on top."

I crawl in beside her and am pleased as fuck when she turns to wrap herself around me.

"Sorry," she mumbles in my chest.

"Sleep, babe. Big day tomorrow remember?"

Within minutes I hear her breathing even out, but I lay awake until morning—thinking about that damn Toyota.

"Where do you want me to put this?"

"Bring that one to the basement. I'm gonna buy a smaller one for the living room," Naomi answers Neil, who walks in carrying a large flat screen TV.

Naomi is standing in the hallway of the new place directing where everything that comes in the house should be taken. I have to smile, because my girl has exposed a side to her I haven't had an opportunity to see in action before. She is bossing around six big men, plus Fox who's also a fair bit taller than his mom, like the dictator of a small country. She's organized. I mean organized with a capital O.

When all our friends started gathering in Emma's kitchen this morning for her move—even Seb who had committed to helping for a few hours—she had a script ready to go in each truck with detailed instructions on what to load first and who would take responsibility for each individual room in her house. She claims it's because she can't be two places at once, and this is the only way for her to make sure everything gets here and is placed where she wants it. Not that we'd have a chance to miss that, 'cause every box and large item in her old place is labeled with its origin and its 'new home.' Standing in the hallway, she checks every item and each box against her own list, and when an item is missing from the load, she insists it be first to come in on the next load.

"Fuck, she's scary," Caleb mumbles to me under his breath after she catches him accidentally putting a box intended for the basement down in the mudroom for a minute to grab a quick drink of water. "You'd think she caught me stealing the silver or something, the way she just stared from the doorway with her hands on her hips. Like Mother Superior at a convent school. I swear my dick has been left a stump and my balls are shriveled to raisins."

Mal, who overhears his brother and I, bends over laughing. Little Naomi putting the fear of God into the six-foot-five ex-ranger is funny as fuck. When I look over Mal's shoulder, I see her standing in the doorway directing poor Neil with another box and Fox won't even come near her.

I walk over to her and she throws me a pointed look when she sees my hands empty. Without a word I pick her up over her protests and walk her into the mudroom where I set her on the washer, inserting myself between her legs and kiss the indignant protest right out of her. When I finally pull back I keep her from moving by resting my hands on either side of her hips to box her in.

"Joe. I've gotta get out there, things will go wrong if I'm not there to make sure they put stuff in the right place."

"Doc, you think maybe you're overdoing it a bit? Hell, you scared the shit out of Caleb. Maybe let up a little? They're grown-ass men, beautiful, and with the detailed instructions you provided everyone with, there's no way something could go wrong. A little faith, okay?"

Naomi's eyes have gone big and are starting to water. Damn, don't want to make her cry.

"Did he say something? Is he mad?" she asks in a little voice, no sign of the slightly tyrannical Naomi we've seen all morning.

"No babe, but you can relax a little. I promise we'll get everything out of the old house and in here. On the off chance something ends up in the wrong spot, it won't be the end of the world. We'll come across it eventually, right?" I try. "What is it that has you so tightly wound today?"

"I don't know. I...I guess...I keep expecting something to go wrong, you know? Like this past week has been the quiet before the storm? I just want to make sure at least the move would go off without any surprises." She drops her head to my shoulder and I pull her into a tight hug.

"I've talked to the guys and put a call in to Dooley to keep an eye out for that green Toyota. Neil did a bit of a trace on the partial number you remembered but had gotten no hits before we left. He'll check again when he's done. Can't tell you to stop worrying, but we're on it."

A knock on the mudroom door is Neil asking where to put a ratty old club chair.

"Sorry, Doc, but that thing is butt-ugly," I tell her when we walk into the hallway and see the lime-green stained chair sitting in the hallway.

"I know, but Fox loves it. He says it's comfy for gaming. I didn't tag it, hoping that by some miracle it'd be left behind, 'cause Fox won't let me throw it out, but I see you guys are diligent," she says with something near disappointment on her face.

"I can see why he likes it," Neil says, earning a snort from Naomi. "It's one of those chairs you can hang in all day; lay back with your legs over the side. By the way, when I pulled off the seat cushion, I spotted this sticking out between the armrest and the springs." He pulls a disc case out of his pocket and hands it to Naomi. "*Mario Brothers*. It's an old one. Haven't checked if the actual game is in there."

Naomi opens the case and her mouth drops open. Looking over her shoulder I see the disc inside. *'For Mom'* is written in permanent marker right on it.

"Can't believe it was in the house the whole time."

Emma's come over with a cooler full of sandwiches and drinks for lunch. Seb left a while ago to change places with her at the diner, since Emma volunteered to do the breakfast shift so he could help move. Apparently she had time to fix lunch for everyone here as well.

We're chatting while the guys are back to Cortez for one last load and I just finished telling Emma about the disc.

"You figure that's the so-called insurance your ex left behind?"

"Don't know. Neil was heading over to the office to see what information he can pull off. He did say it was definitely not the game that was supposed to be in that case. It must've slipped out of Fox's backpack after he came back from Phoenix. He says he can't even remember the last time he played it. I'd never really gone for the violent games, which was one of the reasons Fox and I were having problems. I didn't want that stuff in my house, but when he came back from Phoenix, he brought back all the games his dad gave him. That's all he plays these days."

Emma laughs. "Wouldn't worry about it too much. When we were young, boys would play with sticks and toy guns pretending to shoot the crap out of each other. I figure this isn't much different, just on a slightly more sophisticated level. Fox is still just playing cops and robbers."

Huh. Never really thought about it that way, but I guess she's got a point. Cops and robbers.

Emma's gone to the bathroom while I'm tidying up the lunch leftovers in the kitchen, when the muffled ringing of a phone can be heard. Disoriented with all the boxes surrounding me, it takes me a while to figure out it comes from my messenger bag on top of some of Fox's sports equipment in the front hall, and I go to grab it. I'm surprised to find the front door open and go to close it, answering the phone at the same time. I'm pretty sure the guys pulled it shut when they left for their last run, but maybe it didn't latch all the way.

"Hey, it's me. Did you want me to drop the keys off at the realtor's office? The house is empty and since he was going to let the cleaners in anyway, we don't really need them anymore, do we?" Joe points out.

"I guess that'll work, but are you sure you got everything?"

"Babe, we've checked off every item on your list and once we loaded everything I did a final walk-through of the house. Opened every drawer, every closet; there's nothing but dust bunnies left," he chuckles. I love the slightly hoarse sound of his laugh.

"By chance, did you guys leave the front door open?" I ask him and am met with a pregnant silence from the other side. "Joe?"

"Front door was open?" his voice drops an octave and on my confirmation his voice takes on an urgent note. "Emma still with you?"

"Yes? Oh wait, she went to the bathroom. Maybe she went to grab something from the car. I just didn't hear anything."

I move to open the door and look out when I hear Joe in my ear, "Stay inside! I'm on my way." The sight of Emma with a gun to her head is the next thing I see when I look to the left, almost dropping the phone. Behind her is a tall blonde, who still looks all too familiar. It takes me a minute to process, but her arm around Emma's neck, the shaking of the gun in her hand and the madness in her eyes brings home the truly fucked up situation.

"Brenda," I whisper and I can actually hear Joe's intake of breath before he starts shouting to someone with him. Stunned I'm just staring at Emma's tear-streaked face, who is mouthing *'sorry'* when I hear his voice soft in my ear.

"Naomi, tell me what you see, babe."

The sound of his voice gives me strength and I feel myself standing up straighter as I explain the situation to Joe, my eyes never straying from her crazy ones.

"Your ex-wife is standing on the porch, holding a gun to Emma's head."

"Is that Joe? I want to talk to him," the deranged bitch says in a shrill voice, letting go of Emma's neck to hold her hand out for the phone.

"Give it to her, beautiful."

Feeling all kinds of possessive, I don't want her near him, not even on the phone. I'd rather throw the phone at her head but the gun now under Emma's chin stops me. I hand her the phone and her entire demeanor instantly changes. Totally freaky. From a shrill lunatic with hatred in her eyes, she turns into a simpering fool using a grating baby-voice when she talks to my man.

"Joe, how are you, baby? I was going to surprise you, but this is okay too. So glad you're finally talking to me. I've missed your—"

Slowly the pathetic smile on her face is replaced by a turned-down mouth and flaring nostrils as she listens to what is being said to her, obviously not happy with what she's hearing. I don't know how long it will take the guys to get here, but I can see this going to shit before my eyes. Empty handed, there is little I can do, so I slowly start backing toward the front door, hoping that once I get inside, I'll be able to grab something to use. Not wanting to lose eye contact with Emma, I stay in the doorway, reaching toward the pile of sports equipment that was dropped just inside the door. For once I'm glad Fox is a slob, 'cause he's the one who was supposed to find a place in the basement for those. My hand is feeling blindly through balls, nets, gloves and other paraphernalia, when I feel a smooth knob under the palm of my hand. Fox's pride and joy only two years ago, before puberty and Xbox made him a stranger, his Louisville Slugger. With my fingers wrapping around the baseball bat trying to get a solid grasp, I give Emma, who's been watching me like a hawk, a small nod.

"But Joe—" Brenda has been listening to what I assume to be Joe trying to talk her down, and gives it one last effort before she lets out a frustrated scream. She twists to hurl my phone—and with it my connection to the outside world—off the porch. The movement pulls the gun away from Emma's chin and, as if she'd been waiting for an opportunity, Emma twists away and drops to the ground. Before Brenda has a chance to even move, I come at her with the bat already swinging. When she points the gun in my direction, I haul out as hard as I can, managing to hit her shoulder. The shot intended for me lodges itself in the wood of the new porch right by my feet. Not giving her a chance to recover, I immediately swing again, ignoring the sting in my palms from the previous hit. I flinch when the bat hits her to the side of the head, but she goes down like a brick. Emma scrambles over and grabs the gun that has fallen from her hand and sits with her back against the siding of the house, barrel trained on the motionless Brenda. When I see the blood pooling under her head, I let go of the bat and drop to my knees beside her head. *I'm supposed to heal not harm.* With shaking hands I start checking her for breathing and pulse, ignoring the head wound I've inflicted for now. Finding no heart beat and no air moving in and out of her lungs, I immediately start CPR yelling at Emma to get her phone and call an ambulance.

I can't think of anything else right now, this woman's life is in my hands and if she dies, her death will be on my hands as well.

CHAPTER TWENTY-SEVEN

"Feeling better?"

Joe is leaning against the doorway to my brand-spanking new bathroom, where I'm taking my first bath in the humongous tub.

I'd been on the brink of a nervous breakdown ever since he'd pulled me off the porch and into the house, allowing the EMTs to take over compressions. I barely remember the shit I spewed at them, at Joe and at the universe at large; all I remember is being furious for not getting the opportunity to bring back the woman whose life I took. At least so I thought. Word from Drew, the deputy who escorted her ambulance to Cortez, was that sometime during the ride over, the EMTs managed to get a heartbeat. Regardless of everyone's assurance that no matter the outcome, I not only defended myself but Emma as well, morally the struggle I wage is no less now than had she died.

When the cavalry arrived in the form of Joe, Fox and the guys, followed closely by emergency vehicles one of them had alerted, I'd been in a zone and barely registered the continued apologies coming from Emma, who was in tears the entire time. Silly woman feels responsible, because when she came out of the bathroom and saw a woman's silhouette at the door. She didn't think twice to open the door to see who it was. The barrel of a gun greeting her and the threat that one little sound was going to get both her and me shot, was enough to have her step outside to where Brenda indicated. She doesn't realize I fault myself for pulling everyone into my fucked up vortex. When I tell her that later, after the ambulance has left and we are waiting for word on Brenda, Joe hauls me off the couch.

"Enough," he practically growls his demand, "Not gonna sit there and listen to you beat yourself up over a situation that you neither had nor have any control over. If anything, I should've known she was becoming this unhinged. When I saw that green Toyota sitting in the parking lot on the other side of the feed store and realized it had been her, I could've kicked myself for not considering that a possibility. When you mentioned a glimpse of woman at the wheel last night, I actually suspected Jenna. So if any blame is to go around on this, you better include me."

"Bullshit. The both of you better fucking knock it off," Gus bursts out. "Joe, you should know better than anyone how unpredictable and fucked up situations can get without *anybody's* help. And Doc? I get that this messes with your head, but if you hadn't acted, my wife could've been dead. Now that possibility seriously messes with *my* mind."

Gus is interrupted by Drew's call to Joe's phone from the hospital to let him know Brenda's status. That's when I start shaking with relief and Joe takes me upstairs, not letting go of my arm.

Filling the tub, the only time he says anything is to tell me to get undressed and get in, while trying to pull my shirt over my head. That's when I start batting at his hands.

"Would you stop that? I can get myself undressed and in the tub, thank you very much."

A hesitant smile breaks through the tight lines on his face.

"There she is—was afraid for a minute that you'd disappear on me, but I'm glad to see the bite is back."

He pulls me into his chest, his arms banding around me so tight it's difficult to breathe, yet I savor every second of his warmth. I lift my face for a kiss, which he willingly gives into before resting his forehead against mine.

"God woman, that took twenty years off my life. I'm making sure there is no way in hell we'll have any surprises from the past or the present blindside us like that again. Ever. I wouldn't survive it."

"Fine by me," I tell him.

"I'm okay. Better, thanks," she says with a smile.

I give her some space after making sure she isn't going to have a panic attack on me, finding Gus and Emma talking softly on the couch downstairs. Fox must've disappeared downstairs with Neil, because neither of them are in sight. Outside, some lab techs are busy digging the bullet out of the porch and I know Dooley is out front with some guys looking at the green Toyota. Actually, I see him coming up the stairs right now. Opening the door, I dive right in.

"And?"

"Better go inside so Gus can hear too," Dooley says, motioning his head to the living room. "Where's Naomi?"

"She's relaxing in the tub for a bit. Let her be for now," I tell him.

"Might be best. Pretty disturbed woman, this ex of yours, Joe. Looks like she's been living out of her car for quite some time. Dirty clothes, food wrappers and garbage. Fucking thing stinks like a dump. Pardon my French," he directs to Emma who waves it off, being used to much worse married to Gus and around the GFI guys all the time. Besides which she can swear up a good storm herself. "Most interesting thing though, underneath the garbage bags full of crap the lab boys hauled out was a crumpled printout with detailed instructions on how to assemble a simple remote timer. Not only that, but a roll of black electrical tape and some wire-clippers. Have a feeling I know why we haven't been able to pin the explosion on Heffler."

If I had a sick feeling in the pit of my stomach before, I'm downright ready to puke now. The thought that the woman I'd once thought I loved was this far gone, is beyond my comprehension. I had no idea. I get up with the overwhelming urge to see Naomi when Dooley stops me.

"If she pulls through, I'm afraid she'll face multiple charges of attempted murder, my friend."

"Good," I manage to bite off, "Should've stuck her in a mental institution a long time ago."

No matter what, the burden of responsibility is not one that I'd be able to shake off any time soon. I should've kept a better eye out.

"My boys will be another twenty minutes or so and by then the flatbed truck should be here to pick the Toyota up and we'll be out of your hair. Can't predict crazy, Joe," Dooley adds, clapping me on the back. Right.

Leaving Gus and Emma once again I walk Dooley to the door, who tells me he'll be in touch, before heading up the stairs.

"Care for some company?" I ask Naomi who's laying back in the big master tub.

"Always," she smiles a little weakly. We have a lot of collective shit to process, but I don't doubt we will.

"I love you so much," I say, sliding down behind her with my arms and legs surrounding her. She leans her head back on my shoulder and sighs.

"I know and I love you too."

A group of our friends is gathered at the big table at the diner already by the time we arrive. Even Katie and Mattias are here and Naomi makes a beeline to see the baby. Mal engages Fox right away and Gus pulls out the vacant chair next to him, motioning for me to sit down.

Meet us at Arlene's for dinner; 6 PM. Neil's working downstairs - keeping eye on Fox.

The note in Gus's chicken script handwriting was sitting on the kitchen counter when we got downstairs earlier. With boxes still strewn through the house and kitchenware hidden in one of them, Naomi thought it'd probably not be a bad idea to eat out.

"Did Neil tell you?" I ask Gus.

"Called right away and all files have been sent to Phoenix already. Assistant Chief Wayne Carr is pulling in the FBI for this, seeing as the involvement appears to include members of his own police force and extends beyond just his department. This is going to blow up big over there and I think we'll be able to feel the ripples over here."

Neil had been able to decode the files that were stored on the disc he found in the Xbox game this afternoon. Files with meticulous notes kept by James Miller and some copies of notes and emails showing the widespread corruption and pay-off schemes being facilitated with Bancroft, Miller and Associates as middle men. It appears Naomi's ex was getting uneasy with the increasingly high stakes of the game and was hoping for a way out. Too bad he found it at the wrong end of a bullet. His partner, a number of police officers and detectives and a federal judge were implicated with some evidence to back up the claims, but a further number was suspected.

"Frank Bancroft is being picked up before word leaks that something big is coming down, giving him a chance to run. Sounds like he was in the driver's seat for this scheme," Gus assures me.

"What scheme?" Naomi asks, taking a seat next to me and just hearing the last of what Gus said.

"I'll tell you later," I smile at her, happy to be able to at least give her and Fox the knowledge that whatever James had been involved in, in the end, he had tried to make it right. Regretfully, the only people he trusted, and perhaps rightfully so, had been his sixteen-year-old son and his ex-wife. I guess when you spend much of your career paying off or threatening witnesses, city and state officials, going so far as to be an accomplice in arranged hits, all for the sake of buying your wealthy and very criminal clients freedom, you become a little cautious.

"Who's for chili?" Seb walks up with a big pot, setting it in the middle of the large table. Arlene not far behind with a couple of pans of what looks to be fresh cornbread and pretty soon the conversation around the table shifts to the more positive topics of Mattias, my switch to GFI and the new clinic. As it should.

It's dark by the time we head to the new house, and once we get there, I find myself locking the doors behind us without thought, never even considering my own house in Cortez, where I can't even remember the last night I've slept. Not thinking too hard about what that may mean, I follow Naomi and Fox down the stairs to the basement, where Fox stretches out in his ugly greenish-yellow chair and Naomi curls up beside me on the couch to watch a movie.

I can't even tell what the movie is about, my mind is occupied playing out the past weeks and I realize that despite the massive changes in my life, I can't recall a time in recent memory where I was looking forward to the future as much as I am now. Noticing the slight snoring against my shoulder, I find Naomi has fallen asleep at some point, and I wonder if it'd be too soon to suggest I sell my house and just move in here permanently. After about four years of being at each other's throats, we've come together stronger than I'd have thought possible. Funny how dire circumstances can either break you apart or in contrast, forge stronger bonds. Gently wiping the hair that has fallen in front of her expressive eyes now shielded with long dark lashes against her high cheekbones, I'm pretty sure the latter applies to us.

When I look up again I find the credits rolling down the TV screen and Fox staring at me with his eyebrows drawn together.

"You really love her, right?"

"I really do, Bud," I tell him simply.

"Did you love that other woman?"

A bit taken aback by the question, I consider my answer, wanting to be honest with him.

"I did. There was a time I thought I loved her very much too, but it's like comparing apples and oranges. I was your age when I developed a crush on the most popular girl in school and had no chance in hell of ever getting her. When I unexpectedly got the chance barely being an adult, it was like a childhood dream come true, so yes, I fell head over heels. But I couldn't tell you now whether the love I felt was for her, or the promise of her, because let me tell you, the reality of her was not anywhere near that. One of these days I may tell you the whole story, but for now, let's say that was one of those mistakes a person can make that have long lasting consequences. So long in fact, that it almost ruined any chances I ever might have had with your mother, and that would've been a tragedy. 'Cause let me tell you that even on my best days with Brenda in the past, I didn't even come close to being as happy and at home as I am right here, right now, with the two of you."

Fox, who was listening intently the whole time, doesn't say anything. He just nods, his lips firmly pressed together staring at the floor and I wonder what is going through his mind. Ready to go to bed, I slide out from under Naomi to get up, but before I have a chance to pick her up to carry her upstairs, Fox gets up too and walks right into my arms for a hug. Unsure what to do with this, I go with instinct and wrap him up tight.

"Be good to Mom, Joe. She deserves it," he mumbles against my shoulder and it's all I can do not to let emotions get the best of me.

"Always, Bud. She deserves every bit life has to offer, and so do you," I tell him, my voice cracking.

Head down he pulls away and walks to his bedroom door where he turns around.

"Night, Joe. I'm glad you're here..." he looks up from under his eyelids with a little spark in his eyes, "...but not as happy as I am that you're no longer Sheriff." Chuckling he closes his bedroom door, leaving me with a smile on my face. Brat.

I try to keep my eyes closed, listening to them talk. I don't want to interrupt this moment they're having, but I can't stop tears from escaping my closed eyelids. These men are my entire life, and both of them want nothing more than to have me happy. How fucking lucky am I?

I can sense Joe leaning over and he picks me up off the couch.

"I know you're awake, beautiful," he growls in my hair, walking up the stairs with me in his arms. "I could tell from the way your breathing changed."

I press my smile into his shirt, but don't say a thing.

In the bedroom he lays me on the bed and I blink my eyes open watching him very determinedly taking off his clothes.

"You just gonna lay there and watch?"

"I might," I tease, watching him narrow his eyes at me.

"I think you should get naked." He stands at the foot end of the bed, naked as the day he was born with his hands on his sides, his erection jutting out from his body, large and proud, just like the man. With Joe keeping a watchful eye, I sit up and slowly pull my sweater off, throwing it on the floor beside the bed.

"More," he scowls at the tank-top I have on underneath and with a little smile, I pull that over my head as well, sending it the same way the sweater went. Joe's eyes never leave my body, but when I pause again he raises an eyebrow. Knowing what he wants, I reach behind me to release the clasp on my bra and casually let the straps slide down my arms. With nostrils flaring, like an animal sensing the proximity of his prey, he sets his knee on the mattress and slowly stalks toward me on the bed. In a sudden move, he grabs both my ankles and pulls me flat on my back, grabbing for the waistband of my yoga-pants which he painstakingly drags down my body, leaving me in only my plain white cotton panties. Shit. I wasn't exactly in a sexy mood when I got dressed after my bath this afternoon. Doesn't seem to deter Joe though, as he runs his nose along the edge of my panties and down to where a moist patch is already forming. Ignoring the layer of cotton, he puts his lips right over my clit and sucks me into his mouth, the light barrier causing an extra level of abrasion on the already sensitive nub. Arching off the bed, a deep moan escapes me and the responding approval rumbles from Joe's chest, humming around my core. With nimble fingers, he makes my panties disappear, and I mourn the loss of his mouth. Until he pulls his body up over mine and feeds his hard cock inside me, and I wrap arms and legs around him to keep him close. Slow and deep, our eyes connected, it feels like he fucks me for an eternity, with a single-minded intensity that expresses more than words could.

Sated and complete, I'm on the brink of sleep when my mouth starts working again.

"Never leave..." I mumble into the fine hair dusting his chest.

"Not a chance," he returns.

"No. I mean stay here with us." I close my eyes in the dark, wondering where I found the courage to put myself out there like this. Thinking the silence following my words fills the time he needs to find a way to let me down gently. With progressively negative thoughts running through my head, I find myself slowly pulling away from him, until I'm suddenly rolled on my back, my face caught in his large hands and his lips kissing my eyes, nose and mouth.

"I can't believe you asked," he says, making me want to take back my words even more. "I would love nothing more than to stay with you and Fox. To live here and make this a new start for all of us together. I was afraid you'd think it too soon, or would want more time to establish yourself, but Naomi—getting to build this next chapter alongside you is exactly what I want."

CHAPTER TWENTY-EIGHT

"Morning, Jed."

"Morning. Heard you had some excitement again over the weekend?"

I snicker at that. Excitement is a bit of an understatement. Today is Monday, the first day Jed and his crew are back to start work on transforming the old feed store into a working clinic. The noise would be intense the first few days, he's warned us, but after that, we should barely notice them around. Or so he says. We'll see—I'm just excited to see this all come together. A dream I've had ever since I left Phoenix five years ago. Probably longer than that.

"Yes," I answer, "you may or may not find a bullet hole in one of the new boards on the porch." I joke.

"No shit?"

"Nope, definitely not shitting you. Luckily that was all that was shot and all of us and the new windows are still intact."

I follow him out onto the porch, grabbing a fleece of the coatrack. It's really getting chilly, despite the sunshine. He's stopped to eye the hole where the lab techs dug the bullet out of the wood.

"I'll probably be able to fill that with an outdoor wood-filler. You won't be able to tell the difference. But eh...what's with the bloodstain?" He points to the discolored spot where Brenda had lain bleeding just days before and despite the fact that word is she will be alright—at least physically—I can't help but wince at the reminder.

"Well...I may or may not have had to knock someone out with a baseball bat."

Jed turns to me, eyeing the full-length of me from the top of my head to my shoes.

"Huh. No shit, eh?"

"No. She's not shitting you and will you stop ogling my girl." I can hear amusement in Joe's voice behind me as he pulls me back into him.

"And quite a girl you've got. No offense intended." Jed tilts his head at Joe.

"Quite aware—believe me, and none taken."

"Alright, guys. I'm right here, you know?" I remind them, turning so I can pin them both with a stern look, but I find two pairs of mischievous eyes staring back. "Whatever, you two." I throw up my hands and walk off, leaving them chuckling at my expense on the porch. I'm smiling when I step inside.

"How's Clint doing?" I ask Jed when Naomi shuts the front door. The man shrugs his shoulders, a painful expression replacing the amused one that was there a moment before, making me feel like an ass.

"Awake for a couple of days. At least as I understand it, 'cause the first time he spotted me in the room, he barked at me to get out before passing out again. Haven't been back since."

"Ouch. Guess it's gonna take a while to fix what went wrong with you two," I observe.

"Probably, but I'm gonna stick it out. I deserve everything he'll be dishing out. I won't run from it." Both dejection and determination are clear on his face. I don't get a chance to say anything, which is good, 'cause frankly, I don't know what to say, when Jed announces he'd better get to work and leaves me standing on the porch.

This morning after offering to drive Fox to school, I stopped in at Naomi's realtor's office to arrange for my house to be listed. Best way to go is to strike the iron while it's hot; at least that's the way I see it. Naomi asked me to stay and I don't want to leave. With my resignation handed it and a new job waiting for me, I'm not sad to move closer to the people who have become as close as family over the past few years. I don't have a whole lot in terms of furniture; at least nothing particularly special, but I'll let Naomi go through it with me and she can decide what has to go and what she wants to incorporate. The house is plenty big and even with both our households combined we probably would take a while before we run out of space. There's the clinic too. I'm not sure how she wants to have it furnished, but I'm sure we can make use of some of the shelving and furnishings I have. Even just to start out.

I walk to the back of the porch and sit down on the steps there, looking at the mountains in the distance. Feels right to finally set down some true roots in the same soil I came from. I hear the sliding door open behind me and find Naomi handing me a coffee before sitting down beside me.

"Deep thoughts?" She leans her shoulder against mine.

"Just feeling lucky I guess. I was wondering whether it's this particular house or the fact that it comes with you in it, that makes it feel like home. First time in my adult life I've felt that."

"Mmmm. Funny, I was just thinking this morning that I couldn't stand going back to my place in Cortez after the break-in, yet here we've had three major incidents that were technically far more traumatic, and still the house wins." She smiles at me and I tuck her to my side, my arm around her shoulder.

"It's a good house," I observe casually. "Strong foundation. Good clean lines."

Naomi chuckles. "Clean lines, huh? You're big on those these days."

"You bet. Seems like since we first discussed those, we've been able to come a long way."

"True. I've become a big fan of clean lines myself," she says turning her face to me, which I respond to by slanting my mouth over hers in a kiss that leaves no doubt who I'm a big fan of.

"Must you?" Neil comes walking around the side of the house, shaking his head.

"Yes." Is my short and simple answer. "Seems like you have some kind of perverted built-in radar, my friend. How many times does this happen to you?" Naomi starts giggling at Neil's facial expression. Disgust would be too mild a word.

"I don't want to discuss it," he manages, "Let's just say I could probably recognize a large percentage of the Cedar Tree population by the shape of their ass, and I don't even live here. I swear I'm gonna wear a cowbell next."

I throw my head back laughing.

After getting Neil a coffee, Naomi settles back beside me and turns to him.

"What brings you here this morning? Fox is at school."

"Yeah. I know. I want to see if I can upgrade his old laptop and maybe upload that game he likes playing on my computer on there. I'm leaving at the end of the week, heading back to Grand Junction. A few cases have come into the office there and I'm gonna start laying some groundwork on them. I wanted to leave Fox with something and this way we can play online from time to time. I've enjoyed spending time with him. He's a great kid."

"Awww, that's so sweet," Naomi coos, moving away from me and wrapping her arms around Neil in a full on hug. The damn pain in my ass is sporting a big satisfied smirk on his face when he looks at me. Right.

"Okay. That's enough," I say, pulling her off and throwing him a *'back-off—MINE'* look. Unfortunately, he looks anything but impressed. *Bastard.*

"Fox'll be pumped you're doing that for him. Thanks," I say through clenched teeth.

"My pleasure. It's the least I could do for the kid. He's been through a lot." Now he's pulling a damn puppy face, and it looks like Naomi is lapping it up; she's moving in for another damn hug. Over my dead body. I growl and tighten my arm around her waist so she cannot move making Neil laugh at my expense.

"Anyway, I'll get to it then. Thanks for the coffee, Doc," he smiles at Naomi, who practically melts under the flash of his pearly whites.

"Buzz off, Neil," is my contribution.

When he is out of earshot she turns to face me. "What. Was. That?"

"He was eye-fucking you, beautiful. You can't do that with someone else's woman."

Naomi drops her head in her hands, mumbling, "And here I thought I had a normal boyfriend."

"But you still love me right?" I give her shoulder a nudge and she nudges right back.

"May God have mercy on my soul, but I do."

"Well, that's good. But Doc? I'm not liking the boyfriend bit. I'd much prefer you refer to me as your *man*, or better yet, your husband."

"Husband? Is this a proposal or something?" she says with confusion all over her face. "'Cause if it is, you sure move fast—and—you could use a little work."

I just smile and pull her on my lap facing me. "Let's just say that I want you to know where my mind is going. Once we have our stuff somewhat sorted, and I've had a chance to put some of your suggested practice in, I'll make sure you know I'm dead serious about that proposal."

Naomi slings her arms around my neck and leans her face close.

"And when you do, I'm pretty convinced my response will be very receptive in nature," she replies, smiling against my lips.

EPILOGUE

<u>Two months later...</u>

"What do you think?"

I'm just showing Kendra the final touches in the form of a few prints for the wall and some new towels for the PT room.

"Love it. Looks like a fucking spa in here instead of a clinic. Such a relaxed vibe. You did good." She turns to me with a pleased smile.

Kendra will start with three afternoons a week and as business builds up here, she plans to build down her clients in Cortez; and move those who want to stick with her over to the new clinic.

Both of us have been eager to open the doors ever since Jed and his crew finished with the structural work two weeks ago. It looks amazing. Nice and bright with an eclectic mix of comfy furniture in the front waiting room, making it different from your standard doctor's office. There is a front desk that was built against the side-wall, not just for a receptionist, but also for Kendra and I to do some work from. We were set on having a treatment room each and a small eat-in kitchen and bathroom. With space at a premium, the choice was made to have a full-sized PT room built and drop a separate office for each of us. As an alternative, we each have a small desk in our treatment rooms when we need the privacy for phone calls and meetings, but for office work and file storage, we share the huge front desk with whoever will be a nurse/assistant. I'm actually working on getting Stacy, one of the nurses from Cortez Memorial, to join us here.

I love my treatment room which is the bigger of the two, since I'll also be doing minor procedures in there. Jed wanted to start on the old upstairs storage loft right away, moving perhaps offices up there, but I didn't want to spend my last penny without leaving a buffer to live off for a while if necessary.

When Joe's house sold after a month and he offered to invest his money in the clinic, I told him to hang on to it for now. He's already paying most of the household bills and insisted on taking over mortgage payments, claiming it was only fair since I'd paid a decent chunk down on the house. It was his *condition* on moving in; as if he needed much convincing.

In twenty minutes, most of our combined friends and Kendra's family will be here for an open house and we're a little behind schedule.

Fox and Joe decided there wasn't near enough beer, so they went to get some more and Kendra and I are supposed to be setting out some appetizers. We've been kinda distracted admiring all the new gizmos and gadgets as well as the occasional decorative touches, and forgot about the clock for a bit. Time to focus on the food, 'cause pretty soon this place will be packed.

I'm furious. People have started arriving and Joe and Fox aren't back yet. I've tried calling each of them a few times already but neither is answering. Either they left their phones in Joe's truck or they're ignoring me; I don't even want to think about the possibility something might have happened 'cause I've had enough of bad luck for a lifetime.

Every time the door opens, my head whips around to scan who enters. Beth and Clint showing up is a great surprise and I wish I had more time to sit and chat with them, but new people seem to be coming in all the time.

When the last ones to get here are Gus and Emma, I'm near tears. Gus wraps me in his arms, congratulates me and then whispers, "A bit of faith, Doc." It's enough to allow me to mingle and smile.

I catch up with Mal, who came in with Caleb, Katie and my little guy who seems to be stealing the show. Mal's also a fairly new import in Cedar Tree and we're laughing about a few of the drawbacks of small town living, namely that everyone knows everything and often before you do, when Kendra walks up.

"Introduce me?" she almost purrs and I'm doing a double-take. Kendra, who is one of the crassest women I know, save perhaps Arlene. Oh, or Beth. But anyway, Kendra is batting her eyelashes at Mal. Not making this shit up, and I'm almost immediately reminded that Joe's not here, because this would be something I'd love to point out to him. But before I have a chance to make the introductions, the murmur of conversations around me stills. I follow the various heads turned to the back of the clinic, to see Fox and Joe coming in from the mudroom—both dressed in tuxedos. I'm sure my mouth has hit the ground at the sight of my handsome men dressed to the nines, but for the life of me, I'm at a loss as to what is going on. Both of them walk right up to me and appear to ignore everyone else, big smiles on their faces when Joe starts talking.

"I thought it only fair that the person who was crucial in bringing us together again after I fucked up something in a way I thought was beyond repair, would be standing beside me when I ask you a question."

"Language," I mumble on automatic response, hearing the muffled laughter around me, but having eyes only for the man in front of me who winks in response.

"I wanted to make sure all our friends, who are also our family, were present. I needed the support of the man who will always be the most important man in your life by my side too. Naomi, I knew over four years ago when I first met you that you were someone special. That you were someone I needed to get close to. I had no idea at the time that my feelings for you would run quite this deep. And not just for you; I've grown to love your son as well. There is no better future I can imagine than one with both of you as a permanent part of my life."

When Joe sinks down on one knee in front of me, the tears that already started rolling down my face unchecked, are now nearly blinding me. I'm wiping furiously so I won't miss a thing.

Fox steps up behind Joe and puts a hand on his shoulder as Joe grabs hold of one of mine.

"Beautiful? With Fox's okay, I'd like to ask you to be my wife."

That fucking smile. Those bright blue eyes only focused on me. Have mercy.

"Yes!" I think I must've yelled as I throw myself in Joe's arms, who falls backward with me on top giggling through my tears. The tapping on my shoulder is Fox, who stands there holding up a box with a ring.

"Mom. You knocked the damn thing right out of his hand."

"Sorry," I say, but don't really mean it, 'cause seriously? Who cares about a damn ring when I have everything I could ever want in my life with these two men in front of me?

THE END

ABOUT THE AUTHOR

Freya Barker inspires with her stories about 'real' people, perhaps less than perfect, each struggling to find their own slice of happy, but just as deserving of romance, thrills and chills, and some hot, sizzling sex in their lives.

Recipient of the RomCon "Reader's Choice" Award for best first book, "Slim To None," Freya has hit the ground running. She loves nothing more than to meet and mingle with her readers, whether it be online or in person at one of the signings she attends.

Freya spins story after story with an endless supply of bruised and dented characters, vying for attention!

Freya

https://www.freyabarker.com

http://bit.ly/FreyaAmazon

https://www.goodreads.com/FreyaBarker

https://www.facebook.com/FreyaBarkerWrites

https://tsu.co/FreyaB

https://twitter.com/freya_barker

or mailto:freyabarker.writes@gmail.com

ACKNOWLEDGEMENTS

I want to thank a group of women, brought together by a love of reading—of books, a lot of whom I have not a chance to meet face to face yet. These women whole-heartedly support everything I do. I only have to ask, and sometimes that isn't even necessary. My girls from Freya's Barks&Bites—you know who you are—I love you buckets!

Thank you also to my beta-readers. I ask you to be brutally honest with me and without exception you do more than I expect from you. Time after time after time. The quality of my books is in large part due to your relentless eye for detail, and I can't thank you enough! Love each and every one of you!

A big hug and thank you to my partner in crime at Rebel Edit&Design, Dana Hook, who is my go-to-person in the industry and who knows how to keep me grounded, motivated and 'real'. There are no words to express what you mean to me.

Thank you to Vanessa Leret, who came on board as an independent editor for RE&D and who took on the task of editing Clean Lines and has exceeded expectations by miles! A wonderful, warm, intelligent and very, very welcome addition to my team. Already I adore you, Vanessa!

Thank you to Pam Buchanan, who provided the best assistance a girl could want at the Detroit Mashup Author Signing. I had a fantastic time with you Pam, and am down for a repeat or two! Pam, you've become a trusted friend who is not afraid to speak her mind and give it to me straight between the eyes. There is a special place in my heart for you!
Thank you also to DM Earl, who was my table partner at the first ever signing for both of us, and she made it an experience never to forget. Love you girl, and make sure you hang on that 'DUKE' of yours, he's priceless!

To Ava Manello, who together with Colette Goodchild managed to pull of the event to end all events! Tattooed Bad Boys in York, United Kingdom was an experience I can't wait to repeat. Ava, I adore you and can't wait for you to visit me in Canada, if only so I can stand by the gate with a welcome sign in my hands and grin on my face.
The amazing British fans who welcomed me (some with tears— xox Vickie) and even brought me food, gifts and left wonderful notes in my book. I could feel your love and appreciation in my soul!

My PA, Leanne Hawkes, who despite impressive work obligations and persistent sickness, managed to keep up her tireless attempts to bring my books to a bigger audience. Love your face!

And finally all you amazing readers – the ones who have been there from the very first book, to the newly introduced; you make writing so meaningful. Whether I read your words of appreciation or have a chance to meet you in person, you always manage to motivate me to do more—do better. And I thank you from the bottom of my humble heart.

327

ALSO BY FREYA BARKER

CEDAR TREE SERIES:

SLIM TO NONE
HUNDRED TO ONE
AGAINST ME
CLEAN LINES
UPPER HAND
LIKE ARROWS
HEAD START

PORTLAND, ME, NOVELS:

FROM DUST
CRUEL WATER
THROUGH FIRE
STILL AIR

NORTHERN LIGHTS COLLECTION:

A CHANGE OF TIDE
A CHANGE OF VIEW
A CHANGE OF PACE

(Coming soon!)

ROCK POINT SERIES:

KEEPING 6
CABIN 12
(Coming soon!)

SNAPSHOT SERIES:

SHUTTER SPEED
FREEZE FRAME
IDEAL IMAGE
PICTURE PERFECT
(coming soon!)

www.ingramcontent.com/pod-product-compliance
Lightning Source LLC
Chambersburg PA
CBHW060859210726
48293CB00006B/1871